# PAIN KILLER

By *RKMcKean*

R.K. McKean

Lexi —
Aloha!
Such a beautiful
young lady — A Joy to
meet you — may you
always Remain in love
with Jesus!
Your Brother
Randy

Theatron Press

Reviews —
ipibooks.com
Amazon

About the author: **R.K. McKean,** a graduate of the University of Florida, has lived in such diverse places as Paris, Boston, Munich, Tokyo, Bermuda and the DC area. He is the author of *Radical Faith — 10 Faith Secrets* (translated into Spanish and Indonesian) and *Radical Love — 10 Love Secrets* (translated into Spanish, Russian and Indonesian). He has delivered motivational speeches in over forty nations and presently lives on Maui with his college sweetheart wife and their dog Missy.

Theatron Press
is a secular imprint of
Illumination Publishers.

*For Kay, the one love of my life*

*who, in this endeavor, was my support,*

*my inspiration, my encourager, my*

*advisor, my initial editor and my honest critic.*

*I would never want to make the journey of life*

*without you.*

*All my love, all the time.*

Hurt people hurt people.
Pain always has a consequence.
Monsters always have a face.

*RKM*

There are those who avoid light at all costs,
who scorn the light-filled path.
When the sun goes down,
the murderer gets up—
kills the poor and robs the defenseless.
Sexual predators can't wait for nightfall,
thinking, 'No one can see us now.'
Deep darkness is morning for that bunch;
they make the terrors of darkness their companions in crime.

*Job 24:13-15, 17 (MSG)*

# PROLOGUE

Early September has a slight chill in the air that can't be held back. The leaves are just beginning their life cycle of colors. They will soon be on fire in brilliant reds and yellows. The world's masses come to New England every year to share in this extreme glory of nature. There is still green on the trees but the time of change is close and inevitable. Later comes the rapid fading into the ever-darkening rusts and browns. Then the leaves fall to the ground. Dead. They silently wait to be buried in white, frozen layers of snow.

The winters can seem endless but the promise of rebirth and renewal keeps people hopeful during the pain of the cold, dark months. Some move to the area only to find themselves quickly losing the battle with the bitterness of January's below zero wind-chill temperatures. They escape by running away. In doing this, they miss the beauty and splendor of the promised new growth and the promised new life that always appears, given enough time.

# 1966

Rain, rain, go away.
Come again some other day.

———————

Pain, pain, go away.
Come again some other day.


Rain. Wind. Thunder. Lightning. The swish, swish, swish of windshield wipers. Faster and faster the rain falls, attacking the road, the car, the ability to see. A black van veers into another's lane. Brakes squeal. Vehicles hydroplane. Metal slams into metal. Unforgettable crushing, crashing sounds combined with pitiful, painful screams reach into the darkness of the cloudy night.

Everything stops. No movement. No screams. Extreme blows to the head and body have resulted in silence. It's quiet except for the pounding rain. Broken glass is scattered across the newly laid black asphalt. Plastic and metal pieces are strewn around what used to be precious possessions. Blood is pouring out of open gashes and deep cuts in the fragile flesh of human bodies. People are misshapen, bent in precarious positions. Death hovers closely.

Sirens blast through the wet, thick air. Red and blue flashing lights seem to appear from nowhere. People are working frantically to save the lives of an unconscious mother and father. Already, the van driver has no heartbeat. A child recently awakened in shock from severe head trauma, stares at the wreckage from the open door of an ambulance. He can hear the first responders say, "They're gone. There's nothing more that can be done for them." He sees the body bags being zipped over his parent's faces. The boy is scared. The boy is angry. The boy is devastated. The boy will never be the same. The boy is in pain.

# 1969

"Hey Granddad, why are you always on my back?" screamed TJ. "I'm not hurting anyone doing what I'm doing, so just lay off me!"

"Listen young man. As horrible as the circumstances were on why you came to live with me and your Nana, you do live under my roof. And, as my Dad used to tell me, if you live under my roof you will live by my rules," said Granddad, great calm in his voice.

"But how's a little alcohol and weed gonna harm me? Everyone's doing it. It's the sixties. Sex, drugs, and rock n' roll! That's the theme of the decade," said TJ.

"First of all we both know it's not a little of that stuff, right? I know losing your mom and dad at eleven years old has not been easy for you but you're going to have to deal with the pain and the loss in some other way. Always remember that your dad was my son. I feel a lot, too. You're fourteen now and a sophomore in high school. You could be doing some amazing things but you're not. And you know, there's a lot more to life than getting high! You won't be with us that much longer. I'm trying my best to help you heal and get ready for life. I'm sure I don't have all the answers you need but I do know what some of the answers are NOT. You can't come in at all hours stumbling around, swearing, and making a mess of this house and your life. I won't let you disrespect and demean my wife. These things are just not acceptable. Get some of those Proverbs I've shown you into your heart and then into your life. *They're for doing what is right and just and fair.* As I've told you many times before —perfection never, progress forever. You need to move forward with your life, TJ. Are you hearing me at all?"

"Yeah, I hear you, Granddad. Just another sermon. I hear you loud and clear!" shouted TJ as he walked out and slammed the door behind him.

# Part One

# KING OF PAIN

# CHAPTER
# 1

The monster was a bomb waiting to explode into the lives of a number of very specific people. Determined. Deadly. Dangerous. All of this was hidden deep within. No one knew about the pain and anguish it had endured. How pain is expressed to keep individuals functioning in an insane world can be as different as hot is to cold. No two people ever handle pain in exactly the same manner. Some ignore it. Some seek professional help. This new monster planned to deal directly with the source of its pain. It was a terror threat but no one knew there was any reason for fear. The monster was alone in life. It had no spouse. It had no children. Its parents were dead. It had no siblings. What was there to lose?

In the early morning stillness and in the cover of a moonless sky, the monster was making its first move to kill its pain by making its first move. It was dressed in black. Dark sacs under its eyes were proof of too many sleepless nights. The monster's body was hard, tight, and strong. It had been created that way through years of running and lifting. It was detail-oriented. It had carefully planned every move, every moment of this night for months. The time was finally right.

*I've got to move fast if this is going to work. I can't stop. I can't hesitate. It's got to be now ... now ... now!* The monster was searching for the courage to keep going and to do what it had come to do.

After cutting a hole in a glass door large enough for it to enter the house, it moved quickly and silently up the stairs. It entered the master bedroom. It moved with purpose toward the sleeping man.

*Alone and asleep. Just as he was supposed to be. This is good.* This is very good. The words were echoing through the monster's mind as it willed itself closer to the huge, mahogany Tommy Bahama four-post bed. Then it stopped and stared into the man's face and felt itself colliding in both a beginning and an end. Finally they were face to face. Even asleep, Joe Hiller was handsome. He was a big, muscular man. His large dimensions could be discerned even covered with a sheet and blanket. A few age lines were creeping onto his face but the silhouette of the younger man as seen in a particular photograph was recognizable.

Rage was now racing through the monster. It proceeded to open a large plastic Ziploc bag that contained a dark green washcloth moist with chloroform. It held the washcloth tightly on the man's face until the kicking and struggling had ended. The monster spent the next two hours alone with Joe Hiller in undisturbed silence, freeing itself of its pain. Joe liked being first. Now he would have the privilege of being the first again. The first to die.

Joe's home was on Rivo Alto Island, one of the Venetian Islands on the Venetian Causeway in Miami Beach. It was a beautiful and exclusive area surrounded by Biscayne Bay. It just wasn't so beautiful tonight for Joe.

When Joe awoke, he found himself nude in his bed. His arms and feet were tied and stretched to each corner post. His head, arms, legs, shoulders, waist and mouth were wrapped tightly with silver-gray duct tape. He was immobilized. The monster had brought with it a small, black backpack. It contained all that was required. A high-priced glass-cutting tool. A rope. Three rolls of duct tape. An eight-inch garden hand bypass pruner. A syringe. A needle. Vials of lidocaine. An IV kit. The monster had taken the rubber surgical gloves out of the bag and slid them on before entering the home. The monster had done the same with a pair of surgical slippers. There was also the chloroform-soaked washcloth, returned to the plastic bag. A second smaller plastic bag was empty. That would be filled later.

"Finally waking up, Joe? I've been waiting for you so we could get started. I want you to experience some of my pain," the monster said in a low, firm, steady voice. "I want you to die, but not too fast. I want you to experience the knowledge, the sight and the terror of life leaving your body."

The monster worked with quiet precision. Joe's eyes were wide with fear as his heart pumped at an extreme rate. He felt confused. He felt exposed. He felt the sickening feeling of a living nightmare throughout his entire body.

"Let's start with the IV drip. Now Joe, this works a little differently than others you may have seen. It's not going to drip something into your veins. It's going to draw your blood out. I certainly hope you don't mind the use of the rather large umbrella stand I found by your front door to collect your ten pints of blood. I wouldn't want to make a big mess on your lovely oak floors in your beautiful home. Let's see, I'll just need to reverse the flow and then you'll get to watch as life slowly leaves your body. This is going to be quite something. This is going to be better than the movies, Joe."

The monster found an acceptable vein in an arm and after trying only three times, was successful. The monster attached the tube and adjusted the flow to allow the blood to start dripping out of Joe's body.

"And what's next, you might be asking yourself? Well, let's fill this syringe with lidocaine. It's a numbing drug, Joe. You may have had it at your dermatologist. This is going to sting a bit on the tops of your feet. Now, let's give that a few minutes and you won't feel a thing in those ten digits."

After giving it a little time, the monster took the garden pruner and went to work. One ... two ... three ... four ... five ... six ... seven ... eight ... nine ... and ... ten. The big man struggled against the ropes and tape without producing any real movement. He felt pressure and heard a clipping sound but was unaware of what was exactly being done to him. The amount of blood was okay. The blood loss was less than what had been imagined. The monster stood over the shocked body and smiled. It slid a full-length mirror from the corner of the bedroom and tilted it in such a way so that the dying man could see himself. All his toes had been cut off.

"This is so much less than you deserve, Joe. You'll have a few hours to think about what you've done with your life. The lidocaine will begin to wear off and soon the pain will start to build until you feel like you're exploding inside. Hey, Joe, do you even know why this is happening to you?" asked the monster. It then bent down and whispered the letters "T – H – C" into Joe's ear. With that, it carefully left the room, removing all traces of its presence. It left only the bedside light on so Joe could witness his own demise. The second plastic bag was no longer empty. It held the toes.

"Have a *GREAT* night," said the monster, a satisfied smile on its face.

It went down the stairs, back through the cut glass hole into the outside darkness. It headed for its rental car and drove back to its hotel with the radio blasting. On the radio was quite the appropriate song for this occasion. It was a 1983 Police tune ...

*I have stood here before in the pouring rain,*
*But it's my destiny to be the king of pain.*

As the monster listened to the words that seemed to be written about itself, it decided  more deeply than ever to complete its attack plan. The song actually had the effect of emboldening the monster to finish what it had started. It also decided to spend a few more days in the warm Miami Beach sun before catching its plane back home. After all, it was Labor Day Weekend.

---

Behind the duct tape, Joe silently screamed and struggled in wide-eyed horror as he saw himself in the mirror. All he could see was his own pale-gray reflection. He was looking Death in the face as he remembered what T.H.C. stood for and was all about. He was also thinking of the number ten. The pain was killing him.

# CHAPTER
# 2

TJ Maverick was sitting alone in his study doing some quiet thinking instead of having the forty-two inch plasma TV tuned to Monday Night Football. He would get to that later. After all, it was the first regular-season game, with the New York Giants battling the Denver Broncos at Invesco Field at Mile High in Denver. These were not his teams but still, it was football. From his antique English partner desk, TJ was staring at his floor-to-ceiling built-in bookcase, which contained his favorite books and his many family photo albums. He especially treasured the photo albums. They contained so many incredible memories. There was a dark brown, wood-paddled fan slowly turning in the center of the twelve foot ceiling. On one wall was a portrait of TJ and his wife. This was done in pastels and given to them as a wedding gift from a college buddy who happened to be an art major. On another wall were many framed pictures of his two children as they were growing up through their different ages and stages of life. On the far side of the room was a small couch, two wingback chairs and a round coffee table. In the corner were TJ's three prized guitars and an electric drum set with a stool.

*Men need a cave,* TJ thought. *At least that's what Mars and Venus have to say. True or not, I love my cave. It's my place to get away. My place to think. My place to meditate. My place to just hang out. My place to take the Gators to their next victory. My place to hope against hope while watching the Red Sox late at night. Maybe hope plus dumb luck is needed, given the fact that the curse of the Bambino is still in effect for trading Ruth to the Yankees after the 1918 World Series victory. What an incredibly stupid move! Eighty-three years! Oh well. At least it's my place to feel every hit and tackle of the New England Patriots. My place to plan. My place to organize life. My place to write and play my music. The Beach Boys had a song, "In My Room". Well, I have MY room!*

After paying some bills, TJ continued with his self-evaluation.

*Probably a few too many hours spent doing the sports thing. I need to take some time to write down some of my thoughts. After all, a person's got to get out into the open what's on the inside or run the risk of overloading and unbalancing the delicate emotional system. Isn't that what I used to tell my clients and now teach my students?*

After quickly checking the score of the game, TJ took out a romantic card he had bought earlier in the day. He had spent twenty whole minutes at the Hallmark store finding just the right one. He started typing a short note on his computer to slip inside the card.

> To Suzo:
>
> I'm going to miss you while you're gone. I know it's only for five days but that's too long. I love that we've always written to each other in notes, letters and cards. I remember the many notes I would find under the windshield wiper on my car back when we were in school together. I hope you read this card and note while you're on the plane and read it again before you go to bed while thinking about me. I'll be thinking about you.
>
> I'm excited about what's coming up for us in just a few weeks. It's almost our 25th anniversary get-a-way. Just you and me for 10 days of fun in the sun. I need that time. We need that time.

We've been moving so fast in different directions and missing each other lately. I've done the research. I've got the plane tickets, the villa in St. Barts, the jeep rented and some good books to read – a Baldacci, Patterson and, for something to make me laugh, a Hiaasen. I've also got that book you've always said you were going to read, *Caribbean* by Michener. No better time for you to read it than while we are there! The name of the villa is 'Sea Forever'. Kind of a cool name! It's close to the main town of Gustavia, with some great French restaurants and shops. We can go hiking to the beach at Colombier. It's supposed to have quite a view on the way to it. On one of the days we should explore the whole island. I'm told that there's no way to get lost since the island is only eight square miles in size. Our villa is a one-bedroom place on a hill with a western view so we can have drinks and watch the sunsets every night together. Nice! And it's supposed to be only a short walk down the hill to the closest beach, Gouverneur. The place has a balcony, a garden shower, a small infinity pool and hot tub. It's all very private. An island tan sounds good. I just love looking at you with nothing on. A small bikini is nice but all skin is definitely better. That's my vacation!

This trip will give us some time to talk even if I'm not always great at that. You're often saying I don't talk enough and that I don't express how I feel. Well, that's probably true. A psychologist who doesn't like to talk about his own feelings. Now that's quite something! I just talk about everyone else's, I guess.

Surprise! I'm going to write you a little poem for our anniversary. Now, I know what you're thinking. And yes, it's been quite a while since I wrote you a poem. No time like the present to rekindle an old tradition.

You're in my heart and my dreams so come home to me quickly.

All my love, all the time —

TJ

He sealed the card with his note in it and wrote, For Suzo — Open On Plane, on the front of the envelope. *Now that puts the pressure on. I better get started on that poem,* TJ thought.

TJ picked up the pen again and started writing some of his thoughts. After a while, his words and feelings started to flow freely even as he scratched words out and then found new ones that seemed to fit better. A few hours flew by. In the end, TJ entitled his poem, "Remember".

## REMEMBER
## TJ Maverick

Girl —
>>do you remember when you were small?
>>do you remember when everything was new?
>>>>the first day of school —
>>>>the first time away from home —
>>>>the first time you wondered who you were —
>>>>>I remember.
And —
>>do you remember when you were growing up?
>>do you remember the feelings you used to have?
>>>>your first date —
>>>>your first kiss —
>>>>your first love —
>>>>>I remember.

And —
>>do you remember ever being scared?
>>do you remember the times you cried?
>>>>about the way you looked —
>>>>about the way you felt —

about the way you loved —
I remember.

And —
do you remember our first date?
do you remember our first kiss?
the place —
the feelings —
the uncertainty —
I remember.

And —
do you remember our walking and talking?
do you remember our holding hands and praying?
about you —
about me —
about us —
I remember.

And Girl —
do you remember the feelings when I said "I love you"?
do you remember the feelings when you said "I love you, too"?
I remember.
I will always remember.

*Well, that's not too shabby. Maybe a little more work is needed but it's late. There's always tomorrow,* TJ said to himself. He was having a hard time keeping his eyes open. Time had slipped away. It was almost two in the morning. Before hitting the rack, he checked the outcome of the game. Denver took it as they played in their new stadium for the first time. It was 31 to 20. A loss for the Giants or any New York team was always welcomed. Boston and New York had never learned to play together nicely. They had history.

TJ walked silently up the stairs to the master bedroom to join his already sleeping wife.

# CHAPTER
# 3

Thomas John Maverick lll, or TJ, crawled slowly out of bed on a Tuesday morning. He was named after his father, who had also been named after his father. To keep everyone straight in the family the nickname of TJ had been devised. And so there was Thomas, Tom and TJ. TJ's dad was a corporate lawyer. TJ's granddad had been a minister and university professor in missions. His granddad had served as a missionary in Germany after World War ll. TJ's family had a long New England history, starting with John Maverick, who was born in England and educated at the University of Oxford, and later moved to the Massachusetts Bay Colony in 1630. He then became the first minister of the First Parish Church of Dorchester. One of his sons, Moses Maverick, founded Marblehead. Maverick Street, Maverick Cove, Maverick Court and Moses Maverick Square are all named after him. And so as life passed from generation to generation, it was TJ's granddad who impacted his life in many deep and profound ways by planting into TJ's DNA a desire for truth, a standard of morality and a love for people. He loved to use quotes from the book of Proverbs to make his points. These things did not take root quickly. TJ had hit some very bad times before he embraced any ancestral wisdom.

TJ was a psychology professor at the highly ranked Boston College. Presently it was listed as thirty-eighth in the *U.S. News & World Report* survey of colleges and universities. For years he had been a noted child psychologist who had written several best-selling books but he traded his busy practice in for less pay to have more time with his own family. He didn't want the ever growing "emergencies" of others to keep stealing his time away from those he considered his treasure. His treasure included his wife, Suzanne, or Suzo for short; his son, Ethan; and his daughter, Skylar. For some unknown reason, everyone in the home had ended up with a nickname. It was TJ, Suzo, E and Sky. E originally was called ET for Ethan Thomas but in 1982 the ET movie came out and the letters took on a different meaning. So, ET became just E. Still, big sister would use the ET term at times to get his attention or to get back at him. Kids will be kids even if they're in college.

After becoming a teacher, TJ found a new calling that he came to quickly embrace. He didn't just teach; he had a passion to teach. He was deeply committed to transferring his understanding of human development and behavior to others. He was thrilled to see so many college faces light up with self-discovery, self-awareness and self-knowledge. He could almost feel the personal growth in confidence and conviction of many of his students. This made him feel satisfied with the professional aspect of his life. He knew with certainty that his life's work was important and significant.

"Morning, Suzo – are you packed and ready for your trip to La-La land?" asked TJ.

"Well, I'm getting there, I think," replied Suzanne.

"Do you have to go and leave me like this? With both kids away in college it's going to be too lonely here without you. Just tell your boss you have more important things to do like making love to your incredibly handsome husband!"

"Sure. Like my boss is going to buy the *incredibly handsome* part," said

Suzanne as she rubbed her undressed body next to his.

TJ was forty-six years old. He wore his dirty blond hair short, because he had started to lose some off the front and top. He had the *Sting* look that exuded an older rock star vibe. Black was his favorite color. Almost everything on his side of the closet was black. Black jeans. Black tees. Black socks. Black dress shirts. Only one white one. Two black suits. A number of black sport coats. A long, black wool coat. Three black-leather jackets. His favorite was the Hard Rock Paris leather jacket. There were also black western-style boots and numerous other pairs of shoes, most of which were black. Of course there was more in the closet and dresser drawers; he just didn't wear much else. He would often say, with a smile on his face, that he was always ready for a funeral. He had hazel eyes, a pointy Maverick family nose and a wide mouth. When his kids wanted to give him a hard time, they would affectionately call him Jaws like the James Bond bad guy. The backstory for being made fun of in this way was when he put up $100 on a bet saying he could throw a black, rubber racquetball up in the air and catch it in his mouth in three tries or less. After finding a few takers, TJ was able to swish it on the first try as easily as Bird was able to swish it when the Celtics were world champions. Thus, *Jaws* was born! He was six foot, two inches tall. He weighed in at 185. He was a good-looking guy in a rough kind of way.

"I've got a dozen more things to do before I can get out the door, TJ. Could you fix a small breakfast for us? I don't want to eat the airplane food. It never tastes great and it just sits on my stomach the whole time I'm flying. It's a long flight from Boston to LA."

"No problem, Suzo. As you wish," said TJ in his best *Princess Bride* movie voice. *The Princess Bride* was on the Maverick family's top-ten movie list. The whole family had many of the lines memorized. *As you wish* was the quote most often used.

TJ was a good athlete in high school but never a star. He played some football as an outside linebacker. He loved music and had learned to play the guitar and the drums. Earlier in life, he had acquired certain abilities through a tragic car accident where he lost his parents and sustained a serious head injury. The trauma to TJ's head had affected him neurologically making it intellectually easy to be good with most things including his music. He could get lost in the moment writing songs and working them out on one of his acoustic guitars. Banging on his drums was a favorite pastime. It would actually help him keep his anger under control which had been a huge weakness earlier in his life. *Wipeout,* by the *Surfaris,* was a classic favorite for him.

TJ also loved hanging out with his kids. He had invested much time to make the relationships close, real and, hopefully, lasting. When his son, Ethan, was beginning high school, they started lifting weights and working out together. This had become a bond for them. It had also saved TJ from the forty-something flab. He actually became stronger and more in-shape than at any other time in his life. He had done it to spend time with his son, but it had pumped a good measure of extra life into his body.

"Eggs and toast are on the table. Hurry, they're getting cold," yelled TJ from the kitchen. "And what do you want to drink?"

It was a spacious house but TJ didn't like using the expensive intercom system. Too many buttons. He just liked to exercise his voice.

"My usual will be good. A Diet Coke. Make it a caffeine-free one. And can you pour it in a thin rimmed glass with just a little chipped ice? It tastes better that way," Suzanne replied on the intercom from the upstairs master suite.

"No problem, Suzo. For you, anything!"

TJ was intelligent, even brilliant, but he failed to apply himself as he could have during his much wasted, by being wasted, high school years. And so he felt lucky getting accepted at a couple of state universities. His choice became the University of Florida. For him it was love at first sight. The campus was an expanse of beauty with palm trees and large, majestic oak trees dribbled in grey Spanish moss. There were ponds scattered around the campus, impressive red brick buildings and inviting places to hang out like the Plaza of the Americas. He loved the Florida Field stadium which was later nicknamed *The Swamp*. It was the home of the Florida Gators. Steve Spurrier had won the Heisman Trophy in 1966 as their quarterback before continuing his playing career in the NFL with the San Francisco 49ers and the Tampa Bay Buccaneers. TJ thought it would be great being at a real football school in a stadium with 62,800 other screaming fans. And, being into music, he fell in love with the hundred-foot Century Tower housing the unusual sixty-one bell instrument, a carillon. It was the signature sound of the campus. And so it was an easy choice especially when realized that it was warm year-round, which was nice in itself, but there were many pretty girls who didn't need to wear a lot of clothes. It was also a long way from home and it was in the top-ten party schools in the U.S. as rated in *Playboy*.

Fortunately, after finding himself and finding Suzanne, he turned his life around and excelled in undergraduate studies. He went on to receive his Master's Degree from NYU and then went to Harvard for a Psy.D or Doctor of Psychology, specializing in child psychology. That would usually take five to seven years to complete but TJ had finished in four. He was a guy who never got lost in all the philosophical and intellectual rhetoric of the New England educational community. He was intuitive, sensitive, and quite pragmatic. He related to people easily and, in return, many liked him and called him a friend. He was loud. He enjoyed a good practical joke. He took photos of all family events and artistically placed them in album after album. He loved how his kids would come home from college with their friends and pull out the albums. They would spend hours reliving and sharing the good memories.

As with many in the emotional-help field, TJ initially went into psychology to figure himself out in a deeper way and to help work through his personal, painful ghosts. The accident that had taken his parents' lives left him with deep emotional scars. It had also left him with a cracked skull and a severe concussion. Although very rare, instead of causing brain damage it caused him to become an acquired savant. TJ had acquired a photographic memory, the ability to put puzzles and patterns of all kinds together and a much increased IQ. The average score on an IQ test is 100. Most people fall within the 85 to 114 range. Any score over 140 is considered a high IQ. A score over 160 is considered a genius IQ. TJ's score increased from 121 to 162.

In his profession, he was there to help his patients and his students enjoy and embrace life. He wanted them *to suck out all the marrow of life,* as Thoreau once penned at Walden Pond. This famous pond was located just a few miles from the Maverick home in Lexington where the "shot heard round the world" was fired, beginning the American Revolutionary War. TJ was always the life of any party but being a partier had gotten him into some very dark places earlier in his life. In his high-school days he was especially combative, aggressive and angry. He found escape in self-abuse through alcohol, drugs, and cutting. And, he had been suicidal more than once. It took a combination of epiphanies that became defining moments in his life to help lead him to a solid foundation for life. The first of these occurred late in his senior year of high school when he was diagnosed with Hodgkin's Disease. He was hit hard when the doctor told him he had cancer of the lymph nodes and that the enlarged lymph node was the size of a baseball located between his heart and his lung. Having thoracic surgery, a laparotomy and rounds of cobalt radiation forced him to do some deep thinking about his life and the direction it was taking. Following all of this, he started to make some decisions that changed, and probably saved, his life.

"What's the best way to the airport right now? There are just too many delays with the Big Dig. It seems like the roads keep changing every day. I just can't be late. I can't miss this plane!" said Suzanne, as she gulped down her egg, toast, and caffeine-free Diet Coke.

"Don't worry, I was planning on driving you into Logan and I can also plan to pick you up on Saturday. My classes were cancelled for today. I just have some office work that needs to be done along with a few appointments with students. I'll take 128 up to 93 and into the city. Then the Callahan Tunnel to Logan. I'm afraid 90 will be slow and the new tunnel isn't open yet. It's still early before the big-time traffic hits so we should be okay."

"And when were you going to tell me this good news of driving me to the airport?"

"Just didn't want to give you a false sense of security, Suzo."

"Maybe so, but it would have been nice to know."

"Well, maybe so. Let's look at it this way. By dropping you off you'll save a little time but we still need to hit the road soon. I'll finish the clean-up and you finish with whatever you need to do. Let's be in the car in fifteen minutes, all right?"

"Sounds like a plan."

Suzanne was a great wife, mom and senior editor with Beacon Press, a publishing house with a long and illustrious history. It had been in continual operation since 1854, with offices located on Beacon Street in a very desirable and prestigious part of Boston. Suzanne had a special ability for knowing what would sell and what would not. Also, she was extremely gifted at putting big deals together, handling the large egos, the artsy emotional extremes along with the greed tendencies of both writers and agents. In LA, she would close her biggest deal to date.

TJ and Suzanne met during the winter quarter of their sophomore year in a Hemingway class at the University of Florida. They were, and continued to be, tried and true fans in the Gator nation. She was five foot, seven inches tall with shoulder-length blonde hair. She had just recently joked about not being absolutely sure of her true hair color after so many years of blonde colorings. Like all people, Suzanne had insecurities about herself but at the same time knew how to exude confidence. And although getting older was not desirable to her, she didn't just quietly endure it. She found strength to try new things. A mid-life crisis? Maybe. She had joined a start-up rock band as a back-up singer for some night gigs and became a redhead for a period of time around her fortieth birthday. The kids thought this was quite cool. She even came up with a clever name for the group, *Band In Boston*. The rock band lasted. The red hair was short-lived. Soon after the hair experiment and during a shopping expedition to the Burlington Mall, TJ had spent a frustrating hour trying to find her in the Christmas crowds. He then realized he was looking for a blonde instead of a redhead. He had actually walked right by her a number of times. After that he insisted she return to being a blonde. He told her he had married a blonde for a reason. That he liked blondes. That he only looked at blondes. That last statement had led to a lively discussion of who else he was looking at! Nevertheless, she went back to being a blonde.

"Five minutes, Suzo," TJ yelled up the stairs as he went back to his study for a quick news update.

Although Suzanne was forty-seven years in age, she looked like she was in her early to mid-thirties. The low cut, skin-tight jeans and short shirt fad worked just fine on her. She was all curves and smiles. TJ thought himself a lucky guy as he met other mid-forty aged women who looked very different. Those were women he sure wouldn't want to wake up next to in the same bed! He thought too many people swallowed the lie about age and increasing weight, believing there was nothing you could do about it.

So Suzanne was quite pleasing to the eyes. She had a rounded-at-the-tip nose, and high cheekbones. Her eyes were large, blue, and captivating. Her full lips gave her an air of seduction. Her long legs were eye-catching. They had made TJ look many more times than once in the Hemingway class, especially with hot pants being the rage. Her breasts were small but just right from TJ's point of view. To TJ, she was like a runway model. She wore only light make-up. To accessorize, she liked platinum jewelry that was simple in style. If there were stones, they would be diamonds and sapphires. She turned heads everyday but would usually be too focused to notice.

On this day, she wore a charcoal suit. The skirt stopped two inches above the knee. Her blouse was off-white, silk and sleeveless. She wore grey stockings with black, Italian leather heels. Around her neck was a platinum chain with a beveled, one-carat Tiffany diamond TJ had given her on their twentieth anniversary. Around her right wrist was a platinum tennis bracelet of sapphires, a tenth-anniversary gift. The left wrist was decorated with a delicate, silver watch, her one-year anniversary gift. It wasn't worth much but it was priceless to Suzanne. It had been given to her by TJ when they couldn't afford much of anything since they were both in grad school. Just before their first anniversary they found out Suzanne was pregnant. And so, on the back of this adored watch was inscribed the words *Future Greatest Mom.* These words made the watch so valuable to Suzanne. This was faster than they had planned to have children but it turned out perfect for them. In one sense, they grew up with their kids. They married soon after receiving their four-year diplomas when TJ was just 21 and Suzanne was 22. And so, they were still quite young when Skylar Lynn was born. Additionally, on her right ring finger was a white gold, antique ring bequeathed to her from her 102-year-old German grandmother. On her left ring finger she wore her half carat-diamond solitaire engagement ring and a wedding band of diamonds and sapphires. These cost TJ almost all the money he had at the time but, to him, it was worth it.

"Let's go," TJ echoed into the house from the door leading into the garage.

"Okay, let's go," Suzanne happily replied from the garage, already sitting in the front seat of her silver Audi A4.

They were on their way. On time.

---

"Well, here we are, Terminal B, American Airlines. Hmmm. We made it in forty-three minutes. Not bad. Now, when should I plan to pick you up?" asked TJ.

"I come home on Saturday afternoon around three. My last appointment is a group dinner thing on Friday night. I left the exact time and flight number next to the kitchen phone along with a little card for you. I'll call just before I get on the plane so you'll know if it's on time."

"Sounds good. Have a super productive time and get that book deal signed, sealed, and delivered. I can't wait to open the card you left for me and here's one for you. Please don't read it until you're in flight. Now give me a good kiss. I love you, Suzo."

"I love you too," Suzanne said as she opened the door to get out. "I left good food in the fridge for you so you could eat something nutritious while I'm away. Please don't just go to the S & S Deli every night and eat those wings you love so much like you did the last time I left," she said while grabbing her bag from the back seat. "Well, I've got to run. Bye, TJ, and thanks for the ride," she quickly said as she blew another kiss at him, closed the door and walked away.

Suzanne was the love of TJ's life. Their first date had not gone so well, at least from TJ's point of view. He was stomach-ache sick with the 'Gainesville grippe' and he thought she was out of his league. Still, he hoped for the best. He had borrowed his friend's cool black Trans Am for the occasion. They went to Manero's for dinner which was an intimate and inexpensive Italian restaurant. The emphasis for TJ was on *inexpensive*. The place was popular with many of the UF students. There were red-checkered tablecloths with candles in the middle of each table placed in empty wine bottles. As the wax melted down from each candle, the wax formed a beautiful rainbow of colors on the bottles.

When the night was over, TJ figured there would be no second date. After all, he was just a dorm rat living in South Hall trying to make ends meet. She was a drop-dead gorgeous sorority girl, Delta Gamma, from a well-to-do Miami Beach family. If the truth were told, TJ was somewhat insecure being around Suzanne. This is what really made him have doubts about her. But to TJ's surprise, after the first date she was still very friendly in class. She was always taking a seat next to him and walking out with him. And so, there was a second date about a month later.

This time they had rented inner tubes and floated down the Itchetucknee River together, a totally spring-fed river flowing at the rate of 212 million gallons per day. The water is sparkling clear and is always seventy-two degrees. They chose to do the longest route and so for three hours they slowly floated, seeing turtles, egrets, white-tailed deer, ducks, and even a Great Blue Heron. At times, the fish would come right up to them as they drifted together in the crystal clear water that averaged being five feet deep and twenty feet wide. It was an unusually hot, sunny day for early March in North Central Florida, which made it absolutely perfect. In fact, this date was over the top magical for TJ. Was it the little yellow bikini Suzanne was wearing or just the comfortable talking, honest sharing, and easy laughter for an entire afternoon? He wasn't totally sure what pushed all his buttons but they were all pushed. Hard.

After dropping her off that night, he decided she was the one. The one for him. The one for life. TJ never had another date with any other girl. He found out later that Suzanne had made a similar decision about him after their first date. He had always been amazed by that.

# CHAPTER
# 4

The lines were pleasantly short in the terminal. Suzanne checked her small, black hard-shell suitcase and carried her laptop and necessary paperwork in a sleek, light grey, leather shoulder bag. Never wanting to carry more than one piece of anything through airports, she also used the laptop case as a purse.

After getting through the security lines quickly and easily she proceeded to gate B-32. There she waited while reading the beginnings of a few manuscripts on her laptop, hoping something would dazzle the imagination. After thirty minutes of skimming through the different pages, Suzanne could see there was nothing even remotely good, according to her personal rating system. Her gut feelings.

She had been booked in Business Class but found herself moved up to First Class. Angela, her personal assistant, often found upgrades and special perks to make traveling a little easier. Suzanne entered the Boeing 767 plane with the boarding call for the first-class passengers. She was in row 1, seat B. There was no one beside her and only a few other people were scattered around her throughout the First Class and Business Class sections. In fact, the whole plane had very few people in it. There were only eighty-one passengers on a plane that could carry one hundred and fifty-eight.

*Just my lucky day,* she thought. *First class food. I should have skipped breakfast after all. But, this is great. Extra peace and quiet. And hopefully some good sleep before I'm on the go in LA.*

"Hello, my name is Sara. If you need anything during the flight, please just let me know. Right now, would you like some orange juice, coffee or anything else to drink before take-off?" asked the young, attractive flight attendant.

"Just some water right now, please, but with no ice," responded Suzanne.

"Okay. I'll be right back with your water."

The passengers filed by. Many looked a little disappointed they weren't allowed to take one of the many empty seats in either First or Business Class. Everyone stored their hand luggage in the overhead compartments or under the seats in front of them. They went through the seatbelt spiel and were finally off, using runway 4R at 7:59am.

As soon as the plane was off the ground and in the air, Suzanne removed TJ's card and did her usual routine. She read it through fast, almost in a hurry to learn its basic content. Then she read it again very slowly taking in his heart. It closed with *"All my love, all the time.".* This was typically how TJ had closed out his cards and notes ever since he had told Suzanne he loved her. It never failed to make her smile.

Suzanne's marriage wasn't perfect. There had been times of stress, disappointments, and disagreements. On top of that, TJ struggled with the demons of his past if triggered in just the right way. When those infrequent, dark periods of anger and depression would come, she was there to help him though them. TJ referred to Suzanne as his rock. She was his safe place. But to his credit, even during his hurting times, TJ had rarely raised his voice in any argument or disagreement. His tendency was to just get quiet and be still, as he felt the pain of his past. Earlier in his life, he would get angry and explode at the people around him. He was just not that person since knowing the love of

Suzanne. So, even in the hard times, she felt she had a dream life. After all, she had married the man of her dreams. And, she knew that TJ adored her and adored their kids and adored the life they had made together. He took time for each of them. He tried his best to stay connected to each of them. He was not always successful but Suzanne would point him in the right direction when necessary. After finishing the note for a third time and dreaming a bit about the famous French island of St. Barts, Suzanne suddenly noticed a situation that didn't look right. It had danger written all over it.

They were only 15 minutes into the flight, when the two men who were seated directly behind her in seats 2-A and 2-B got up, even before the seatbelt sign had been turned off. They were at the door of the cockpit forcing their way in. At the same time, there was an uproar behind her of some sorts. What she couldn't see were the two flight attendants who had been stabbed and the passenger in 9-B who had his throat slashed. What she could see was the captain and first officer leaving the cockpit under duress. One of the men who had been seated behind her sat himself down at the controls. They now had a new pilot. Suzanne's head was praying fast and Suzanne's heart was beating even faster.

"I have control," said the new pilot, a dark-skinned man, speaking in what sounded like a Middle Eastern language to his compatriot who had been sitting beside him in seat 2-A. The 2-A man was standing just outside the cockpit holding some kind of knife-like weapon in his hand. The blade was held close to the original pilot's throat.

A few minutes later, the new pilot addressed the passengers and crew members. The time was now 8:23 in the morning. "We have some planes. Just stay quiet and you'll be okay. We are returning to the airport." One minute later he continued, "Nobody move. Everything will be okay. If you try to make any moves, you'll endanger yourself and the airplane. Just stay quiet."

Suzanne didn't know what to do so she did nothing at all. She was frozen with fear. As she looked around at the faces she could see from her seat, everyone looked terrified. *TERRORISTS*, was the word screaming through Suzanne's mind.

At 8:33, the pilot came on the speaker one more time with increased urgency in his voice, "Nobody move, please. We are going back to the airport. Don't try to make any stupid moves!"

# CHAPTER
# 5

S kylar was sleeping in on a Tuesday morning. She had stayed up late finishing a paper that was due for her 11a.m. class. Sky was in the first weeks of a dual Master's degree at New York University for Library and Information Science. She loved the city. She loved her school. She loved the fact that she had overcome her fears four years earlier as she arrived as a freshman in New York City to live out her dream. She had applied and been accepted to five top universities but this is where she wanted to be. If you can make it here, you can make it anywhere!

Sky lived in a fourth-floor apartment located at 126 First Street. This was within easy walking distance to one of Sky's and her dad's favorite places to eat and hang-out together when he was in town visiting. The place was Katz Deli. The pastrami was to die for although Harry and Sally, from the famed 1989 movie of the same name, had also found Katz's food to have an orgasmic quality. Sky lived in her apartment with four other girls. Two were twins from California named Shari and Kari. They attended the prestigious Joffrey Ballet School. They had been affectionately renamed Diva 1 and Diva 2 following the first time the other roommates saw them dance. They were amazing. The other two, Summer and Rayne, were undergrad NYU students.

Rayne had been best friends with Sky back at Lexington High School, although a year behind her. They had bonded while both were doing the drama thing. They were the ones who had leading roles in all the plays and musicals. Summer was the lone New Yorker. She was a bit rougher and wilder than the other girls but was also a great protector for the group. She didn't have a gun-carry permit for nothing!

Two years earlier, Sky and Rayne had stepped out one evening to check out a fun and fashionable SoHo club. While there, they met Summer, Shari and Kari. After a boring hour they left the club and went out together to grab some tasty New York-style pizza. That lasted for many hours with laughs and smiles and stories all around. The group of five became best friends with each other almost overnight. A short while later they found an apartment and moved in together.

The apartment was small. It had three tiny bedrooms and two tiny bathrooms. The kitchen, dining room and living room were all crammed together as the one other room in the apartment. Sky's room was the size of a large closet but she had it all to herself. There was a twin bed and a petite desk with an attached bookshelf. The kitchen was just big enough to turn around in. In the sitting area was an olive green couch and a brown, leather chair. The rug, lamp, decorative items and furniture were all from the Pottery Barn. There was also a round maple dining table with five matching chairs under a black hanging lamp that looked like it had been there since the Port of New York had opened. There was no elevator and no central air. They did have a big-screen TV in one of the corners which was mostly used for movie nights. The girls had thought themselves fortunate to have found this apartment for only $3,200 per month.

Skylar was slender with shoulder length, streaked-blonde hair. She was five foot six. She had high cheek bones, a wide smile, and a Maverick nose. She was athletic and artsy. More than that, she was confident, smart, and going places. She genuinely cared about people. She was a beauty but not stuck-up about it. She was like her mother in so many ways, but Sky was not resentful of that. On the contrary, she cherished that fact. She adored both her parents and had an ongoing conversation about everything with her mom, Suzanne Maverick.

At 8:50 a.m., Sky got a call from her boyfriend, Sean. He lived at 777 6th Avenue, apartment 14G.

"Yeah, hello," in a sleepy voice.

"Are you seeing this? It just happened. You've got to see this!" said Sean almost shouting.

"I didn't get to bed until 4 a.m. Call me later, okay?"

"No. Get up, Sky. Something's happening. Are your roommates there? No one's at the World Trade Center area for any reason, are they?"

"All had early-morning classes today. I'm alone. What are you talking about?" said Skylar now pretty much awake at this point in the conversation.

"Looks like a plane hit one of the Towers. It's on every news channel. I'm seeing it out my window. Get up and see it for yourself."

"Okay, got the news coming on. Oh my goodness! It looks really bad. Is my brother still there with you? You know he sometimes goes for coffee and to study at the Starbucks in the World Trade Center before his classes since it's close to Pace," said Sky, worry and concern in her voice.

"No he's not here. Not sure where he went. I called you first to make sure you were all right. Let's both try to reach him as quick as possible. If E is there he needs to get away from that place fast!" said Sean emphatically.

"Good idea. I'm going up to my roof for a live look. Call me back if you hear anything. I'll do the same. I'll also call my parents."

"Okay. Talk to you later," said Sean.

Skylar threw some clothes on, grabbed her cell phone and went to the roof of her building. Many of the other tenants of her building were already there, looking over toward the World Trade Center. It seemed as if everyone in the City was camped out on the multitude of rooftops. She called her parents and left a short message saying she was fine and that she was trying to get hold of E. Ethan wasn't answering his phone.

Sean was on his phone trying to reach Ethan too, but also got no answer. While he was still looking intently out his huge floor to ceiling window the unthinkable happened. A second plane glided through the sky and exploded into another tower of the WTC. On the rooftop of her apartment building, Sky watched in horror as she saw the same thing. Shocked and scared, they both hit the speed-dial for Ethan. All they got was a busy signal. It was 9:02 a.m.

# CHAPTER
# 6

Pace University was not Ethan's dream school. He wanted to go to NYU, the school his dad attended for a Master's program. He also wanted to join his sister at NYU to bond their friendship, since they had been apart for the last three years. And as a personal goal, he wanted NYU so he could be a part of the prestigious Tisch School of the Arts. Ethan had higher entrance scores than Sky but it was three years later when he had applied. By then, the TV show *Felicity* was at an all-time high. The series about a young girl's college experiences in the Big Apple as she attended the fictional school of UNY, the University of New York, was highly-rated and so highly watched that the number of people wanting to attend the real New York University jumped to sky-high numbers. And as the number of applicants increased, so had the entrance standard of NYU. So Ethan settled on Pace University, planning to transfer after his sophomore year to NYU. Pace was located near the World Trade Center. He was having his Public Speaking class from 8:30 until 9:20 a.m. This was *waaay* too early for class. At least that's how Ethan felt about it. He walked into his classroom drinking a tall, which is really a small, cup of herbal tea from Starbucks in the commercial concourse in the WTC.

Ethan was five feet, eleven and a half inches tall. He was still hoping for another half inch. He weighed in at 165. He was all muscle. His self-imposed diet was extreme. No gluten. No dairy. No non-organic fruits or vegetables although this wasn't always possible, so at least he demanded fresh fruits and vegetables. No beef unless grass fed. No poultry unless free range. No farm-raised fish. His father had told him to add one more 'no' into his list by saying that it would be *no fun* eating like this all the time. E had read the book *Fast Food Nation* in 10th grade and then vowed to never eat fast-food again. That was the beginning of his new lifestyle. He would no longer even walk into a McDonalds with the rest of the family. He said the grease lingering in the air was bad for his lungs and that it made his face slimy. But no one could criticize the results of his radical choices. His body fat was almost non-existent and so he was quite cut. Ethan had longish, healthy blond hair, the prized sunken cheeks, a squared face and perfect skin. More than a few people commented that he could easily play Brad Pitt's younger brother in the movies.

He was also quite talented. He played the drums and the acoustical guitar much better than his dad. He wrote songs. He always had a lead part in the school musicals. He was also a model, doing print work and TV work during his middle-school and high-school years. And because of these early life opportunities, the dream to become an actor had been born. Back in the eighth grade on his first go-see, or job interview, he had been chosen to be the Nabisco boy for the year on their national television commercials. He basically sat on a giant Oreo cookie with a very pretty, dark-haired girl his own age and together they flew through the air on the cookie. During the next few years he had made more money off the residuals from these commercials than his dad, TJ, or his mom, Suzanne, were making as working adult professionals. It had become a family joke.

Suddenly, while sitting in his classroom, Ethan, along with the whole class heard some kind of explosion. Ethan glanced at his watch for the time. It was 8:46 a.m. Looking out of the classroom window he could see smoke starting to rise from one of the WTC Towers. He was thinking he had just been there earlier in the morning. Many, including the professor, made their way over to the wall of windows to stand and watch. It was a strange scene.

———

Sixteen minutes later as the class was settled down and back into the lesson, another explosion occurred, causing more smoke and more fire to come from another tower. No one seemed to move for a long time. Although all cell phones were required to be turned off and put away during class, many came out; students were making calls. A few got a connection. Some went straight into voice mail. Most calls only got a recorded message saying the call could not go through at this time so please try later. Or, they just got a busy signal. Ethan tried to call his sister, Skylar, and his parents. He couldn't get through to either of them.

"Anyone find out what's goin' on?" said Ethan to the whole class.

A girl with dark make-up and piercings in her nose, left eyebrow, ears, and tongue had just finished talking to her parents. She responded from across the classroom. "Yeah, two planes have crashed into the towers of the World Trade Center. They think it's terrorists. No one knows for sure what's really happening. There's a lot of confusion," she said rapidly in a machine gun like cadence.

Some of the students left right away. Others, including Ethan, stayed glued to the window. Class was definitely over.

———

A short time later, with a few students still watching from the classroom windows, they could make out tiny images of people jumping from the windows of the towers that were above the impact point of the planes. This wasn't a movie. This was really happening. A few of the students started to tear-up. Some were in shock. No one would ever be the same after witnessing this horrific sight.

# CHAPTER
# 7

T J had dropped off Suzanne in plenty of time to catch her 8 a.m. flight. The traffic had been okay coming into the city at six in the morning. Now, the traffic was bad coming out of the airport and funneling into the Sumner Tunnel. It got worse on the city side with the Big Dig mess and work day traffic in full swing. The Boston Big Dig had been going for ten years with another five until completion. It would be the largest and most costly public-works project in the United States, costing tax payers twenty-two billion dollars. This was due to much corruption, incompetence, and many overruns. The project was secured for Boston by the controversial senator Ted Kennedy. The plan included placing the elevated highway that cut through downtown Boston underground. It was to be replaced with green space bringing the beautiful waterfront and the city back together. The plan also included building a tunnel to the airport, the Ted Williams Tunnel, named after the Red Sox "Thumper" who was one of the greatest hitters in baseball history. With the tunnel being an addition to Interstate 90, a person could literally drive from the East Coast to the West Coast without a single turn. And so, in the midst of all this confusing construction mess, instead of going directly to the Boston College campus, TJ decided to do some work from the house before going in. Besides, in the rush of the morning, he had forgotten his laptop, which contained important information he needed.

To pass the time, TJ had brought along some CDs that contained some of his favorite songs. He put one in and cranked up the volume. His son, Ethan, had made them for him for his 45th birthday. The CD was sixties and seventies songs that TJ thought to be the greatest era of Rock 'n Roll music as long as you took out the disco disaster junk. Some of the songs were soft love songs and some were more edgy. From the Beatles to Bread to Queen to Led Zeppelin to Journey to Chicago to Lynyrd Skynyrd, each song had memories attached to it. It was a true *Sentimental Journey* although that song was a forties song sung by Doris Day, her first Number One song. TJ was singing out loud and enjoying his music as he headed back on 93. The music was playing so loud there was no way for him to hear his phone ring. On the way he noticed, more than once, people checking him out during the bumper-to-bumper traffic slowdowns as he sung with passion, intensity, and exaggerated hand gestures. He just smiled and kept on singing. Right before getting to the interchange at I-95 and I-93 he came to a dead stop due to some kind of accident. He couldn't exit off and he couldn't move forward. TJ was thinking of the other routes he should have taken to get home. Almost two hours and three CD's later he was past the problem of an overturned semi with multiple cars bent and busted almost beyond recognition. This accident had completely blocked the highway. *There was no way to survive that crash,* TJ thought. It stirred up some latent feelings. At the same time, things like this reminded TJ of how fortunate he and his family were. Although quite late for work, he found himself feeling happy, knowing he and his family were safe.

Arriving home he put the silver Audi sedan in the garage beside his new, black 350Z. The Z was his car but he had taken Suzanne's to get to the airport. He knew it was more comfortable for her and also the luggage space was better by far. Actually, she didn't like the Z at all. It was difficult for her to get in and out since it was such a low car. The door was heavy and it tended to not stay open especially if the car was on any kind of incline. Suzanne's legs had felt the crunch more than once. But she was happy that TJ was happy with his new toy.

*One more reason to come home,* thought TJ. After all, his car was fun to drive even in Boston's notorious traffic. Coming into the house from the garage and walking through the kitchen, he noticed the message light blinking on the phone. *Must be a quick good-bye message from Suzo.* He pressed the button and listened. There was one short message from his daughter.

"Dad and Mom, this is Sky. Just wanted you to know I'm all right. Not sure what's going on but I knew you would worry. I'm going to call E to make sure he's safe since he hangs around the World Trade Center a lot. I'll try your cell phones as soon as I hang up. I love you and will call again soon."

TJ had no idea what she was talking about. He looked at his cell phone and saw he had missed the call from Sky. *Probably couldn't hear it with the music so loud.* He quickly turned on CNN and started to figure it out in a hurry. It was 9:55 a.m. He called both his kids but couldn't get through to either of them. He went back to the television.

"This is CNN reporting to you live from New York. America is under attack. The first plane, believed to be American Airlines flight 11, hit the North Tower at 8:46 a.m. A second plane reported to be United flight 175 struck the South Tower at 9:02 a.m. Just minutes ago, at 9:45 a.m., a third plane crashed into the Pentagon. We are still not sure ... Oh, my God! It's falling! The South Tower just collapsed! I can't believe it! Again, occurring at 10:05 a.m. Eastern Standard Time, building number 2 of the World Trade Center, the South Tower, has collapsed."

TJ collapsed on his couch in his beautiful, serene home, watching the screen in silence and disbelief. He was stunned. He was powerless.

He felt hopeless. He felt like a man who had just been punched in the stomach, kicked in the head and held underwater, all at the same time.

"Tower number 1, the North Tower, is also in trouble and could come down at any moment," he heard the talking head say.

The second tower came down twenty-three minutes after the first one. Grey ash was exploding into the air. Instead of the *shot* heard round the world it was the *shock* heard round the world. It was 10:28 a.m., Tuesday, September 11, 2001.

Ethan watched from his classroom as 2,749 people were murdered. But, he didn't know.

Skylar watched from the top of her apartment building as 2,749 people were murdered. But, she didn't know.

TJ watched from the comfort and safety of his living room as 2,749 people were murdered. But, he did know.

American Airlines, flight 11. It left Boston at 7:59 a.m. from Gate 33-B on runway 4R. It was going to LA but made an unplanned stop in NY. It contained ten thousand gallons of jet fuel as an accelerant. On this beautiful day in September, one hundred and six floors of concrete and steel came crashing down floor by floor on top of each other.

All dressed in black? Yes, he was. Always ready for a funeral? No!

*THERE'S NO WAY TO SURVIVE THAT CRASH* was the thought crashing through TJ's mind.

Suzanne, the love of TJ's life, had not just been murdered. She had been obliterated. From dust to dust, ashes to ashes, took on a whole new meaning.

# CHAPTER
# 8

Funerals and memorial services are always tragedies. They are about loss and separation. Even when belief in heaven and an afterlife are in the hearts of those in the crowd, it's not easy for the ones left behind. Grief is a real thing. There is no way around it for anyone. Facing it is heroic in every circumstance. The demeanor of Ethan, Skylar and TJ was stoic and sad. They were holding on to each other with some kind of invisible cord while holding on to their individual emotions by shutting them down. As they faced the crowd of family, friends, and spectators, their reddened eyes and fallen faces exposed the truth of the disaster that had crashed and exploded in their hearts.

TJ rose from the front pew of the old New England church building located just off the Battle Green in Lexington. He took from his coat pocket the folded notes he had written the night before. Then he addressed the crowd as he strained to control the eruption of the emotions that expressed his heart.

"It's been seven days since saying good-bye to Suzanne at Logan Airport. I didn't know at the time that I was saying good-bye to her forever. I would have held her and told her how much I loved her and I would have never let her go. God gave her to me for twenty-seven very precious years. It's been that long since we met in a class at the University of Florida. Suzo was a beautiful woman inside and out. She was my home. She was my life. She made me happy. Her smile and her touch made me always feel life was worth living. I'm sure she wasn't perfect in your eyes, but she was in mine. She had much more life to live. She was only forty-seven years young. We were married for almost twenty-five years and she was an extraordinary wife and mother. She gave me Sky and E, who are two incredible kids. I can gaze into their eyes and clearly see Suzo.

"I went down to New York to be at Suzo's real burial place. Everything for blocks was caked with a grey soot and ash. I walked alone through the streets surrounding the WTC, even though there were thousands of others doing the same thing. It was solemn. It was silent. There was no laughter. No shouting. No real noise. It was a funeral parade of desperate men, women, and children seeking an answer and a loved one. I, along with all the others, were walking and praying and thinking. People were showing their respect for those who had fallen in a war of terror we didn't even know we were fighting. At certain places there were notes hung to express sorrow. There were also the notes crying out to find someone lost in the rubble. I left no note. There was no hope for my Suzo to be found.

"I tried to remember our good times in the City. We lived there soon after we were married while going to grad school. The city-life was new to both of us; at the time we thought it was a dream come true. Later, living here in Boston and with our children going to college in New York, we would go to visit them as often as possible. We were always so proud of them.

"Suzo and I saw *Les Misérables* three times through the years and left with both tears and smiles each time. We were so moved by such a noble theme. Truly, to love another person is to see the face of God.

"I came home with my memories but I didn't come home with my

Suzo. I'll keep the memories close. I can't stop looking at our family photos. I appreciate all the love and support so many of you are giving to me and to my kids. We need that right now. We are hurting and we feel pretty helpless. We'll get stronger in time but we are quite weak right now. I can't look any more at the images of the crash into the towers. I only see and feel my wife being obliterated. It's all so very painful. As you can see, I have a lot to work through inside me.

"I remember Suzo's smiles that drew me to her when I was first getting to know her. She was a people person. She knew how to connect and how to stay connected to all kinds of people. No one was a stranger very long around Suzo. And she had so many friends. She liked to say she had three kinds of friends. Friends for a season, friends for a reason and friends for life. I'm glad to say I fit into her last category.

"She liked to give me a hard time about my driving, about not eating breakfast and for straightening pictures around the house. I'm going to miss all those little things. She was my friend and my lover. In fact, she was a great lover. I'll just leave it at that since there are kids in the audience, especially mine.

"She made everything feel special. I remember my fortieth birthday. She devised a plan so I would be surprised, which she said was hard to do with me. She got me up real early and told me there was a mouse in the basement. I came running down in my pajamas and was met with a loud 'Surprise' shout by thirty people in their pajamas, robes and slippers. She said she had seen something like this on an old rerun of *The Dick Van Dyke Show.* I was genuinely surprised. Maybe shocked would be a better word. She was a true memory-maker.

"She made me a better man through the years we had together. In fact she was a major part of my salvation from a deep-rooted anger against life. I was angry at everyone, including God. She calmed my pain stemming from the senseless loss of my parents in a car accident that occurred when I was young. I was out of control with alcohol and drugs in my teen years as I was trying to escape my pain. She made me strong. She had faith in me, faith in her children and faith in God. She was my rock. I will admit I am struggling now and in turmoil again as this new attack of loss and pain rips and explodes in the very core of my being.

"I wrote a song for our wedding and I want to share with you a portion of it. The words captured what I was thinking and feeling on that day and what I still feel today. The song was entitled, "Our Dream Will Last Forever."

> *As you were walking down the aisle*
> *You looked so beautiful.*
> *And now—*
> *Standing close to me*
> *White lace and satin*
> *You are all I see – You belong to me.*
>
> *Our dream will last forever*
> *For our words are always true,*
> *Our dream will last forever*
> *For our lives have been made new.*
> *Our dream will last forever*
> *By making one from two,*
> *Our dream will last forever*
> *'Cause I'm in love with you.*

"For Suzo and me, our forever wasn't long enough but she was certainly my dream come true. And so, Suzo, I just want to say to you again ... I'm in love with you."

There was silence and quiet tears as TJ sat back down. Following TJ were his kids, who shared about their mom and some of their best memories. It was touching and it helped to bring some closure to a chapter in a life that could never be re-opened. They did the drive to the cemetery where there was no casket, but just a simple headstone. There was a little talk and prayer by the minister. Then they went home.

After hours of food, drinks, and well-meaning talk, TJ, E, and Sky were left alone in their home. They were completely exhausted. Exhausted physically. Exhausted emotionally. Exhausted spiritually. Their belief system was being challenged by a tsunami of emotion brought on by the devastation of their tragic and unexpected loss.

After many years of control, TJ's anger was starting to get the best of him again. He kept yelling at his kids as they were helping to clean up. Sky and E were shocked and hurt at this unusual behavior from their dad. They decided to give him some space so they hugged each other tightly and went to their separate bedrooms. They closed their doors and closed their eyes. TJ grabbed the bottle of Macallan single malt Scotch Whisky that had been a gift from a well-wisher. He proceeded to his bedroom where he slammed the door, drank half the bottle and then closed his eyes. TJ never wanted to open them again.

# CHAPTER 9

TJ got up very late and very slowly the next day. His head was pounding. He was hung over, angry at the world and feeling numb all at the same time. Sky and E were getting ready to drive back to school in the City.

"Are you heading back already?" TJ asked his kids.

"Yeah, we talked about it this morning. We think it's best since we've already been gone a week. It's going to be an incredibly difficult time no matter where we're located. At least we'll have each other," replied Sky.

"But a few more days of rest and being all together may be best for both of you," said TJ.

"I think you need some time to be alone, Dad, so you can process and deal with everything that's happened. It's not going to be easy for any of us but Mom wouldn't want us to stop living our lives," Ethan said with a sad tone.

"Besides, you're getting really mad at us for no good reason. I don't need that on top of what's already happened," said Sky.

"Well, I'm really sorry about that. I don't mean to take it out on you guys," said TJ, hugging his kids.

TJ got a little something to eat. The kids finished packing and loaded the car. They all hugged and said their good-byes. TJ stared down the road long after the car was gone. He finally went back inside the house.

TJ was trying to figure out his next step. He had been given some information from American Airlines about a grief support group. He thought this would be the thing to do. He also decided to do some writing in what he would call his Suzo Journal.

# JOURNAL ENTRY
## September 22, 2001

Dear Suzo:

 I've decided to take a sabbatical hoping that will give me the space I need right now. I'm trying to make sense of all that's happened to you, to me, to us. I find it hard to do. Please listen to my thoughts for a few moments. Some of them may just be rambling words but I need somebody to listen to me. I wish you were here beside me to help me think through everything. I wish you were here beside me to help me know how to feel and what direction to take.

 In nature, a cycle of life is completed every 365 days. In any given year there are four distinct seasons. In people, there are also cycles of life. People arbitrarily mark the events of their lives in years — when I was fifteen or when I was forty, such and such occurred. Then there are our seasons in life. They are not as clearly marked in time. There may be a season of grief, a season of fear, a season of sadness, a season of bad health, a season of joy, a season of satisfaction, a season of success, a season of failure, etc. And every life season or cycle carries with it certain emotions. Some more than others.

 So much happens to each individual in each year of life. At the end of every cycle is a crystallizing of the strongest emotions in the heart and psyche of a person. That becomes who that person is on the inside. That's the real person. How an individual processes their emotions determines the outcome of their lives. People can't stop emotions, but they can decide what direction to go with them. The emotions either become a positive force or a negative force. In life, we tend to reinforce the good feelings and downplay the bad ones. The pictures we take are of good times and happy times — on vacations, family reunions, at Thanksgiving and Christmas times. We don't stop in the middle of a painful event and say, "It's a Kodak moment. Let me capture your tears on camera so I can remember this sad or bad time." This just doesn't happen. And overall, that's a good thing. But what if a person's thinking and emotions are out of control and are only reinforcing the bad to the point of not being able to see the good?

In any individual, cycles and seasons of life just keep coming even when a time-out is needed. An individual may have just come through a season of explosive pain but regardless of the content of any given season in any given life there's always another season and cycle that follows. If there is a failure to deal successfully with enough seasons, people go into emotional overload. Then they either shut down or explode. Either way, they're broken. That's when people can get desperate and stupid.

With each cycle of life, a person has the freedom to make good choices or bad choices. Depending on the decisions made, a range of results are produced, from a living dream to a living hell.

Suzo, I'm feeling so much pain right now. I'm angry. I'm not seeing a whole lot of good in anything. I know I've got to keep moving forward and try to get to a positive place. I know I have to get better or I'll end up bitter. One thing I'm sure about is that I don't want a 'living hell' or even a 'just getting through life' kind of existence. Like you told me many times — 'Life isn't easy, TJ.'

So what am I supposed to do now? I can't just go back to living my old life. I can't just get up and go to work. I don't feel like dealing with people. I don't feel like teaching. I don't feel like eating. I certainly don't feel like joining the leaf peepers for some kind of reflection with nature. I don't even feel like getting out of bed. Right now, life sucks!

I never thought I would have to do life without you.

All my love, all the time —

TJ

# Part Two

# SUICIDE IS PAINLESS

# CHAPTER 10

T.S. Elliot, a product of Harvard University, wrote the famous line in his Wasteland poem that April is the cruelest month. But, April is not the cruelest month if you live in New England. There are many cruel months. November with its below-freezing temperatures, grey clouds, cold rains and occasional snow storms start to bring on the Seasonal Affective Disorder, or SAD, for many. For TJ, his depression had little to do with the weather. With the loss of Suzanne came the old nightmares of the loss of his parents. So much pain had come alive all over again. All he wanted to do was to deaden the pain that kept erupting. He moved out of his Lexington house and locked it up tight. Without looking back, he settled in the rental property he and Suzanne had invested in back when prices were reasonable. He took only one suitcase of personal belongings and his favorite guitar. The furnished apartment was between tenants at the time, so there was no problem moving in. The property was in the small but famous North End neighborhood of Boston. With people living in this space since the 1630's, it was Boston's oldest residential area. And for the true foodie, this was the go-to place for real Italian food and atmosphere.

The apartment was a two-bedroom place on the top floor of a well-kept building. It was near 193 Salem Street, the address of the Old North Church. This was the church with its high, white steeple from which the famous "one if by land, two if by sea" signal was sent. It was a message to Paul Revere for his midnight ride of April 18, 1775. A great feature and a main selling point of TJ's apartment was the fact that it had a private rooftop deck. From the deck a person could see the confluence of the Mystic and Charles Rivers that emptied into the Boston Harbor. For TJ, the best part about the apartment presently was that the memory of Suzanne was not found in any room, closet, clothing, or picture.

For weeks, TJ could not find much strength to even do the basics of life. He ate very little. He drank alcohol and smoked pot excessively. He didn't answer his phone. He spoke few words to his kids or to friends. He found himself at a place he had thought he'd left behind many years earlier but now seemed to be an even darker, deeper hole. He hadn't been tempted with cutting or doing drugs for so many years and yet he now found that pull almost compelling. Cutting, or deliberate self-injury, had been a way for him to cope with the emotional pain and intense anger from losing his parents in a senseless accident. Although he only cut his unseen inner thighs a few times, it had brought a momentary sense of calm and a release of tension. Unfortunately it was followed by a lot of guilt and shame and the return of his painful emotions. Still, it helped for the moment. That moment was again becoming a greater and greater temptation for TJ even as he knew it made no sense at all. On top of this, the old desire for some stronger numbing drugs was nagging at him. This was also something from his teen years that he thought had been completely eradicated.

There had been three key life-enlightening events in TJ's teen years. The first was his cancer. That was huge. The second was when he had attacked another teen guy in the high school hallway after thinking he had hit on a girl TJ liked. In reality, the other kid had just been asking questions of the girl about a homework assignment. The attacked boy, Christopher Thompson, ended up in the hospital with a broken nose, three broken teeth and a dangerously swollen eye. He was out of school for a month and needed surgery on his nose and dental procedures to repair his teeth. Many, including the police, wanted the 17-year-old TJ to be charged as an adult with assault and battery, especially since he already had a record of angry interactions and fights. Ultimately that decision would be up to the teen boy and his parents. But instead of a police report and an arrest, TJ and his grandparents were invited to the boy's home to talk.

After some uncomfortable conversation about the incident between everyone, Christopher spoke up and said, "I completely forgive you, TJ, and I want us to be friends and to be comfortable around each other."

This blew TJ's mind. He did manage to get out a rather weak, but honest, apology. As a follow-up to this meeting, TJ's granddad wrote a note to the family saying, "We never expected the extreme showing of grace that you offered us. People like you are so very rare. Although I most certainly wish that we had met under extremely different circumstances, I must admit that I really feel that there is a reason why this happened and why you were put in our lives."

Later, this forgiveness thing made TJ do some deep soul searching about the many things his grandfather had been trying to teach him for years from the Bible. This one incident cemented the teachings as real and needed instead of outdated and immaterial.

The third life-enlightening event was his relationship with Suzanne. True love had a way of completing TJ's healing, or so he thought for many years. He had no way of knowing that his overall emotional health and stability would be flawed and superficial when it was challenged with another senseless and tragic loss.

On the night of November 7, TJ tuned into the Country Music Association's Annual Award Show thinking this would take his mind away to a better place for at least a little while. As TJ sat with his seventh beer of the day in hand, Alan Jackson took the stage and said he had recently written a song he would like to share with America. It was a different song from the one scheduled. It would be the first time it was publicly performed. Alan Jackson started singing, "Where were you when the world stopped turning on that September day?..." Almost immediately tears started flowing from TJ's eyes. His pain hit a crescendo as the song ended. TJ emotionally crashed all over again.

———————————

In the morning, after a night of anger, frustration, liquor and weed, TJ stumbled around and looked up the details about the offering of a grief support group he had learned about seven weeks earlier. He had not taken advantage of it yet. He found the information and decided to attend. He knew he needed something.

# CHAPTER
## 11

TJ made his way slowly into the room for the grief support group that was to begin in ten minutes. There were twelve people in a circle of fifteen chairs chatting with each other. They obviously already knew one another. TJ was the new guy and as the new guy he felt a little uncomfortable. He took a seat and proceeded to introduce himself to the people on either side of him. Soon, the leader of the group arrived and introduced himself as Dr. Jack Simmons. He said he was a trained professional in grief and loss who had been hired by American Airlines for the second and final five-week session to help with the tragic loss of loved ones on 9/11. He was also the author of the best seller, *The Journey Back From Loss.*

Dr. Simmons asked everyone to introduce themselves and to share about the loved one or loved ones who had been so tragically lost. Most had lost their spouse or their significant other. A few had lost a sibling or mother or father. And one had lost both his wife and his daughter. That person, a Boston Police Deputy Superintendent, looked a little familiar to TJ but he couldn't quite place how he might know him. When it was TJ's turn to talk, he had a flood of memories streaming through his mind as he shared about Suzanne.

"Suzanne, or Suzo, was my wife. Suzo was my rock. Suzo was my best friend. Suzo was my everything in every way," said TJ with stifled and, at the same time, obvious emotion.

"Thank-you for everyone sharing," said Dr. Simmons looking in TJ's direction who was the last person to share. "And now, let me explain how we are to go together on this mourning journey. I will start with a short lesson each week, giving you some helpful information and then we will have time for sharing with each other. I hope you will feel free to be open about how you are doing on your personal journey back from loss. My hope is that shared pain will bring shared healing. Always know that you are not alone in your grief and that grief serves to help us accept the loss. It's a painful process of accepting and adapting to life without that special person or persons. Also remember that death and dying experiences are common to all of mankind. The therapeutic purpose of grief and mourning is to get you to the point where you can live with the loss healthily. Not everyone's personal path will look the same. You'll have to figure out for yourself what will be most helpful for you. Some may find music to be helpful. Others may find long walks in nature to be good for them. Or, it could be going back to special places or looking at photo albums or starting a journal. Still others may want to find a friend with whom they can deeply share their thoughts and emotions. In the end, whatever helps you move along on your mourning journey is a good and positive thing."

He continued to talk about and describe the intense feelings, emotions and thinking patterns of grief. He shared about normal grief behaviors a person experiences when they have had a loss affecting them psychologically, physically, socially, and spiritually. There could be sadness, fear, anxiety, anger, guilt, self-reproach, loneliness, fatigue, numbness or confusion. A person could feel a hollowness in the stomach, a lump in the throat, tightness in the chest, aching arms, oversensitivity to noise, a lack of energy, apathy, crying, or enduring sleep difficulties. A person could find themselves withdrawing, having difficulty with interpersonal relationships, having a lack of motivation, having problems functioning on the job or being easily irritated by others. On a spiritual basis, he explained, it could lead a person to search for a sense of meaning, having hostility toward God, questioning God or feeling an inadequacy in their value system.

TJ was thinking that this guy really knew his stuff. It wasn't like TJ didn't know this information; it was just so different being on the other side of it. Dr. Simmons' words opened up the hearts and voices of most of the group as they shared what they were experiencing and feeling. It was actually helpful to TJ to be assured that he was not alone and that others were going through similar thoughts and feelings. He did note that his were more intense and desperate and destructive than what others had shared. TJ did not open his mouth in the group but listened carefully and eagerly.

At the end of the group he talked with a few of the men and got their phone numbers. In the midst of these conversations he felt bonded with them and so started thinking about asking them over sometime for a night of poker, pizza, and beers.

# CHAPTER
## 12

It was a beautiful 73-degree sunny afternoon as the plane landed. This was a big difference from the New England weather the monster had left a few hours earlier. The monster arrived at the Orlando International Airport, rented a car and proceeded to drive 19 miles to the small town of Windermere. This was presently the home to many well-known personalities, including Tiger Woods, Phil Mickelson, Shaquille O'Neil and Johnny Damon. The monster checked into a hotel and waited until the cover of darkness.

So much was happening in the mind and the emotions of the monster. The thing it wanted to do most was to alleviate its pain. Coming to Florida again was all part of its plan. After the monster's wife committed suicide, the monster found a stash of secret diaries and pictures she had been keeping. What it found out broke the monster's heart into tiny pieces over and over again.

She was a little younger than the monster. They met when she attended Tufts University for her Masters work soon after completing her undergraduate degree at the University of Florida in 1975. The monster thought her an Italian beauty in every way. She was smart. She was usually thoughtful and quiet but could be outgoing and loud in the right crowd. She always had something going on inside her head that made her strong at times and fragile at other times. With her olive complexion, big blue eyes, long, black, silky hair and a nicely shaped body, the monster's attraction to her was immediate. Her name was Leah D'Angelo.

Driving to a particular house located on Main Street, the monster was enjoying the quiet after-midnight hours. The front of the house was facing Lake Butler, part of the Butler Chain of Lakes composed of thirteen lakes that flowed South, eventually reaching Lake Okeechobee and then the Everglades. The monster proceeded to cut the glass of a large sliding door and move cautiously through the house. This time it had to deal with a wife who was in the den watching TV at this unusual hour. She quickly decided to quietly cooperate fully as a knife was held to her throat and a chloroform-soaked cloth coved her mouth. The monster blindfolded, gagged and immobilized her with duct tape. This was all accomplished without her ever laying eyes on the monster. It then proceeded to the master bedroom located on the other side of the house. It found Troy Wilson sleeping like a baby. The monster knocked him out with another chloroform-soaked cloth, removed his bed clothes and tied him up with rope and duct tape.

"What the hell do you think you're doing?'" the terrified Troy screamed when he woke up.

"I'm dealing with my pain, so just shut your mouth, or better yet, I'll shut it for you," said the monster as it placed duct tape over Troy's mouth.

"I want you to know that it was me that visited your old frat brother, Joe. We had a wonderful time together. I hope you heard about what happened to him because that would give you a good idea of what's coming next for you."

Troy was shivering with fear and trying his best to struggle against the rigid tape. The monster started the IV drip and numbed up both feet with lidocaine shots. Then with a smile on its face, it took out the bypass pruner.

"Hey Troy, do you remember the meaning of THC? Bet you do. And, bet you got really high on it! How about the significance of the number ten? Let's play a little game while you give that some thought. I hope you don't mind if I borrow a little from Agatha Christie.

"Ten little gators went out to dine, one choked on a cherry and then there were nine. *Clip.*

"Nine little gators swingin' on a gate, one tumbled off and then there were eight. *Clip.*

"Eight little gators happy under heav'n, one went to sleep forever and then there were seven. *Clip.*

"Seven little gators chopping up sticks, one chopped herself in half and then there were six. *Clip.*

"Six little gators all alive, one kicked the bucket and then there were five. *Clip.*

"Five little gators by a frat door, one got pushed in and then there were four. *Clip.*

"Four little gators going on a spree, one hanged herself and then there were three. *Clip.*

"Three little gators out on a canoe, one tumbled overboard and then there were two. *Clip.*

"Two little gators foolin' with a gun, one shot the other and then there was one. *Clip.*

"One little gator left all alone, she overdosed and then there was none." *Clip.*

The monster placed the ten toes in the plastic bag and held them up in front of Troy's face. Troy's eyes got watery and his breathing became erratic. The monster collected its paraphernalia from the room and put it all in its backpack, not noticing the small object that fell out during this process.

"Well, I guess this is good-bye, Troy. And when I say good-bye I mean FOREVER!" said the monster.

The monster left the house and walked to its car which was parked a distance away. It drove back to its hotel and enjoyed an undisturbed and satisfied sleep.

---

All Troy could hear was the dripping of his blood as the beige wall-to-wall carpet was turning red.

Drip. Drip. Drip. Drip. Drip....

# CHAPTER
## 13

The first to arrive at TJ's apartment from the grief group for the initial poker night was Chip Thompson, the Boston Police Deputy Superintendent of the Criminal Investigative Division, which oversaw all investigations including homicides. He was the one who had lost both his wife and his daughter on 9/11. He had looked somewhat familiar to TJ at the first grief group meeting but he couldn't quite place him. After the third meeting, Chip, in the midst of all that was bad and sad, thought he would have a little fun with TJ.

"Excuse me, Dr. Maverick. Could I have a private word or two with you?" asked Chip.

"Sure, no problem. What's up?" replied TJ as they moved out to the hallway to a secluded area.

"Please put one hand on the wall and one hand behind your back. No sudden movements please. Now let me have your other hand so I can cuff it also and be sure to move it down slowly. I am arresting you for assault and battery. You have the right to remain silent. Anything you say can be used against you in court. You have the right to talk to a lawyer for advice before we ask you any questions. You have the right to have a lawyer with you during questioning..."

"Hey, what's this all about ... STOP THIS NOW! ... I haven't done anything wrong," insisted TJ.

"If you cannot afford a lawyer, one will be appointed for you before any questioning if you wish. If you decide to answer questions now without a lawyer present...."

"Okay, I know the spiel. I've watched *Law and Order*. What gives?" asked TJ.

"If you decide to answer questions now without a lawyer present, you have the right to stop answering at any time. Do you understand what I've just said to you?" said Chip.

"Yeah, yeah. I understand. Assault and battery? What are you talking about? I haven't done that!" insisted TJ.

"Oh yes you have. There are many witnesses to what you've done... to ME!" said Chip breaking out in a big smile and a big laugh.

It finally dawned on TJ that this was the kid he had beaten up back in high school. He went by Christopher back then and he looked different now. He had lost his hair, was wearing glasses and he had beefed up considerably. He also had a different first name that he had acquired. The nickname of "Chip" was given to him by a group of college buddies who thought he had a bit of a *chip on his shoulder*, since he was always willing to get into verbal fights over politics. The name just stuck.

"Just having a little fun with you, my friend," said Chip.

"Well, I have to admit you had me going there for a minute. Can you take the handcuffs off me now? But, before you do let me say that I'm sincerely sorry for what I did to you and I want you to know that your forgiveness and mercy impacted my life and helped me move forward in a positive way. So, thank-you and please forgive me," TJ said.

"Those words mean a lot. Thanks! Know you have been completely forgiven for all these years. But about those handcuffs, I just don't know. They look real good on you," said Chip as he was laughing so hard that tears were forming in his eyes.

After this interaction, they gave each other a big man-hug as they enjoyed the moment, remembered the past and felt the pain each was dealing with in the present. A special bond of friendship had begun.

The second to arrive was Darius Mitchell. He was the FBI Special Agent who oversaw Boston's field office, which was one of fifty-six such field offices in the United States and Puerto Rico. Darius and his division covered the states of Maine, Vermont, Massachusetts, New Hampshire, and Rhode Island. His wife had been aboard Flight 11 as she was flying to LA to care for her mother who was to undergo open-heart surgery. Darius was a tall, imposing figure — an African American who had played football for U Mass Amherst. He was their star tight end until he blew out his knee in his junior year.

The final two arrived at TJ's door at the same time. They were Marco Mancini, the Metro Editor for the Boston Globe, and Dr. Frank Spear, a retired cardiac surgeon who had been affiliated with Massachusetts General Hospital. These men had also lost their wives in the crash.

"Well, everyone is here and so I want to officially welcome you to my humble abode. We are here to eat, drink, and play cards. That's it. We are not here for a grief therapy session although our shared pain has brought us together," said TJ.

"So where's the promised food and drinks?" asked Darius.

"Hold your horses, everybody. The best pizza in the North End, from Galleria Umberto's, will arrive soon. While we're waiting, there's plenty of Sam Adams and Corona in the fridge so just help yourselves. And for dessert, the cannoli of your choice from Mike's Pastry. If you've never had them then you've never had a real cannoli. Best in or out of Italy. And I've got a great selection: plain ricotta cheese, chocolate ricotta, Oreo, limoncello and strawberry. So, let's have a wicked good night together," said TJ with a smile.

The group all got some beers and started to get to know each other better as they were now in a social setting instead of the grief group setting. The pizzas arrived and it was like a horde of swarming locusts ascending on them. The small group bonded quickly and easily, enjoying the food, the laughter and camaraderie. The ten-dollar buy-in for the poker chips meant it was just a fun way to spend an evening playing Texas Hold'em instead of being a serious, high-stakes game. Between the blinds, bluffs, boats, broadways and bullets, it was a brief space in time when life seemed normal again.

As everyone was leaving to make their way home, the five made a pact to do this together on a regular basis. After all, it had been their most helpful therapy session to date.

The last to leave was Chip. He turned to TJ and said, "I'm going to start calling you Maverick or maybe just Mav. Besides thinking it's a cooler name than TJ, I like the idea of starting fresh with you. A new name makes it feel that way. And as the name implies, be a person who blazes their own trail. I also wanted to point out that you don't look too good without the sleep and the food you need. On top of that, I noticed all the different bottles of booze around the place and you can't completely hide the lingering pot odor. Those things can't be good for you. You've got to do what I've got to do. You need to find a way to not be defined by the pain of your loss. You've got to find a way that moves and motivates you forward because of your pain and because of your loss. And one more thing about the new name, Mav. It was the call name for Cruise in *Top Gun.* He came back strong after losing his best friend, Goose, and so it could inspire you about being able to come back strong after losing Suzanne. I know it's just a movie and I know it's not exactly the same but we all need some inspiration, so watch the movie again."

With that said, Chip walked out and TJ shut the door. Before trying to get some sleep, TJ took out his *Suzo Journal* and began to write.

# JOURNAL ENTRY
## December 7, 2001

Dear Suzo:

It used to be I was sleeping all the time but lately it's been hard to stay asleep. It's probably going to be another sleepless night so I thought I'd spend some time talking to you instead of lying in bed with my eyes and mind wide open.

It's Pearl Harbor day today. It's a day of painful explosions like the explosions of pain I feel every day. Good news! I did just have a little respite tonight. I had a good Friday-night time with a few new friends playing cards but, I have to say, I now feel a little guilty. I feel bad about having had a good time without you. With that confession out of the way, I wanted to tell you a few more things that are going on in my head. I'm sure that not everything is correct in my thinking right now but here's where I'm at.

There are things a person can't forget — try as they will. There are some things a person can't forgive, or won't forgive. God has his unforgivable sin. Maybe each person has their own unforgivable sin, too. It's this particular sin committed against them that causes an emotional freeze or an emotional upheaval to occur. It's something that can't be moved past. Or, at least it's very difficult to move past.

In this world everyone gets emotionally messed up. The question is not if you're damaged but to what degree you're damaged. Some come through life better than others. It's usually those who are emotionally hurt later in life instead of early in life that come out less damaged. But no one gets through life unscarred. And when the damage to a person reaches a particular critical point, it can wreak havoc. Some lose it completely. They go off the deep-end and often take others with them. Others just slowly learn to cope. They adjust. And then there are those who deaden their pain with promiscuous sex, pornography, alcohol, drugs, sleep, or media. That's a solution but the cure can be worse than the disease. Eventually, all tend to alleviate their pain by closing themselves off from the source of their pain. The source is usually certain people, certain places, or certain situations.

And then there are those who have been hurt who become "blamers." They blame God or they blame others for their loss, for their pain or for their difficult life-situation. This leads to bitterness, which leads to unhappiness. It's good to note that people can bring pain on themselves stemming from their own actions and decisions. Learning to take personal responsibility is not an easy lesson but it is a necessary lesson to successfully move through life.

And so the truth is all people are emotional cripples to some degree, limping through life. Emotional upheaval has to do with a break of trust or an irreplaceable loss. We're wired this way. There's no escaping our genes. This is who we are. There are also many great actors or liars who have learned to walk, talk, and live in such a way as to hide their emotional limp. The problem is, we get fooled by those actors and so we think there's something abnormal about ourselves. But the truth is that walking with a limp, with pain, is normal in this life. It's normal for everyone.

Suzo, without you, I live in pain. Does it last a lifetime? Why did this have to happen? Why do bad things happen to good people? If God is in control then why do things go so wrong at times? Granddad taught me that God is a God of love, but I'm not feeling the love right now. Since you left me all I've wanted to do is to deaden the pain I feel. I've been doing it with a lot of sleep, pot, alcohol, and TV. I know that's not good. I was told by a guy tonight that I needed to learn how to move forward after the pain of my loss and that I needed to be motivated by the pain instead of being defined by the pain. That's easier said than done but I know it's true.

Well . . . I guess that's enough for now. I feel better being able to share my thoughts with you. Thanks for listening again. Goodnight, Suzo. I miss you more than words can say. I miss your laughter. I miss you kidding around with me. I miss you helping to organize my life. I miss your wisdom in so many of life's situations. I miss your helpful criticisms of me. I miss watching a movie with you. I miss eating popcorn with you. I miss talking with you about the kids and about the future. I miss your touch. I miss your body. I miss your love.

All my love, all the time —

TJ

# 1971

Leah D'Angelo arrived at the college town of Gainesville in early September. It was the home of the University of Florida. She arrived with many hopes, dreams, and a huge appetite to experience life. She wanted to figure out who she was and who she would become. She wanted to find herself. Leah was seventeen years old but would turn eighteen in just a few weeks so she felt like her whole life was ahead of her. She had long, straight, black hair that accentuated her five-foot, six-inch stature. She was athletic, one of the best long-distance runners for her high school in Winter Park, an affluent small city located next to Orlando. On her arrival day she wore short jean cut-offs, showing off her long legs, and a white peasant blouse with blue stitching. With an inner excitement that was about to explode, Leah almost ran to her new home, a small dorm room in East Hall. It was for women only and was located close to the football stadium.

She had been a "good" girl in high school. She respected and appreciated her parents and had a healthy desire of not wanting to disappoint them. Religious conversations among the family were only little snippets of information that could not ever be called detailed. And yet, Sunday church attendance had been expected. She had grown up hearing about needing to fear God and needing to say no to sex, drugs, alcohol, and smoking. She had managed to say no to all of these except an occasional drink at some of the parties. She was creative, intelligent, hard-driving, and full of excitement about her future college life. At the same time, she was somewhat insecure about how she looked, even though everyone said she was quite striking. She was not pleased with her body due to her small bust size, which was great for being a runner but not so great for attracting boys. She also was insecure because her face had some scarring from acne. These left her always comparing herself to the other girls around her. In her mind she usually came up wanting.

Before the first week of classes there was Rush Week with

the sororities and the fraternities. With a pleasing and outgoing personality Leah was given bids, or offers to join, from three sororities. She ended up choosing to become a part of the Delta Gamma girls. The sorority house was located on SW 13th Street and had a large white anchor near the front entrance. As a freshman she was required to live in the dorms but she would move into the sorority house in her sophomore year.

Her first days of classes were hectic and a little unsettling as she walked the sprawling campus trying to find her classes while dodging people and bicycles. She found it was complete bedlam at the Florida Book Store buying the needed books and supplies for all her classes. During the first week, she stepped out into the street, not seeing a biker coming down the road. She was almost knocked down as the boy on the bike valiantly tried to quickly maneuver out of her way. As he hit the brakes the bike skidded in some sand and brushed up against Leah. This left Leah standing in shock and the bike and the biker laying on the ground in pain.

As the boy picked himself up and rubbed his scraped and bloody knee he said, "Are you all right?"

"Yep ... I think so. I didn't see you coming — so sorry about that," said Leah.

"You must be a freshman. Bikes are a big deal around here so you've got to keep a lookout for them all the time. By the way, my name is Joe Hiller. What's yours?" asked the boy.

"I'm Leah. And yes, I'm a newbie here so I'm trying to learn my way around. I guess I'm not doing such a great job at it," said Leah.

"Don't worry about it. We all had to go through the same thing. I'm in my third year so I've learned the ropes. I live back there on Museum Road just before you get to Fraternity Drive, in the SAE House. It's the one with the Lion out front. I could help you get to really know the campus and have you meet some great people if you want. Let's exchange numbers and meet up sometime, okay?" asked Joe.

"Well ... sure. Why not?" Leah said with some hesitation as they scratched numbers on some paper and exchanged them.

---

October came quickly. Homecoming was a time to let go and enjoy life. The Gator Growl on Friday night was energizing and fun with the guest of honor being Pat O'Neal, a UF grad who had made it on Broadway, television, and the cinema. The parade was at noon on Saturday and it included the Gator Skydivers and the new Homecoming Sweetheart, Margaret Montgomery. This was special for Leah since Margaret was the president of her Delta Gamma sorority. She could say she knew Margaret.

The opening kickoff for the big game against Maryland was in the afternoon. The stands were packed, with loud cheers of a victory, with the record-setting John Reaves as quarterback. James Edmondson, the man known as Mr. Two Bits, moved among the crowd with his famous *two bits, four bits, six bits, a dollar, all for the Gators stand up and holler!* He began the cheer in 1949 at the season opener against The Citadel after the crowd had booed the players and the coach even before the kickoff. This was because the Gators had lost the last five of six games in the previous season and were not expected to do any better in their new season. James took it upon himself to try and turn the morale around and got up and led the fans in a cheer about adding up bits. The Gators won the game and the tradition was born. As the fourth quarter ended at the 1971 Florida Homecoming game, the crowd went absolutely crazy: Florida, 27; Maryland, 23. It was time to party!

Leah had become friends with her hit-n-meet biker, Joe. They had often hung out together over the past five weeks. More than once, Joe had pushed her to have sex with him but she had pushed back on that idea. Still, she liked the attention and the thought of sex was very much on Leah's mind. She had turned eighteen and was asking herself if it was time to fully become a woman.

*Would it be so bad if my first time having sex was just with a good friend? I'm not madly in love with Joe but he seems to be a nice guy. What's it going to be like? It could be the best night of my life!* These thoughts were racing through Leah's head while holding Joe's hand trying to get through the crowd of happy UF students all trying to leave the stadium at the same time.

---

The night was wild and crazy all around campus. The streakers were out doing their thing. The Homecoming Dance was a packed gathering on the north lawn of the Reitz Union. The band *Weston Prim,* was playing loud and long. The frats had their own parties going on and going strong. The alcohol was flowing and the sweet scent of marijuana was in the air. Music was playing and everywhere there was dancing, with smiles and sweat.

Joe brought Leah to his frat house to celebrate UF's victory, although the party would have been happening even with a terrible loss. Leo the Lion sat in front of the house and had been painted orange and blue — the official colors of UF. The tradition was to paint Leo for special occasions like Homecoming, the 4th of July, special philanthropy events, or a sorority's color when they were paired up for an activity. There were many rumors floating around campus concerning Leo the Lion. Older frat brothers said it was to be used as a way to discipline new pledges by having them sit on it for hours in the hot sun. It was also rumored that it would change colors when a brother took a girl's virginity. The lion would end up the color of the girl's underwear. These were just rumors, though, like the one that said if you graduated from UF a virgin, a brick would fall out of Century Tower.

Joe got a beer for himself and Leah. It was the first of many during the evening. Leah was letting herself go on this Homecoming night. When they weren't engaging with random people in the crowd, they hung out around Joe's best friends, Troy and Pete. After a few hours of talking, dancing, and drinking Leah wanted to go home and get some rest but Joe insisted they have one more drink and a couple more dances together.

"Okay, but just bring me a Coke and I'll stay for a couple more dance numbers. I'm really tired from the day. I got up early to run this morning and I'm feeling it big time especially with all the alcohol I've consumed. I know I've had way too much! It's been great being with you but I just need to crash," explained Leah.

"Sounds like a plan. I'll be right back with the drinks but you're going to go with some rum and Coke," said Joe.

After gulping down her drink and spending more time on the dance floor, Leah was feeling funny. She was light-headed and not feeling in control. For some reason all she could think about was a line from the poem, *The Love Song of J. Alfred Prufrock,* that she was studying in her English class. She kept thinking the words *like a patient etherized upon a table ... like a patient etherized upon a table ... like a patient etherized upon a table.* Leah felt drowsy and confused yet with a sense of freedom.

"Leah, don't worry. I'll let you lie down for a few minutes up in my room. You'll feel better in no time," assured Joe.

"Sure. That would be nice of you," Leah said, slurring her words a bit.

Then Joe called through the crowd, "Hey Pete. Find Troy. It's THC time!"

Everyone around who heard this thought the little group was going upstairs to get high when they heard THC, short for Tetrahydrocannabinol, the principle psychoactive constituent of cannabis. Only Joe, Troy, and Pete knew exactly what it really meant. A few others who had found out some of the real meaning were told to keep their mouths shut ... or else!

"Open the door and get her in quick. I'm the one who's been setting her up for this so I'm first. Everyone good with that?" asked Joe.

"Hey dude, she's your catch. You did the hunting so you get the trophy. So you think she's really a virgin?" said Troy.

"No doubt in my mind from all she has said and not said to me. Every time I tried to touch her she pushed me off so I'm thinking the cherry's going to pop tonight," said Joe with a leer.

The three boys proceeded to remove Leah's clothes while noting she was wearing red underwear. By this time Leah had only slurred speech and her mental function was greatly impaired so she couldn't fight the boys off. Soon she was able to observe what was happening but was completely unable to move. Each one took their turn, starting with Joe, as the other two watched. The watchers were ready to keep her quiet if necessary although the loud party music was drowning out most of the sound.

After all the boys had finished with Leah they sat around for a while making rude, crude, and lewd comments about her. Having been motivated by lust, aggression, and a desire for power and control, they had no genuine feelings or concern for the girl. She was just there to be used and abused by them. The boys were full of themselves and full of liquor as they celebrated and high-fived each other.

Then Pete exclaimed, "Well that was an unexpected awesome event for Homecoming! And Joe, you racked up some digits."

"Yep. So be sure to add ten to my overall score. Now we've got to get her dressed and out of here. We'll dump her somewhere around her dorm area. There's that grassy area between the dorm buildings they call The Beach that could work. People will think she's just had too much to drink. Someone will find her and help her to her room. She'll sleep it off and be confused but, most importantly, she should completely forget about everything. The night will be a total blur for her. That Rohypnol stuff I put in her drink works great every time," said Joe with a sly smile.

———————————

The next day Leah's bed was spotted in red and the lion was anonymously splashed with a heavy dose of new paint ... red.

# CHAPTER
## 14

The monster was at home trying to figure out its next step to alleviate the pain that kept surfacing and exploding. After the suicide death of its wife, Leah, it read and reread the diary books it had found. She had been writing entries in these since her high-school days. After many years with Leah, the monster was only now getting to fully know her. After all, a person becomes who they are through the experiences they have had. If a person never shares what they have been through, both the good and the bad, then that person can never really be fully known. It wasn't until the eve of their twenty-fifth wedding anniversary that Leah spoke truthfully about the traumatic episodes that had damaged her. She told about how she had been abused and how she had responded to that abuse. This had only been done in a broad-stroke kind of way but now with the diaries the monster had detailed situations and feelings, precise locations and dates, specific names — and photographs.

These previously unknown diaries and photos had been hidden in a plastic storage box carefully placed at the back of her closet under other plastic containers that were filled with clothes and keepsakes. After she died, the monster went through all of Leah's things, trying to hang on to her in every way possible. When it came to certain parts of what she had written in her diaries, the monster was enraged.

> *On Homecoming night I was raped. I had sex for the first time and it was not with me saying "Yes." In fact, I don't know what I said. I can't really remember any details. I know I went to the Homecoming parade and game. I know I was with my friend, Joe. I know we went to his SAE frat house party. But after that I only have a clear memory of waking up in my bed the next morning feeling miserable and seeing some blood on the sheets. I don't really know how I got there. My roommate said she saw me laying out on the grass between the dorm buildings when she was coming in and that I was completely wrecked. She said I smelled of alcohol, cigarette smoke, and pot. She also said that my clothes were very disheveled. She told me she got another girl to help me get to my room and into my bed. I don't remember any of that. Joe says he lost track of me at the crowded party. Pete says he saw me heading out the door sometime after midnight thinking I was tired and going home. I do remember wanting to go back to my dorm room. Joe said he was pretty much out of it as it got later into the night. He said he was totally wasted when the party ended somewhere around 2 a.m. I feel guilty. I must have done something wrong which caused this. I must have somehow brought this on myself. Maybe if I hadn't been drinking so much or maybe if I hadn't been wearing that really short skirt. Someone must have gotten me as I was coming back. Or, maybe when I was alone in the darkness laying in the grass. I feel like I'm a bad person. I know my parents would be mortified to hear about this. I feel so much shame and guilt right now. I'm not going to tell anyone about this ... NEVER EVER!*

The monster had always known there were things that made his wife emotionally fragile, but it was shocking when it first learned of the horrible violations Leah had encountered. The monster knew it didn't have a full picture of her life during the years they were together because it had only received certain truths about Leah's life history on the installment plan ... truth revealed a little at a time. In stressful situations a truth might leak out. There had been one particular occasion when a certain life-history truth came to light. When it happened, it was hurtful and damaging to the trust in their relationship. She hadn't been honest at all.

# CHAPTER
## 15

The evening drive from New York City to Boston was brutal. It was bumper to bumper traffic trying to get out of the city and then stop-and-go traffic up the I-95 corridor. There was also light snow flurries whipping around in the wind with strong gusts of below-freezing air. It was not a pleasant drive for Skylar and Ethan.

"So how's it going to work this time with us going home? Thanksgiving time was rough to say the least," said Ethan.

"I don't really know. Obviously Dad's world is completely shaken. You know he's drinking and smoking and sleeping a lot. He's like a different person from what I've ever known him to be. He's still hurting bad but so are we," said Sky.

"Yeah, I know. I'm not sure how to help him. It's like I think he should be helping us more with it all but here we are needing to help him. Is that right?" asked Ethan.

"I don't know what's right anymore about this whole mess. Sometimes I cry. Sometimes I study and study and then study some more just to keep my mind occupied. Sometimes I almost forget it all really happened."

"Same here," said Ethan.

"Mom's gone and she's never coming back. Nothing will ever be the same and that makes it all freaking bad!" said Sky with a loud voice.

Sky and E were quiet after that for much of the drive. Both were tired from exams. Both were looking forward to seeing their dad. And, both were apprehensive about seeing their dad. They needed a helpful and positive Christmas break.

Arriving at the North End apartment, they parked the car, unloaded the suitcases, took the elevator and made their way to the door. TJ was waiting with open arms, a big smile and a big hug for his kids.

"So glad we get to spend Christmas and New Year's together. I've missed you two so much and I think this time together can be good for all of us. Love you both so much!" said TJ.

"Great to be home with you," said Sky and E in unison.

"So don't completely unpack. Tomorrow we're taking the ferry over to Nantucket. A new friend, who is a retired cardiac surgeon, has given us the Christmas present of using his beautiful vacation home for a few days. It's going to be cold and windy but we'll have a fire going 24/7. There's some great restaurants he has recommended for us. The beach is just a block from the house so we can have some good walks and talks together. He told me there are plenty of good books on the shelves and many fun games to play. It will be a new place for some new memories together. How does that sound to you?" asked TJ.

"Wow! I was not expecting this. But it sounds good to me. What do you think, Sky?" said Ethan.

"Well, as long as we can go back to our real home sometime during our visit. I want to feel as close to Mom as possible. There are so many memories back in the Lexington house for me," stated Sky.

"Sure. Whatever you both want to do. I'm sure you'll want to hang with some of your old friends at times also," said TJ.

TJ was putting on his best face for his kids. He was trying hard to make this first Christmas without Suzanne as good as possible for himself, for Sky and for Ethan. He hired people to clean the apartment, got rid of the pot, and put the alcohol at the back of the upper cupboards. He even decorated a small Christmas tree to give it a holiday feel. He was not ready to move back into their home even for a few weeks. There was still too much pain associated with it for him.

For the holiday, TJ behaved himself and did his best to emotionally give to his children. They shared meals. They shared movies. They shared gifts. They shared memories. They shared laughter. They shared feelings. They shared each other with each other. On January 2, they all had a little reprieve from reality. It seemed like old times watching and rooting for the Gators, which had always been a family-favorite thing to do. Florida was in the BCS 2002 FedEx Orange Bowl with the ol' ball coach, Steve Spurrier, doing the thing he did best. Winning. Florida easily defeated the Maryland Terrapins, 56 to 23. Together they enjoyed their popcorn, pizza, and wings. They just didn't have the woman they all loved and needed. Still, all in all, it was the best possible Christmas and New Year's celebration they could produce, given the lingering sadness and grief from the loss of a mother and the loss of a soul mate.

They said their good-byes with long hugs.

---

The night after Sky and E left, TJ reached into the back of the upper cupboards and pulled out his bottles. He got hammered and stumbled off to bed.

# CHAPTER
## 16

"Hello Maverick, this is Chip. Hope you're feeling good and doing good today."

"Yeah, I'm good today. What's up?" said TJ

"Well, Darius and I would like to get together with you sometime for lunch. In fact today would work for both of us if you're up for it," said Chip.

"Sounds serious. You have second thoughts about arresting me?" laughed TJ.

"Nope. Nothing like that. Darius actually has a proposal for you to think about. I'm just coming along for the ride. So, could we meet at Legal Sea Food at Copley Place? Let's say at noon?" said Chip.

"Must be something really good or something really bad if we're going to a five-star restaurant like Legal's. It's the kind of place to either get engaged or get dumped thinking delicious food makes the good news taste better or good food makes the bad news go down easier. Also having a crowd around either adds to the celebration feel or lessens any possible negative emotional outburst. You know, we coulda just gotten some grinders and frappes, but Legal's it is. See you at noon," replied TJ.

"Hey, don't worry. It's all good. Trust me. See you there, Mav," said Chip.

It was already ten in the morning and TJ had just rolled out of bed a few minutes before the telephone rang. He was still taking a break from doing much of anything. He was on his supposed sabbatical, although he wasn't getting any writing or research done. He had just experienced another rough night but he didn't want to mention that on the call with Chip. The poker group met together a few times over the past month and a half and the friendships were deepening. Trust was being built between the different personalities. Everyone in the group had started following Chip's lead calling TJ "Maverick" or just Mav. TJ didn't mind it. The New Year had been rung in but TJ wasn't feeling very new. He wasn't having a lot of success moving forward in a positive way from Suzanne's death.

# CHAPTER
# 17

"Thanks for meeting us, Mav," said Chip cheerfully.

"Hey, no problem. You can take me out to Legal's anytime you feel the urge," said TJ.

"I appreciate Chip making the phone call to you as I was in meetings all morning. And thanks for being able to make it on a moment's notice, Mav. But who said we were paying for your meal?" asked Darius with a big smile.

The restaurant was starting to fill up with the lunch crowd. The pleasing smell of fresh seafood filled the air. They were seated next to a large floor-to-ceiling window looking out to the Back Bay district. A bitter cold wind was blowing through the streets of Boston at the end of January. TJ could see people wrapped up in scarves, hats, gloves, and heavy winter coats. Some had Patriots, Red Sox, Bruins, or Celtics gear as part of their ensemble. They were moving fast, trying to get into the warmth. The warmth was found in maze-like, multi-use developments connected by glass-enclosed pedestrian bridges and walkways. These kept people out of the winter cold or out of the summer heat. The Prudential Shopping Center, the Copley Place Shopping Center, the Hynes Convention Center, along with the Marriot and the Sheraton hotels with all their extensive spaces and ballrooms were all connected. There were some smaller boutique hotels in this maze as well, along with an abundance of all kinds of eating establishments. And, the fifty-two story Prudential Tower, known as the Pru, was also a part of this ingenious web. It stood as the tallest building in Boston, at 907 feet, including its radio mast. Another tower was under construction but it would be much shorter. And to make it an easy in-and-out, there were underground MBTA or "T" stations connecting to the massive complex of buildings above them.

TJ was reminded of bringing in the new millennium on New Year's Eve just two years earlier by dining with Suzo on the top-floor restaurant of the Prudential Tower known as the Top of the Hub. They had an unmatched panoramic view of the city's skyline, delectable food along with exceptional live entertainment, and a dazzling fireworks display in the harbor as the clock struck twelve. TJ was thinking that it certainly lived up to its reputation of being Boston's most romantic dining experience. But more than that, he was thinking that Suzo had looked so elegant and so radiant and so ready to live life for the next thousand years.

"Excuse me, gentlemen. I would be happy to take your food and drink orders. If you need more time deciding on your meal, I can just do the drink orders now," said the young waitress.

They all ordered a Sam Adams Boston Lager draft. TJ ordered the scallops with cheese and crumbs, Chip got the New England baked haddock and Darius went with the lobster stuffed with crab and shrimp. They each got a cup of the famous Legal New England chowder and, to split among them, an order of Rhode Island-style calamari. This specialty was prepared with hot peppers and garlic. All put together, it was a feast they were looking forward to.

"Okay, let's get down to business," said Darius. "Maverick, I've a job proposal to give you. It's for some consulting work and it's just a three-month contract. And in case you're wondering why you're sitting down with both of us, it's because we work together on some cases. And now that I've gotten to personally know Chip and we're all friends, it seemed like the right thing to do. Although the TV shows tend to pit the FBI and the police departments against the idea of working together, it's just not always true. It's better to have a good working relationship with each other if we're dealing with the same territory. Then, we can share what we know and hopefully get the bad guys. I'm not so concerned about who gets the credit as long as we get the criminal."

"Mav, I'm here more out of my concern for you. We're all struggling with what happened to our lives but you've come off the rails. You and I have talked about it. When Darius mentioned to me his need for a criminal profiler during our last poker game, I thought you could be a good fit. I also think it's something you need to try. You're not engaging in your old life and so you need to engage in something new," Chip said with honest concern.

The beers came and everyone took a few big swallows.

"So what's this new gig all about? A criminal profiler? What exactly is that and why would I qualify?"

"Good questions, Mav," said Darius. "Let me explain a bit. The objective of profilers is to develop a psychological profile of a subject based on the available evidence. A profiler looks at the clues left behind at the crime scene while looking at the nature of a specific crime. Then they deduce the probable traits or characteristics of the responsible criminal. Profilers may visit crime scenes or they may only assist at a distance by reviewing and analyzing the evidence."

"I've got to say that this sort of blows my mind. I would never have guessed that this is what our lunch was going to be about. At this point, I'm just not seeing it, but what would be my specific duties and responsibilities?" TJ asked

Darius proceeded to pull out some folded sheets of paper from his inside suit pocket.

"I've brought a list with some more info that you can take home with you as you think about all of this. Let me hit the bullet points in a way to answer your question. The duties and responsibilities would be:

- Visiting and analyzing crime scenes
- Analyzing evidence
- Reading reports from investigators and, possibly, other analysts
- Studying human behaviors and characteristics
- Developing psychological profiles
- Writing reports
- Providing court testimony
- Working with FBI agents, police officers and detectives
- Teaching

"I don't necessarily see formal teaching as part of this three-month consulting job but you never know. You would certainly be teaching those involved in the investigation on which direction it might be best to undertake a search. So what do you think so far?"

Three cups of steaming New England chowder arrived, along with the calamari. They all took some time to step back from the conversation and savor the flavor of what was in front of them. They kidded each other about some bad plays with their poker games and had a few laughs. After a few minutes, the conversation went back to being serious.

"You asked me what I thought. I don't really know. But you still didn't tell me why you think I'm qualified to do this," said TJ.

"Let me take this one," said Chip. "First of all, what Darius didn't tell you is that he just lost a very effective profiler and he's got no replacement at this time. So, you're needed. He also didn't mention that the open case that just came his way has the University of Florida involved to some degree and, having attended there yourself, you know the territory. And then it's who you already are in so many ways. You've been given a gift to put puzzles or pieces of information together, along with a photographic memory. You've got a high intelligence, which is another gift you've told us about stemming from your childhood accident. You've got the right degrees, Doctor Maverick. You've got years of experience working with kids with emotional issues. And let's face it, so many bad and evil behaviors are a result of what did or didn't happen during that growing-up period of life. Besides all of this, you're intuitive. You've got teaching experience. You're respected and well-known in the field of psychology. You've got good people skills. You're likable. And, I think I'll stop there so you don't get the big head!"

The food came and the conversation turned to small talk among friends. The food was consumed like lions with a fresh kill. The bill was paid by Darius, who said it was a business expense. He told TJ that he had until February tenth to decide if he wanted the job.

"So, before we break-up this party," said TJ. "I just wanted to say thanks for believing in me. And I'm going to really consider all you guys have said today. This time has meant the world to me. Thanks so much."

They all left, knowing they would have to leave the warm maze of shops, hotels and restaurants and confront the Boston cold. A new layer of bright white snow had begun to fall.

# CHAPTER
## 18

T J left the meeting both encouraged and depressed. He was genuinely thankful for the faith his friends had in him but, at the same time, their words about being off the rails rang true. He wasn't functioning well professionally, with his kids or in his own head. There was so much more going on inside of him that was not being dealt with honestly. He made it home just as the snow started coming down heavy and wet, making the roads treacherous.

He went into his apartment and immediately pulled out the hard liquor bottles. It was five o'clock somewhere but it wasn't even close to that in Boston. He also went to his zip-up travel toiletry bag that was kept in the bathroom and took out an almost full bottle of OxyContin. This medicine had been left over from an excruciating back issue he had a year earlier. OxyContin was a time-released, long-acting formulation of the drug Oxycodone, an opioid used to treat pain. TJ was now treating a different kind of pain. He knew that taking too much of this could cause a high that could lead to abuse and addiction but, at the moment, he didn't care. He had taken the pills with him before leaving his Lexington home and had already crushed a few and snorted them. It gave him a high marked by euphoria along with a sense of well-being. It was a pleasant emptiness. He felt more content, even happy. It was comparable to a heroin high because the drug worked in the same way. When mixed with alcohol, the high lasted longer. If he took the whole bottle of pills, TJ knew his pain could be over forever.

TJ poured himself some whiskey in a large glass meant for water. He didn't do anything with the pills. He just placed them on the coffee table in front of him along with the whiskey bottle in reach for the next pour. He grabbed the clicker and found a station with the 1970 movie *M\*A\*S\*H* just starting. When the movie got to the faux suicide Last Supper scene, the actor Ken Prymus started singing the theme song "Suicide Is Painless." Although TJ knew he was watching a comedy about death and that the movie was not endorsing suicide, it started TJ thinking some of his dark thoughts. Some of the words kept playing in his mind.

*Suicide is painless*
*It brings on many changes ...*

*The game of life is hard to play*
*I'm gonna lose it anyway ...*

*The pain grows stronger ...*

*Is it to be or not to be ...*

*Suicide is painless*
*It brings on many changes*
*And I can take or leave it if I please ...*

The words, *I could take or leave it if I please,* kept running through TJ's mind. He knew he had a choice. To be or not to be. Words originally in Shakespeare's *Hamlet* as the prince contemplated suicide while bemoaning the pain and unfairness of life as well as acknowledging that the alternative might be worse. TJ tried to think about other things.

He knew the history of the movie's hit song and it brought a smile to his face. The director of the movie, Robert Altman, tried to write the words for the song and just couldn't do it. So he asked his 14-year-old son, Mike, to write it. The teen did it in five minutes. Then Johnny Mandel composed the melody. The father was paid $70,000 for directing the movie and his son ended up making a million dollars in song-writing royalties. The people who sang the main version of the song for the movie were just uncredited session singers. They were only paid their salaries. It was funny to TJ how life worked out. He remembered a favorite scripture of his granddad's about this. He walked over to a certain drawer and pulled out a Bible. He looked up Solomon's writing in Ecclesiastes 9:11. He started reading it out loud: *I have seen something else under the sun: the race is not to the swift or the battle to the strong, nor does food come to the wise or wealth to the brilliant or favor to the learned; but time and chance happen to them all.*

Time and chance. American Airlines flight 11. TJ put the Bible down next to the bottle of pills and the bottle of alcohol, thinking it had been too long since he had read it. At one time it had been a habit that he had embraced from his granddad and then from Suzanne. He was thinking he needed to open it up again.

When the movie ended he stared for a long time at the bottle of pills and the bottle of alcohol. He cursed and shook his head knowing Suzo, his granddad, and his kids would be disappointed in him. All of a sudden, TJ got up, flushed the pills down the toilet, and poured all the alcohol in the apartment down the drain. He then took out the papers Darius had given him about the profiler position and he started looking them over. Instead of coming off the rails he wanted to get back on track.

# JOURNAL ENTRY
## February 8, 2002

Suzo:

Thanks for meeting me again. It's the anniversary of our first date ... February 8. Because we went to that little Italian restaurant, tonight I did a delivery order of lasagna (which is what I had on our date!) and a piece of tiramisu. I had a bottle of Chianti Classico to wash it all down with. I'm told it has super spicy acidity and sour cherry flavors. Honestly, I can't really taste those specifics but what a great meal! The only thing missing was you.

And some good news ... we had a great victory last week with our Patriots in the Super Bowl! Our team was in the battle against the Rams. It was Kurt Warner and "The Greatest Show on Turf" offense against the second year Tom Brady, our new quarterback. We almost didn't make it to the Big Show but, thanks to the obscure 'tuck rule' in a previous game against the Raiders, we were there! The halftime show with the Irish rock band, U2 honored you, the victims of 9/11. I deeply appreciated the honest and sincere expressions of love. But it made me miss you all the more.

Now back to the game. With just a minute and thirty seconds left the score was tied 17 to 17. Without any time-outs, Brady took the Patriots down the field and set up a game-winning 48-yard field goal by Adam Vinatieri just as time on the clock expired. So this was the first Lombardi Trophy for the New England Patriots. It was beautiful! If only you had been with me.

So here's where I'm at. It's now been almost five months

since I lost you and it seems like the pain never goes away. I'm still thinking it must stay in the emotional makeup of a person forever. To lose your first love is unforgettable. To lose the love of your life is absolutely devastating. Time helps but time does not completely heal. Staying busy helps but staying busy never lasts. The end of the day always comes. And, even when you're exhausted, the quiet darkness may be met with eyes wide open. It's impossible at times to turn off the mind, the memories or the emotions just because the clock or the body says it's time to sleep. Of course, a person can medicate themselves with alcohol, drugs, pornography, television, etc., and become numb to life. As I've told you already, I've done some of that stuff but still the pain stays alive within. It's always lurking, waiting to reappear. Memories can get stirred. Fading shadows can become stark reality again. Pain can be resurrected at any given moment. It may come through a simple word, a familiar smile, a voice, an old photo, a television show, a certain sound, a song, a news report, a movie.

The resurrected pain can be a short emotional ripple or it can explode into huge waves of emotion that keep crashing and breaking against us until it leaves in its wake nothing but destruction and devastation. It may start as a few gentle rain drops but it can end as a Category 5 hurricane. I find that the event of the emotional storm can pass quickly, but the reawakened pain can remain for quite some time.

I think there exists no permanent solution. There is no perfect cure in this life. Life is pain. Who said that? Oh, a Princess Bride line ... something like "Life is pain, Highness. Anyone who says differently is selling something."

Yes, life is pain. And, pain is life. To learn to live with pain is to learn to live life. Life is the ability to cope with pain. Therefore, pain is not all bad. In fact, I believe pain can push people to become better and more of who they were created to be. Pain offers either personal growth or personal destruction. In the end, each individual chooses one or the other. No one remains the same with pain. There is the kind of pain we were made to endure and there is the kind of pain we were not made to endure. The pain we were not made to endure emotionally damages us beyond repair. We humans are extremely bendable but we are also breakable.

The old M*A*S*H song "Suicide is Painless" just isn't true. It does bring on many changes but not good ones. And it's not painless! The terrorists who committed suicide have brought so much pain into the lives of so many — including me. You can't compare pain. You can't tell a person it's not that bad compared to some other person's pain. You can't tell a person it's time to just be over it. It has to be endured by the individual. Physical pain tolerance is different for everyone. Emotional pain tolerance is also different for everyone. I find my tolerance or threshold for emotional pain low right now. I feel so mad. I can't shake it. I can't leave it behind. It comes with me wherever I go.

How do we live in a world full of pain? Maybe it's a matter of learning to live above the pain by living to alleviate the pain in others. We have to get our minds off ourselves. The only way to do that is to think of others. This certainly will bring more challenges into our life. It might even bring more pain into our life but it's not the personal, irreparable kind of pain. It's the pain that, to some degree, helps and

heals. It can be like the surgeon's scalpel. It initially causes pain but it leads to healing. It ultimately saves lives. I
think helping others can start to cure the tragic, unrelenting
pain of grief, of loss, of abandonment, of betrayal, of abuse.
I think it can keep a person alive as they go through the
journey of living. I think it could keep me alive. I have to
confess that I've had some more dark thoughts lately. I've
also had a three-month consulting gig offered to me. Some
new friends think I'd be good at criminal profiling, given
my background, education, and professional training. They
need some immediate help and maybe this would be good for
me. I don't really know what's best for me but I'm willing
to try something completely new.

At least that's what I'm thinking and feeling right
now.

I pray I can sleep tonight. At least when I'm asleep,
I'm numb to the pain for a few hours of unconsciousness.

Goodnight, Suzo.

All my love, all the time —

TJ

# 1972

Leah was finishing her freshman year at the University of Florida. She had changed from the light-hearted girl who had arrived on campus nine months earlier. She had been so full of life. So confident. So excited about what the future would bring her way. Now, she kept more to herself, as she lacked faith in herself. She no longer found the same joy in running and working out as she had in the past. Loud noises easily startled her. She felt alone, thinking no one could understand how she felt. She felt guilt, believing she did something wrong that caused her to be sexually assaulted. She was full of shame, thinking she was a bad person because this happened to her. She believed the people around her would think poorly of her because she was attacked. Something had emotionally died in her on that Homecoming night. The rape had hijacked so many of her dreams of love and romance. Her resolve to hold to a certain moral standard had been stolen. She now medicated herself with heavy doses of alcohol and drugs.

Before Leah went home to Winter Park for the summer, she started liking a guy who was completing his junior year. His name was Lincoln Hart; they met at "The Library." This was not a place for books and studying; it was a place for drinks and dancing. Because the legal drinking age was eighteen the place was always busy. It was a favorite with UF students, as it allowed them to truthfully say to their parents they had been at *the library*. Lincoln lived off-campus in an apartment complex on SW 13th Street and was staying in Gainesville for the summer quarter. They visited each other throughout the summer months and became emotionally and sexually involved. They started to refer to it as their Summer of Love. Of course this was a reference to the social phenomenon that had occurred during the summer of '67 when 100,000 young people invaded San Francisco's neighborhood of Haight-Ashbury. It encompassed hippie music, anti-war protests, hallucinogenic drugs and free love. For Leah and Lincoln, their Summer of Love was all about free love with some pot and alcohol thrown in. The intense lovemaking was surprising to Leah because she had said to herself after the rape that she would keep both her mouth and her legs shut.

When the new school year started, Leah moved into her Delta Gamma sorority house. She stayed there during the week but she spent every weekend with Lincoln at his apartment. The sex was usually good and, somehow, she felt comforted and less insecure about her body and about the past by being wanted. She slowed down on alcohol and drugs as she replaced them with her new medication. Sex.

Lincoln was tall with shoulder-length, dirty blond hair and a Fu Manchu mustache. He had wide shoulders and a strong upper body developed through years of physical training. From the time he was little, he had been on both the swim and basketball teams. The upper portion of his nose had a small bump due to being broken on two different occasions. After all, elbows in the face were not an uncommon occurrence in the world of sports, especially on the basketball court. Leah thought he had a Robert Redford kind of charisma about him. She was drawn to him, as were many other people, especially girls. She would catch them taking second looks quite often. At first, the relationship for Leah was built on a physical attraction and on a physical need but she had eventually fallen in love with him. He made her feel protected. He made her feel happy. He made her feel free. She was even starting to believe her past could be put in the past.

Back in July the movie *Butterflies Are Free* was released and Leah and Lincoln had seen it together. It became one of Leah's top-ten movie favorites. The plot revolved around a blind man living in San Francisco whose over-protective mother disapproved of his relationship with a free-spirited hippie girl. Twenty-seven year old Goldie Hawn played the role of the hippie girl. Inspired by the message and popularity of the movie, the Florida Players decided to do this as their first play of the new school year. They chose a talented Goldie Hawn look-alike to take the leading role. She happened to be in the Delta Gamma sorority and was a friend of Leah's. Leah had loved the movie and could hardly wait to see her friend in the UF production.

The play was running for six nights at the beginning of October in the beautiful Constans Theatre. Tickets were 75 cents for students and $1.50 for non-students. Leah arrived early with Lincoln to get the best seats. Recently, Leah had felt they were drifting apart, but couldn't figure out why. They had been getting into a number of ugly arguments. It seemed like the disagreements and the feelings never really got discussed and resolved. Lincoln was just satisfied with having sex. All the seats were filled as the lights were turned down and the play began.

At the end of the play, the audience gave an enthusiastic standing ovation. Leah also thought the play was excellently done and that her friend had carried off the free-spirited acting role splendidly. Of course she knew her personality was a lot like that without any role-playing. The only thing that was a little crazy was when a streaker ran across the stage. But still, after a short laugh from the audience, everything went as planned.

As soon as she could, Leah went back stage with flowers in hand. She wanted to hug and congratulate her friend on a great performance. As she was returning to the auditorium she spied Lincoln in a corner with one of her sorority sisters. It was actually someone she had introduced Lincoln to when he had come to pick her up for a date. They were in some kind of a serious clash. They were so into their conversation that they didn't notice Leah approaching.

"So when are you going to tell her about us?" asked the girl.

"Hey, we were just having a little fun together, right?" said Lincoln.

"What are you talking about? You said you loved me and that I was the one for you. Remember that?"

"Well, I was just being in the moment," smirked Lincoln.

The girl used some choice words and shoved Lincoln as hard as she could against the wall. With an angry, screwed-up face she pushed her way through the crowd as she raised her middle finger at him. Having heard the gist of the conversation, Leah came up to Lincoln set and ready for a major confrontation.

"What the hell is going on, Lincoln? You screwing that? I thought we were a real thing," said Leah.

"Hey, you weren't around and she came on to me and … and who said we were exclusive? Remember it was our summer of love. That's free love … butterflies are free!"

Leah turned around, just wanting to get away from him. By the time she hit the door she was full of tears, full of anger and full of pain. Her emotions were flip-flopping with the thin line between love and hate. The degree of love and passion she had carried for Lincoln was now turning into that same degree of hate and desire for revenge. He had lied. He had cheated. He had broken trust. He had broken her heart. She was physically shaking from the shock. And it was all happening so quickly. Her jealousy was raging as the pain of betrayal was taking root inside her already fragile and damaged being. If her name had been Booth, Lincoln would be dead.

Outside the theater Leah just started walking. Her mind turned to her sorority and she yelled out, "What a great sisterhood. So much love, care, and concern for one another!" As she continued walking she found herself on Museum Road in front of the SAE House. The lion in front of the house was its usual white. There was nothing special enough going on to commemorate using special colors. It was 10:30 at night and they were having some kind of party. The music was loud and people were hanging around inside and outside the place. She had not seen or spoken to Joe for a long time. They had grown apart, as he became too busy to spend time with her. She had felt pushed away but didn't know why. As she stood on the sidewalk in front of the fraternity house, she was intensely angry and all she could think about was getting back at Lincoln. She was a person in love who had been jilted and betrayed and so she wanted to hurt Lincoln the way he hurt her. She wanted revenge. She wanted to be cruel and vicious. She thought she would sleep with somebody, maybe Joe, and then throw it in Lincoln's face.

Leah entered the party, passing up offers for beer from the many available kegs. Instead she grabbed the shots that were being passed around. Everyone was dressed up. Fortunately, Leah had just been to the play, so she fit in with the crowd. She noticed there were two photographers at work. One was in a corner taking photos of couples using a professional looking black background while the other one roamed the party getting candid shots of the crowd. Leah also noticed there seemed to be plenty of people going stag so she felt comfortable. She figured it was just some kind of typical fraternity celebration. She proceeded to put down five shots one after the other and started to feel the effects quickly. But she didn't stop. She took some kind of mixed drink that was being offered and started gulping it down. From across the room, Joe was surprised to see Leah. He went over to her.

"Hey girl. What are you doing out on this beautiful Saturday night all alone?" said Joe.

"Just out for some fun. You got anything to help with that? I'm open to suggestions. In fact, I'm open for anything tonight — maybe anything with you!"

"Wow! That was really unexpected. I'm sure something can be arranged. I'll be right back so don't go away, okay?

"I'm not going anywhere," said Leah feeling the buzz and starting to slur her words a bit.

Joe left and found his buddies Pete and Troy.

"You guys won't believe this but remember that virgin girl we did at last year's Homecoming? Well, she's back and I think we should give it to her again. In fact, for some crazy reason, I think she's actually asking for it. What do you guys think?" asked Joe.

"You know I'm always up for a good time," said Pete.

"I'm in," said Troy.

"All right! So, let's do a Tangerine Ops this time. Five digits each!" exclaimed Joe.

Joe went to his room and got a sugar cube that contained Lysergic Acid Diethylamide —LSD, a drug popularized by Ken Kesey, and the Merry Pranksters. Tom Wolfe illuminated their undertaking in his book, *The Electric Kool-Aid Acid Test*. Joe had loved the book.

Feeling revved-up, Joe started singing to himself, *Picture yourself in a boat on a river, with tangerine trees and marmalade skies.* As he sang, he emphasized with a sly grin the word, tangerine. This was the beginning to the song, *Lucy In The Sky With Diamonds.* Although the Beatles claimed it wasn't about LSD, people found that hard to believe. Their claim was that Julian, John Lennon's son, came home one day from nursery school with a drawing of a girl named Lucy who was one of his classmates. Julian described the picture to his Dad as, "Lucy ... in the sky with diamonds." With that as inspiration, John and Paul wrote a song using psychedelic terms. They said they never noticed the LSD initials until it was pointed out later. Joe returned and found Leah in the crowded party room. He offered her another drink, which was mixed with the sugar cube he had "I think this will make you feel happy. It should help take you on a trip into another world," said Joe.

"And that's what I need right now. It's safe, right?" asked Leah.

"I will always keep you safe. No worries, Okay?"

"Okay."

Leah took the drink and started swallowing it as Joe led her up to his room. After a little time had passed with some trivial conversation, Leah was feeling some kind of sensory alteration. Things were happening with her sense of smell, touch, taste, sight, and hearing simultaneously. All her faculties were off kilter. It was a strange and new experience for her. She had never taken an hallucinogen before. Her eyes were widely dilated. Time seemed to just drag along. She saw ripples with colors of the rainbow moving around the room. Everything was melting together from all her senses. Leah felt she was experiencing a oneness of existence. But in this oneness, there seemed to be a number of floating faces in the room.

The boys had slightly torn her dress as they unbuttoned it. They practically ripped off her panties. They had their hands all over her as they each entered her. She had become unaware of her surroundings and unaware of what was being done to her. She reached into the air trying to catch the numerous psychedelic butterflies hovering around her. She softly sang to the music that was magically playing in her head. She felt the effects of the drug come in waves until it intensified to a peak. For hours the line between perception and imagination was blurred.

When the three were done with her, they got her up, put her back together as best they could and then, all together, walked her down the hall and down the stairs. At the bottom of the stairs there was a boy who had come into the frat house only to drop off some books to a friend. As he was leaving, he saw some guys struggling to guide a girl down the stairs. As they neared the bottom he started helping them out. The girl could hardly stand up on her own so they sat her on a nearby couch. The three guys quickly walked away and blended in with the crowd. The boy stayed to make sure the girl was okay, since she was stoned and out of it. He asked her if she needed any help to get home. She never coherently answered. After a while, the girl got up, shoved the boy away and staggered out the door going down Museum Road in the direction that would take her straight to the Delta Gamma sorority house. The boy left too, but headed in the opposite way.

---

A few weeks later, Leah found herself pregnant.

# CHAPTER
## 19

The monster was home sitting in front of the fireplace and enjoying the warmth. It had a long day at work and was tired. The bigger problem was exhaustion from, night after night, not getting good, sound sleep. Ever since Leah's confession night and then finding the hidden writings of its wife, it had images and thoughts that kept running through its mind, especially when its head hit the pillow at night. This was also true many years ago after a visit with an obstetrician but now it was so much worse. The monster knew the whole truth. Trauma. PTSD. Post-Traumatic Stress Disorder. The monster knew it was a real condition.

Each night the monster would re-read some of Leah's writings. It knew they were cries for help that she never let anyone hear. It would look at the pictures she had kept in her secret box. It studied every detail of each man. These were the faces of the men who had robbed him of his wife. These were the faces of those who raped without remorse. Two down so far. There were more to come. He opened the box, picked up the diaries, and began to read.

# R.K. McKEAN

*I went to the play, Butterflies Are Free, feeling happy and hopeful. The night stole those feelings away from me. As I came out of the frat house, or should I say the lion's house, I felt like I was floating in the air as I made my way back to my sorority house. After a few hours of coming out of the liquor and whatever drug I was given, I examined myself in the mirror. My dress was ripped. Two buttons were missing. My underwear was torn. And, I was bruised and in pain where there had been obvious, forceful sexual penetration.*

*What I know: I know I was so incredibly angry and hurt from the cheating betrayal of my boyfriend. I know I ended up at the SAE house. I know I wanted revenge. I know I drank all the hard stuff I could put down. I know I spoke with Joe who I still considered my friend even though we had lost touch. I know I wanted to punish Lincoln. I know I carelessly offered myself to Joe. I know I asked for something to mellow me out. I know he must have given me something in my drink that did a lot more than that. It took me to another world. I'm guessing it was LSD. I had never felt the way this mix of alcohol and drugs made me feel. It was good and it was bad. It made me forget my pain for a while but it allowed people to do things to me I never consented to. I know I saw faces around me when I was in Joe's room. I know people were touching and groping me everywhere. All I can think of is the phrase, "Throw her to the lions!" I know I was raped AGAIN! I know it was a gang rape.*

*Since I wasn't totally sure of who was involved with what had happened to me, I went in search of the photographers who were at the SAE party. I had my suspicions. I needed some proof so I could tell myself I wasn't going crazy with what I was thinking. I found out who the shutterbugs were and tracked them down. I asked to see all the pictures that were taken from that night. They were more than helpful when I told them why I needed to look at them and what I suspected. That I thought I was raped.*

116

*The one who was moving around in the crowd taking candid shots had one of me, in the background of a photo, going up the stairs with Joe. CONFIRMATION. I was right about that. I know we talked for a while in his room. I know I zoned out but I can still remember seeing glimpses of faces, seemingly floating, around me. I saw Joe. I saw Troy. I saw Pete. I didn't remember seeing others but there could have been more in that room. HOW MANY MORE? I hate to think about that! In another photo there were four guys holding me up as I was coming down the stairs from the bedrooms. I recognized Joe, Troy and Pete.*

*I also found a photo of me being seated on a couch with four guys all around me. These were the same four who were at the bottom of the stairs helping me stand up. Again it included Joe, Pete and Troy. The other guy I'd never seen before. Lastly, I discovered a photo of just me and this unknown guy sitting together on the couch.*

*So I believe they all raped me and then left me in an alcohol and druggy stupor figuring I wouldn't remember what took place. I bet they raped me at Homecoming, too. I suppose they gave me some other drug at that time so I couldn't remember what really happened. I'M SO STUPID! Joe. A friend? He's as silent and deadly as a lion. He's hunting for easy prey — girls like ME! He befriends them. He ambushes them. He attacks them. He abuses them. And he's not alone in his offensive, aggressive violations. How many victims have there been? WHAT AM I GOING TO DO NOW?*

The monster threw the diary on the floor with a loud thud. Again it was thinking that at least it had taken out two of the guys who had created in Leah mountains of excruciating pain. Joe and Troy. A beginning. Not an ending. The monster slowly walked into his dark, lonely, piled-up-dirty-dishes kitchen for a bottle of beer. There used to be so much joy and merriment in this part of the house. It used to be Leah's bright, sparkling clean chef's kitchen. It was a place of sweet smells of all kinds of Italian foods. The monster loved how Leah loved to cook and it loved enjoying her creations. Just hanging out and enjoying good food and good talk with Leah was a fulfilling and satisfying life.

Before getting the beer, it first opened the freezer and took out two plastic bags. Ten frozen toes were in each bag. It held them and promised itself that they would have more company soon. It furiously threw them back in the freezer and then grabbed a beer. Going back to the fireplace and its lounge chair, it picked the diary up from the floor and opened it to read another excerpt.

> *No one's going to listen to me. No one's going to believe me. I tried talking to the fraternity house mother, a women named Dorothy Whitlock, but she emphatically declared she had no time for me. I thought about going to the campus police. I thought about going to the president of the fraternity ... but then I remembered Joe Hiller is in that position! I even thought about talking to O'Connell, the president of UF. But, money talks. Power rules. The families of the three guys I believe abused me are all connected, powerful, and rich. I've checked them out. Each family has donated an outrageous amount of money to the university. One of them even has a building with their name on it. I've been quietly told that if any trouble comes their way, it just goes away. And then trouble comes my way!*
>
> *And how could I ever prove they initially raped me? And this last time I, admittedly, was out of my mind emotionally and drinking to get drunk. And beyond that I asked for the drugs and I even said I was open for anything. People saw me drinking and heard me talking. I'd be the slut in people's eyes. Even if I could prove a sexual assault took place, the blame would probably be on me since I was looking for it and was even asking for it! Just got to keep my mouth shut!*

As the monster was finishing the beer, it quickly flipped through a few pages of the diary and then started reading some more of Leah's thoughts.

*It's confirmed. I'm pregnant. I can't believe it! I'm only 19! What am I going to do? I feel alone. I feel depressed. I feel desperate. What would my life be like as a teenage single mom? What about all my plans for my life? How would my parents feel if they knew I was pregnant? It would probably be a shock for them just to know I'm having sex. BUT WORSE. The first question would be, "Who's the father?" Then I say, "I don't know for sure." EXPLOSION! My explanation: I was mad because my boyfriend, who I was sleeping with every week-end, betrayed me with one of my sorority sisters. So I wanted revenge. I decided to sleep with anyone available as payback. So I got drunk. Then I was drugged and gang-raped. So, I just can't be sure who the father is. And, most likely it's not my scum-of-the-earth boyfriend because we usually used protection except at the beginning and that was many months ago. End of explanation.*

*I knew that the student newspaper,* The Florida Alligator, *ran some articles about abortion at the end of last year. It caused an upheaval on campus. There were protests and arrests. And there was a trial dealing with First Amendment Rights after there was a mimeographed insert placed in each newspaper in the middle of the night with a list of abortion clinics. It all led to the Alligator no longer being supported financially with student fees and being split off from the university. It became a private, off-campus newspaper. I didn't get involved in the controversy because I believed it was never going to be an issue for me.*

*At this point I know very little about the actual abortion process except I would have said I was against killing babies just a few weeks ago. But now, maybe not. Is this the best way to deal with my predicament? I remember my speech class back in high school when we were assigned a debate about abortion. I had actually been put on the side to advocate for it but in so doing, I developed a conviction that it was morally and ethically wrong. I got convinced that a fetus was a human life. I found out that the fertilized egg became a real person with a unique genetic make-up. I understood that as early as a few weeks after conception, the skeleton was formed, the sex was determined and the heart began to beat. But, I sure don't want to marry Lincoln (as if he would be willing!) and I sure don't want to be a single mother. So, is it really all that bad? Maybe I've been wrong. Maybe it's not a real, living human being until it's born? A women's body — a women's choice. Right? This is what I hear all the time.*

*I found and read the series of articles in the archives of past issues of the Alligator. It was interviews of UF students who had undergone legal and illegal abortions. Most felt good and satisfied because they had it done. They said the procedure was relatively safe, easy, and painless. They were relieved that they could just go on with their lives. No encumbrances. No upheaval. No dealing with rejection from family. No facing the possible finger pointing or the looks or the stares. No having it talked about behind their backs from supposed friends and acquaintances. One girl spoke about some physical issues that occurred after her abortion but pointed out it was an illegal one. Only two girls shared about their guilt and their emotional nightmares from what they had done.*

*I know enough to know it's illegal in the state of Florida. The article said it was forbidden under an 1868 statute and that it was only legal in New York, Hawaii and Puerto Rico. I know getting an illegal abortion would be more dangerous and possibly life threatening if I ended up in the hands of the wrong people. I remembered that in a particular edition, there was an insert that printed the addresses of known abortion clinics. So, I discreetly asked around for a copy of that list. It wasn't hard to find.*

*SOMETHING BAD! I'm having fleeting thoughts of suicide.*

*What's that song from the movie M\*A\*S\*H? "Suicide Is Painless." I have my doubts about it being painless! It certainly isn't painless for those who are left behind. Is abortion painless? Is it painless for the baby? Is it painless for me years after I do it? I hope so because I'm seriously thinking about having it done. I can almost feel the relief already.*

The monster returned to the refrigerator for another beer before looking at more writings from Leah's diaries.

*I just talked to Lincoln and told him I'm pregnant. He asked if I was sure it was his! WHAT A LOUSE! I assured him it could only be his. NOW I'M A LIAR! I told him I needed and wanted an abortion and that he needed to pay the $150 for it and also the cost of the plane ticket. He said he would pay half of it. He said he had a friend who had a friend who could help me out with the details. I met with this friend of a friend. She seemed nice. She told me she had connections with an abortion clinic in New York. And, she told me to NEVER tell anyone for any reason that I had an abortion. She said I might marry someone who goes into public service and that this information could be used against him in some way. Or, it could be used against me depending on the profession I entered. I said I would keep my lips sealed ... FOREVER!*

# CHAPTER
# 20

I t was just a 15-minute drive from TJ's North End apartment across the Charlestown Bridge, then past the Bunker Hill Monument and onto the Tobin Bridge and into Chelsea to the FBI office on Maple Street. At the entrance a large, concrete wall-like structure had been created for the sign. The black and off-white large letters boldly proclaimed, FEDERAL BUREAU OF INVESTIGATION — BOSTON DIVISION. There was a huge FBI seal mounted on the portion of the wall that was black, a reminder to all that the FBI was with the Department of Justice. And the seal's banner had three defining words on it. Fidelity. Integrity. Bravery. TJ could see they definitely wanted people to know they were present, available, and ready to do whatever needed to be done at any given moment. The building had the same off-white exterior as the signage wall along with black columns that made it look very austere. It was a simple rectangular building with a lot of glass, and didn't seem like anything particularly special to TJ. It seemed stark and bare.

TJ pulled into the parking lot and hesitated to park, not knowing if he was considered a visitor or a member of the FBI club. He decided on member. As he walked to the entrance he shivered, but not because of the mid-February cold. It was the feeling of the start of a new life that sent a shock through his whole body.

Inside the sterile building, TJ found himself at his first day of his new job with the Boston Division of the FBI, being introduced as their newest criminal profiler expert. He had to inwardly laugh at the idea that he was any kind of a real expert at this profiling thing. He wasn't exactly a person with a broad and profound competence with his fifteen minutes of experience. He was just hoping to find his way around the building without getting lost and without saying anything that sounded deficient or foolish. He had decided to give this new opportunity his best shot. He didn't want to let his friends down. A proficient profiler? Not now. At least, not yet.

"So let's get started," said Darius.

Darius had a comfortable office with large windows facing east that allowed plenty of morning light even on the many cloudy days of winter. This helped to give the room a cheerful and positive atmosphere even as abhorrent and appalling details of crimes were discussed.

"Maverick, you've been introduced at the staff meeting, now let's go over the particulars of why I wanted you here. By the way, do make sure you do the necessary paperwork for new hires and then pick up your credentials."

"Sure, no problem. It will be done, boss," said TJ with a small salute.

"So here's the case I want you to work on. It's out of the ordinary but the Boston Field Office was requested to use some of its resources on it. Unfortunately we already have all our available personnel overloaded with previously assigned cases. Clearly, the 9/11 investigation has involved many of our people. And you were made aware earlier of the recent loss of one of our best profilers. So, that's where you come in for three months. You can concentrate on this one case. Just give it your best effort and everyone will be satisfied with how the Boston Division responded to the request," said Darius.

"Okay. I get it. I'm covering your butt," smiled TJ.

"That's one way of putting it. Also, you need to decide for your own life if you're going to be a victim or a victor. You need to be busy. You need a new routine. This is your opportunity to move on with your life in a positive way. You get that, right, Mav?"

"I get it. I really do."

"Now let's get into the details. There have been two brutal and bizarre murders in Florida. One in Miami Beach and the other in Windermere which is just outside of Orlando. The first happened over Labor Day Weekend of last year and the second happened in mid-November. Both occurred at the residences of the deceased. Both were broken into using a high-powered glass cutting tool and then the perp entering the home through the hole made in a sliding glass door. There were no prints or hairs or anything else found that could be helpful at either crime scene. Both victims were male. Both were found in their beds nude and tied up with rope and duct tape. Both had an intravenous device that slowly extracted their blood. And both had their ten toes cut off and removed from the scene. Obviously, it has to be the same perpetrator," said Darius sitting back in his black, leather desk chair with his hands folded behind his head.

"So both in Florida. What's that got to do with Boston?" asked TJ.

"That's the right question. At the crime scene in Windermere there was a torn portion of a Patriots football ticket. It was apparently dropped by the perp. The wife was questioned about it. She said they had never traveled to Boston and that they were both Tampa Bay Bucs fans. There were no useable prints on it. The ticket portion did not include any identifiers like seat number or section number. But since it's obviously from Boston, we have been asked to look into it. Honestly, it doesn't make a lot of sense to me. These cases have even become somewhat cold. But, they're connected, and there's a crossing of state lines if the killer is from New England, so we were contacted. Between you and me, I think they're punting the ball to us after making no forward progress."

"Wow. That's a lot to take in. Anything else?"

"Yes. These two men had a past connection but no apparent recent connection. They were both at the University of Florida and were in the same fraternity at the same time. They were there from '69 to '73. The reports said they had a spotless academic and behavioral record. And of course, they both happened to have families that are mega-rich and well connected politically. So now you can see why someone is pushing this to be more aggressively investigated even in the midst of the 9/11 terrorist attacks. I think the powers that be are trying to say to the parents they are pulling out all the stops. To me it's like the ol' Boston College Hail Mary play pulled off by Doug Flutie in '84. The percentages are low but at least it's a shot at winning. It certainly worked for Flutie."

"So you're saying instead of the Miracle in Miami you're trying for the Miracle in Boston," laughed TJ.

"Yep. You've got it! The ball is in your hands, Mav. I'm giving you the freedom to go anywhere and do anything that you think would be helpful to getting this investigation headed in the right direction. Given the powerful political pressure factor, you can have all the financial resources that you need. Just don't go crazy on me! Go to Florida or not. Read the crime scene reports. Call or have some face-to-face interviews with anyone connected to the investigation. You were a UF student during some of those same years so you know that territory. Why are the victims nude? Why is the killer slowly dripping their blood out? Why is the killer cutting off their toes? What's the connection between these two guys? Give me your best psych work-up of this butcher, this executioner. Be the criminal profiler I believe you can be!"

"Sounds like I'm getting out of the cold. Maybe I should check out South Beach for any clues first. Perhaps there's a message in the sand identifying the slayer," said TJ with a wink.

"Just get out there, Mav, and do something that keeps these people off my back. And since this case is a little different from our usual protocol, report directly to me. Let me repeat that. Report only to me. That will keep everything clear and simple. Also Mav, call me boss at work but please don't call me that outside the office. We're too close as friends for that. I'm good with Darius."

"Got it ... BOSS!"

# CHAPTER
# 21

TJ decided to take Darius at his word and resolved to fly to Miami but with a stopover for a night in New York City. He knew he had been neglecting his kids by only having inconsistent phone calls that were short and shallow. TJ felt happy about his decision.

TJ met Skylar and Ethan for a late lunch at his favorite spot, Katz Deli. He wanted his pastrami on rye. The kids ordered things that were more nutritious. It was obvious that Skylar had lost weight, even when she didn't need to. She had tired eyes underscored by dark shadows underneath. She was not very talkative but seemed happy to be together. Ethan, on the other hand, was distant mixed with an underlying anger. TJ chose a table off by itself in a corner to give them some privacy. He wanted to talk about the obvious elephant in the room. He was wise enough to start the conversation with a heart-felt apology.

"Thanks for coming and meeting together like this. Although we had a good time together for a few days at Christmas, I know I haven't been who you needed me to be since your mom died. I want to deeply apologize to both of you. Please, please forgive me for my selfishness, my immaturity, and for acting out the way I have. There's no excuse for it. I haven't let you in and I haven't been emotionally or physically available to either of you. I want all of that to stop as of now," said TJ, tears streaming down his cheeks.

Both of the children were taken aback by their father's words and tears. They had become somewhat numb around their dad as they felt the need to stuff and hide their feelings and personal needs to protect him. Although Sky and E had grown closer together over the past few months after tragically losing their mother, the same could not be said about TJ and his relationship with his daughter or his son. They had grown apart like the North Rim and the South Rim of the Grand Canyon. TJ was determined for that to change. This situation made TJ think of Evel Knievel attempting to leap the mile-wide chasm of the Snake River Canyon on his specially engineered rocket motorcycle. Evel had been confident he could do it, but he had failed. TJ felt confident that the jump could be made to close the gap with his children; failure was not an option.

"I forgive you, Dad, but I've been hurt deeply by your neglect and insensitivity. And, I've been so worried about you that I haven't been sleeping or eating well. I've also been having some PTSD issues I've never told you about. Being just twenty-five blocks away and watching thousands of people die as the towers came crashing down has left me with haunting and reoccurring images piercing my mind. I'm thankful I wasn't any closer but, still, just four subway stops away was a killing field worse than Pearl Harbor — and Mom was in that field," said Skylar with tears now pouring down her face.

"Again, I'm so, so sorry I haven't been here for you. I was mainly thinking about what I was going through instead of being aware of what you were going through, too. It breaks my heart to see you like this. I'm here now. How can I help?" asked TJ.

Jumping in at this point was Ethan. "Dad, I've been pretty mad at you. Here you are, the great psychologist and you just checked out. You checked out from us. You checked out from yourself. You checked out from life. I could smell the pot and I could see all the alcohol in the upper cupboards when we were home at Christmas. I want it to be all good between us again but it's going to take some time for me to get there."

"Fair enough. I get it," said TJ.

"Dad. E. We need each other if we're going to get to the other side of this tragedy. Let's start rebuilding and reconnecting. Consistent phone calls and visits are a must. Let's all believe we're going to find the way to never forget Mom even as we make new memories that lead to good feelings about each other," said Sky.

"That all sounds great to me," said Ethan, softening a bit.

"And who's the psychologist around here now? How much do I owe you, Sky, for this session?"

They all laughed and cried together. They got some strange looks from some of the other customers but they didn't care. They started to enjoy their food as they enjoyed simply being together. TJ filled them in on his new gig with the FBI and why he was going to continue his trip by going down to Florida. The kids were both impressed and skeptical.

TJ also went into an explanation about finances. With the loss of Suzanne's salary, he didn't want them to be worried about their college expenses. He explained that there was the September 11th Victim Compensation Fund that was created shortly after the attacks. Seven billion dollars were in that fund. The amount of money given to the families who lost loved ones would depend on the projected amount of money a person would have made in their lifetime. He explained they would take their present age and salary and analyze it to come up with a number. The range was a minimum guarantee of $250,000 all the way up to $4.7 million and so the average given would be $1,185,000. TJ let them know the Maverick family had been awarded $2.35 million. He explained he had to sign a non-negotiable clause in the acceptance papers for the settlement, which was a promise to never file suit against the airlines for any lack of security or unsafe practices.

Then on top of this there was a million-dollar life insurance policy from their mother's workplace and a personal life insurance policy of $500,000. He let them know that other money would most likely be coming in from good-hearted, everyday people who had donated $528 million to what was called the September 11th Fund.

"That's overwhelming and I'm not sure I needed to know all of that," said Sky.

"I'm sort of feeling that same way, Dad," said E.

"Well, I just wanted to let you know all of what's been going on and for you not to be concerned about money issues. I'm personally not feeling great about all this money. It just doesn't feel right to me. You know there are some who are complaining they didn't get enough. I find that greedy and sad. I feel guilty for having it myself. I've got to figure out how to handle all of this but, for now, it's just sitting in the bank.

When they had finished eating and talking, TJ pulled out four tickets for Les Misérables.

"I have some therapy for us tonight. We've all seen it before but we need to see it again. It has such a noble and inspirational theme and I think we all need to be reminded of it. The music has always moved my heart in the right direction. I've got the best seats in the house, and yes, I even bought a ticket for Mom. She'll be with us in spirit."

When they got to the show they were feeling upbeat and positive. During the show they laughed at times. They cried at times. And, every now and then, each would glance at the empty seat, knowing it was not empty in their hearts. As the musical ended they remained seated while the theater emptied. Their inner spirits were deeply affected by the words to many of the songs. When they finally got up to leave, they hugged and held each other in a way that said they would never let go again. All of them had the hopeful lyrics of the song, *Do You Hear the People Singing?* ringing in their minds: *There is a life about to start when tomorrow comes!*

They had arranged to meet up with all of Sky's roommates and her boyfriend, Sean, for some late-night pizza after the show. TJ was truly happy to be surrounded by people who obviously loved and cared about each other. He had known Rayne for years as a high school best friend to Skylar. Shari and Kari, or Diva 1 and Diva 2, were so delicate, dainty, and delightful that they automatically drew people to them. Summer, the true and tough New Yorker, had a special place in TJ's heart. Somehow her presence made New York City seem safer for the other roommates. Sean and Sky were a little googly-eyed with each other. And it seemed like Ethan was trying to make up his mind between the twins. He obviously liked them both ... a lot.

As the night ended, everyone said their goodnights with kisses and hugs. Each had a packed schedule to keep the next day. TJ was scheduled for Miami Beach.

---

As he lay exhausted on his hotel bed, his mind was thinking some dark thoughts. *I said good-bye too quickly ... I should have held her longer ... We should have made love that morning ... I never should have rushed her ... I never should have let her out the door ... I drove her to her death!*

At the same time, some lyrics from the evening's performance were keeping him from being completely depressed and falling into a downward spiral: *To love another person is to see the face of God ... A heart full of love. No fear, no regret ... Jean Valjean is nothing now, another story must begin! ... There is a life about to start when tomorrow comes!*

# CHAPTER 22

TJ arrived in Miami on time, grabbed a rental car and went directly to the City of Miami Beach Police Department on Washington Avenue. He found himself juggled around from person to person but was finally sitting by the desk of the lead detective, Luis Perez, on the Joe Hiller murder. Luis was a first generation Cuban who was tall and lanky with black hair cut extremely short. He was in his mid-forties and overweight by fifteen pounds. Luis had been on the job for more than twenty years. Working his way up through the ranks to detective was not an easy thing to do, as competition and prejudice were huge roadblocks at times. Here in the late afternoon he looked stressed and overworked as he sat at a cluttered desk in a small cubicle as private as Grand Central Station.

"What can I help you with?" said Luis, not looking up.

"I'm TJ Maverick, a criminal profiler with the FBI from Boston. I have been asked to look into the murder of Joe Hiller. This murder occurred over Labor Day Weekend of last year."

"Yeah, I remember the case. What's a profiler from Boston doing with this? I don't get it," said Luis.

"Well, it's an unusual case as it has a twin up in Windermere, which is just outside of Orlando. I think you know about that. At that crime scene, a New England Patriots ticket was found. Then, apparently, some very influential families put the full press on the right people to have it more carefully looked into. It landed on my boss's desk in Boston and so I'm here to take a look and get a feel for things."

Luis was now looking up into TJ's face. "So, what would you like to know?"

"Everything!"

For the next hour Luis went through all the reports and then had copies sent to TJ by email.

"So what's your best thinking about who and why?" asked TJ.

"Let me be very honest with you. We have a lot of murders in Miami and Miami Beach. Only 50%, if we're lucky, get solved. This one has gone cold. There was nothing left at the crime scene — no prints, no DNA, no hair, etc. We canvassed the neighborhood and no one saw anything out of the ordinary. We checked cameras in the area and got nothing. It's as cold-blooded as I've seen with the toe and blood thing but we have nowhere to go with it. My best guess is it's a professional hit with some kind of message being sent. The perp probably flew in and flew out in a matter of twenty-four hours, never to be heard from again. At least not in the Miami Beach area. I'd say this Joe Hiller guy did something that really pissed someone off. Same with the guy up in the Orlando area. Both of them did something that got the wrong people's attention. You know what I mean?"

"So it's on the back burner, so to speak. Correct?"

"Look at my desk. I've got new stuff coming in all the time. We do what we can do and then we have to move on."

TJ left, discouraged. He went to the crime scene but there really wasn't anything to be seen. After that he checked into a hotel, got some food and read over everything the detective had sent to him. Then he hit the rack.

Early the next morning he drove the 238 miles to Windermere, using the Florida Turnpike. TJ pushed his speed to 80 and made it in three hours. He found and spoke with the lead detective assigned to the Troy Wilson murder. His name was John Cunningham. He was an older white man in his early fifties with a styled beard and a shaved head. Average height. Average weight. Average looking. Not handsome, not ugly. He spoke with a south-slow accent. Again TJ received all the information from the investigation that might be helpful. It was obvious they were perplexed about the case with no real direction to go. Same scenario: no blood, no DNA, no hair — no trace of the killer. The wife who was restrained saw nothing that helped in any way.

Detective Cunningham knew both men were in the same fraternity at the same time in the early '70's but, beyond that, he could find no connection. It seemed unlikely to him that their time together so many years ago would now bring about the kind of vicious deaths they both endured. In his opinion, it had to be something more current but he had no concrete idea of what that might be. They had investigated but found nothing recent that connected the two men. The opinion of Detective Cunningham was there was something illegal, probably drugs, that they were involved with. When TJ asked about his take on the Patriots ticket he just got a shrug.

Once more TJ drove out to look over the crime scene but he found and saw nothing of interest. Famished, he found a Sonny's BBQ and ordered a slab of baby-back ribs with baked beans, fries, and a large Diet Coke. He now felt revived, even though his trip wasn't turning up much. He went to a mid-priced hotel for the night, made a plane reservation to get back to Boston and went to sleep.

He would be home in time for the scheduled card game at Chip's house.

# CHAPTER
# 23

"Good morning and may I have your attention, please. This will be the first report from our newest criminal profiler, Dr. TJ Maverick. He has been previously introduced to you so you know his credentials. I personally invited him to participate in a somewhat non-typical case for a three-month duration because the Boston Division was asked to get involved. Dr. Maverick has already informed me of his thoughts as I asked him to report directly to me. I believe his perspective and logic will be helpful for all of us to hear regardless of which case you have been assigned presently to work. I find his thinking to be intelligent, astute, and penetrating. He is deeply insightful. Some of his methods of deduction and judgement are a bit unique. Most of you know the background of the case in question from the weekly brief. It's the one concerning the two murders in Florida.

"I have also invited the Boston Police Deputy Superintendent of the Criminal Investigative Division, Deputy Superintendent Chip Thompson. I am anticipating the need to establish a joint task force that involves both the FBI and the Boston Police Department with this case. I wanted to get a little head start on it today. Without any further introductions, I give you Dr. Maverick," said Darius.

"Thanks Darius ... I mean Special Agent Mitchell. So these are my thoughts concerning the Florida murders as the lead profiler. I do hope my assessments might be helpful in any present or future case that you find to be similar. I also know that not all this information is new to you but it could serve as a good reminder.

"As an introduction, let me say that, overall, monsters are made, not born. And from my perspective, all murderers are monsters. I understand there is a small proportion of people, about four per cent, who do not have a conscience. We have named them sociopaths. As we know, not all sociopaths are murderers, child molesters, torturers, or cannibals like Jeffrey Dahmer. In fact, most are not. Most are effectively oblivious to us as they learn to appear normal by manufacturing emotions normal people feel. This would include love, regret, and sympathy.

"Fifty thousand people die violently every year in America. Why? The four main reasons are: relationship problems, interpersonal conflicts, mental health problems, and recent crises. People get wounded but not all wounds are visible. We must remember that there's always a history to pain. Stories never begin when they happen. Make no mistake, pain produces monsters. It's how a person handles their pain that ultimately determines their life. Everyone experiences pain in their lives. There are those who carry pain and there are those who cause pain. For example: one half of all females who are murdered are killed by a current or former spouse or partner. Some egregious pain surrounding their relationship triggered murder.

"A small percentage of the four per cent without a conscience are born like that, as their cerebral cortex does not function correctly. But studies show that most sociopaths are produced from their environmental factors such as childhood abuse and neglect. In fact, most murderers are *NOT* sociopaths. And, most murders are *NOT* caused by serial killers. Therefore, the overall truth is that monsters are made, not born.

"Additionally, books, magazines, newspapers, television, and movies produce wrong thinking because of a wrong emphasis. I believe they have it wrong because the general population does not want to see or know or admit the truth to themselves. So often it's a story about a serial killer who tortures animals in their childhood and then goes bonkers (a very technical term by the way!) in some mysterious way. In these narratives, the killer leaves messages for the police involving a particular detective or nemesis because he/she thinks he/she is smarter and can't be caught. Certainly that happens. But it's rare. Somehow people feel better thinking it's some mysterious germ-like thing floating in the air that gets caught by only a few bad people and that's what produces the crazies that murder. Then they can sleep better at night. But it's more often the everyday, normal, next-door-kind-of-person who gets traumatized and then gets angry and vengeful that causes the chaos. The turmoil is mostly the reaction to something or someone. Trauma is anything that overwhelms the brain's ability to cope. It can begin with a hurt or jealousy or abuse or a disturbing shock — and end in murder.

"For the record, I traveled down to Florida (yep, I know, a tough life!) and talked face to face with the lead detectives in both Miami Beach and Windermere. Both feel their case has gone cold. I went to each of the crime scenes although neither was still actually taped-off at this point in time. I asked for and received the crime-scene photos and the police reports. I spoke on the phone briefly to the forensic scientist in each case. I also called the University of Florida to access some of the victims' student records. In addition to all of this, I've been researching past murders with any similarities. So with all that, here are my conclusions so far ....

"One. There is always luck and chance involved in any investigation. Investigations are like puzzles. There are many pieces to fit together. Some puzzles are easy and some are hard. This one is hard.

"Two. These murders were probably done by one individual. A white male. The victims were both male Caucasians around fifty years old. So because of being in that age group any strong relational or emotional association to the victims would most likely be with another Caucasian. Obviously, that is not always the case. It's a best guess.

"Three. The perpetrator is highly intelligent and well prepared. How he entered the homes and how he left them not leaving any trace of himself was a well-executed and smart plan. He does not want to be caught. He's not playing games with the police. He's not purposely leaving any clues behind. He wants to get in to kill specific people and then get out to return to his everyday life.

"Four. He cut the ten toes off each victim. He wanted to cause pain but he also wanted to send them some kind of symbolic message.

"Five. I believe he was punishing his victims. Maybe an eye-for-an-eye kind of thing. Pain given for pain caused. Maybe death given for death caused.

"Six. He slowly drew out their blood. He wanted them to have a slow, painful death while they were able to think about whatever they had done to him or to someone he loves. So he was inflicting pain to alleviate his own pain. By doing this, it gave him a feeling of power and control. But as I've already said, it was mostly done for punishment. Therefore, I don't see this being a drug-related crime or a random crime or a crime of passion. It was premeditated. It was deliberated.

"Seven. The two victims are connected. They both went to the University of Florida and they were in the same fraternity at the same time. It can't be just a coincidence. I think this is a key to everything. This must be thoroughly investigated.

"Eight. In my mind there is no doubt the killer is from the New England area. The only mistake he has made so far is to drop a portion of a Patriots ticket at the scene of the second murder. There is no other explanation for it. A Pats fan going to a cold weather, regular-season game is most likely living in the region.

"Now here's where you might think I'm getting a little funky. I have always used the Bible for truths about people in both my private practice and in everyday life. Whether you believe in God or the Bible doesn't matter. The wisest man living in his time was Solomon, and in Proverbs he wrote truths about the human condition and about human nature. So I'll continue my thoughts with the topic of jealousy.

"Nine. It says in Proverbs 6:34 ... 'For jealousy arouses a husband's fury, and he will show no mercy when he takes revenge.' And in Proverbs 27:4 ... 'Anger is cruel and fury overwhelming, but who can stand before jealousy?' Maybe jealousy is the motive or a portion of the motive. It certainly is something that has been built into the human heart. And, it can be what triggers murder.

"Ten. When we know the motive, we will know the killer."

With that, TJ looked out into the audience and hoped he was now an embraced member of the FBI club. He surprised himself on how much he wanted their acceptance.

"I've got some more digging and analyzing to do. Hopefully I'll soon have some helpful direction to give to the detectives in charge of the different investigations. With the right information we can start putting more pieces of the puzzle together. As each new piece fits together, we'll get a more defined picture of the monster. And with enough pieces, we'll be able to see his face."

TJ finished and sat down. The room was still for a moment and then someone starting clapping and the others joined in. TJ thought he must have done an acceptable job.

The three friends decided to meet in Darius' office for a few minutes away from the crowd.

"Mav, you did an amazing job with that!" said Darius.

Speaking to Darius, Chip said, "I told you Maverick was the man for the job! And I must say he sounded a lot like an investigator along with a profiler."

"Yes, he did. Keep up the great work, Mav," said Darius.

"Yes, great work," said Chip.

"Hey, one thing guys. I need some help as soon as possible. I need a detective who can do some investigative work. The lead D's in Florida are not doing a lot right now and I doubt they'll take a whole lot of direction from me although I'll try to give them some," said TJ.

"Mav, you know my situation. Everyone is crazy busy with all the terrorist stuff," said Darius.

"I think I can help," said Chip. "You mentioned a task force, Darius. Let's put a small one together with Maverick and one of my best detectives from the Boston PD. The man I have in mind just closed a big case so I know he's got some space in his schedule. His name is Justice Jackson."

"Sounds good to me," replied Darius. "What do you think, Mav?"

"Sounds good to me, too. And thanks, Chip."

"No thanks necessary. I'll arrange a meeting."

They gave each other fist bumps and left to have a little celebration over lunch about TJ's successful start. They both said TJ would pay because he was the big winner at last week's poker game.

# CHAPTER
## 24

The Starbucks in downtown Boston on Beacon Street across the street from the Boston Common was jammed with people. The line was long and everyone seemed to have their special concoction that had to be made exactly to their specifications. TJ just ordered a tall, black coffee with no room for cream or sugar. As he was handed his drink, he saw two people leaving from a corner that had two overstuffed, brown leather chairs. He ran over to grab them before anyone else had the chance. He was waiting to meet the other half of what was being generously called a task force. He was waiting for Justice Jackson.

A tall, well-built black man made his way confidently through the double doors of the Starbucks. Justice looked around until he saw TJ sitting in the corner with an empty armchair beside him and then gave a slight nod. TJ waved him over, stood up and they shook hands. They were both sizing each other up.

Justice had a small scar on his chin and a larger one above his right cheek. He had the air of a man who could easily take care of himself. He was wearing black jeans with classic Chelsea boots that were also black. His shirt was a cream-colored waffle-knit Henley worn under a black, leather bomber jacket. A person could get a glimpse of his Glock 17 and shoulder holster if they watched him closely. He was in his late 30's and had a bit of grey coming in around his temples. He had on his left hand ring finger a plain, white-gold wedding ring. TJ took a liking to him immediately.

"Hello, my name is Dr. TJ Maverick, but please just call me TJ."

"I'm Homicide Detective Justice Jackson but call me Detective Jackson."

"Let me get you something to drink before we chat for a while," suggested TJ.

"No thanks. I'm good. And I'm in a bit of a hurry so let's just talk about what you need me to do. You must have some pull if you've got Deputy Superintendent Thompson making this meeting happen for you."

"Well, Chip's a good friend. Back in high school is where I first, let's say, bumped into him. But, it's only been in the last few months that the bond between us has become close and strong. Presently I'm working for the Boston FBI as a criminal profiler and they put me on what they call an unusual case," remarked TJ.

"Why unusual?"

"Because the two murders occurred in Florida which is not exactly the Boston FBI's territory. The only connection to the New England area is a dropped Patriots ticket found at the second crime scene. It definitely didn't belong to anyone in the house of that crime scene. Then a father of one of the victims demanded more attention be given to the investigation. That person is apparently very rich and has influential friends in high places so the request for help landed on my boss' desk. I thought at first it was both families of the victims demanding a deeper investigation but it was just the one. The Wilson family. Troy Wilson was the second victim."

TJ took Detective Jackson through the details of the two murders.

He handed him copies of everything he had received from the Florida detectives. Justice remarked about the toes being cut off and the slow leaking of the blood being bizarre, monstrous, and totally over the top.

"So what are you looking for me to do to help?" asked Justice.

"Well, since the detectives in Florida have shoved this to the back of their desks, I think it needs a lot of basic investigative work. You would know better than me but I was thinking about someone looking into flights taken by a person out of Logan around the dates of the two murders. Or maybe out of Providence or any of the New England airports. I was thinking about someone finding out about cars being rented by a person around those same dates and locations. Maybe it would be good to talk to a few of the most involved and most outgoing frat brothers who would know the victims back in the late sixties and early seventies. And, maybe finding out if these two somehow stayed in touch with each other. I assume their home phones and mobile phones were already checked but I'm no tech geek to know everything that could be done. Then, the more I think about it, I'd like to get a chance to talk to the parents of the two men who were targeted … that is, if they're still alive. Additionally there's the need to figure out more about the men who died by having conversations with officials from the University of Florida. What a person is like in those formative years tell a big story of who that person becomes later in life. I actually was a UF student during some of the same years they were there so that makes me even more curious about what really happened. Now I'm sure there must be more that could and should be done but I'm pretty new at all of this."

"How new?"

"Just started a few weeks ago."

"Great. I'm stuck with a rookie!"

"Not really. I've got plenty of degrees, from high profile schools, many years of working with real-live clients and much time with college teaching experience. So don't sell me short. I'm just new at using my knowledge and skills in my present profiler gig," said TJ, defending himself.

"Okay, okay. Don't get all uptight. I didn't mean anything by it."

"Sorry if I overreacted. It's just that I could tell when you walked through the door that I would like you and I could trust you. So, it would be great if we could become friends, or at least be friendly and respectful during this short time we're working together. I need your expertise, advice, direction, and help. Believe me, I know I've got a lot to learn."

"Fair enough. So just a thought here. Let's remember it was the time of the Vietnam War, heavy LSD use, the free-love explosion with the ever helpful pill, hippies, streaking, the aftermath of the assassinations of JFK, RFK and MLK, sit-ins, violent and peaceful demonstrations, black power, legalized abortion ... and the list could go on. There might be some kind of weird connection to that past history. Maybe they knew something or experienced something at that time and, for some reason, they're just now getting killed for it."

"Yep. Retrojecting could be very helpful. There's a lot going on during that period of time for sure and you may be right on the mark with those thoughts. After all, pain doesn't know time. Or it could be something as simple as both of them being involved with the same girl ... or guy. But, for sure, the perp wanted to be up-close and personal enjoying the pain of his victims. I have a strong feeling it was about punishing them for something they did. In my way of thinking, the person who did these horrible acts needs to pay big time for them!"

"Hey, TJ. Be sure to realize there's a great many unsolved homicides across the country. Plus there are deaths misattributed to overdose, accidents or undetermined causes, which means there are even more murders than the stats indicate. I know there's no question about these being brutal murders but, with you being new and all, let me clue you in on the fact that we can't always find the killers. I'm just saying, especially with such little concrete information to go on, to not get your hopes up too high. You know those CSI shows are a load of crap. It's not so easy or so quick. They wrap up all their cases in a short span of time and that's totally ridiculous! But there are two things those shows do have right — always follow the money and always follow the pain. You see, if we learn the why, then we'll learn the who."

"I wouldn't call that a great pep talk, Detective Jackson."

"Yeah, but it's the awful truth. Take the pretty, young woman, Susan, or Su, Taraskiewicz back in September of 1992. She was the first woman to become a ground crew chief supervisor for Northwest Airlines at Logan. She was found stuffed into the trunk of a car after being beaten and stabbed to death. So what did she see or know? Was it drugs coming in? Was there a credit card scam she found out about? We still have no idea and it remains to this day, ten years later, an open case. As you may already know, Logan Airport has always had problems well before the 9/11 fiasco."

"I know too well about the 9/11 fiasco. My wife was a victim on American Airlines, Flight 11."

"Oh my God! I am so sorry. I had no idea."

They both sat in silence for a period of time not sure of what to say next. Finally, TJ broke the silence.

"Justice. That's an unusual name. How did that get chosen for you?" inquired TJ.

"Big question. I'll try to give a relatively short answer. My dad was deeply into social justice. There's a clue right there! Although Boston is in the North and people had the idea that there was greater equality because of the location, it was far from the truth. My dad was inspired by the Birmingham Movement and so he became a voice for the "Stay Out For Freedom" campaign here in Boston. This was a move to demand desegregation by having kids *stay out* of school. Then there were different incidents that provoked storms of protests. My dad would almost always be in the middle of the turmoil. For instance, there was the beating and arrest of a Roxbury resident and folk singer named Jackie Washington. And in January of '63 there was the strangling murder of sixteen-year-old Daniela Saunders. This was determined to be the work of the Boston Strangler but the murder outraged Black Bostonians and my dad was caught up in the anger and in the fight for justice.

"Then, to top it all off, my father traveled to DC for the March on Washington for Jobs and Freedom. Of course that's when Dr. King gave his *I Have A Dream speech* — August 28, 1963. Most people hold on to and remember from that speech the words: "I have a dream" or "let freedom ring" or "free at last." But my dad memorized and would always repeat a different part of that speech. His favorite words were: 'The whirlwinds of revolt will continue to shake the foundations of our nation until the bright day of justice emerges.'

"Soon after coming back to Boston from DC, he was protesting and was arrested. It was a peaceful protest until the police showed up with clubs, tear gas and rubber bullets. My mother, pregnant with me, was in the crowd. Trying to protect her, my dad pushed a cop to the ground. He was immediately arrested. As they were dragging him away he was shouting those favorite words of his. But when he came near the end of those words, a white policeman hit him on the head so hard that it instantly killed him. The cop was never charged. The last words my mother heard him shouting were: 'THE BRIGHT DAY OF JUSTICE.'

"And so, when I was born, my mother named me, Justice. My father's final word."

"My goodness ... that's a shocking, horrible, and beautiful story all at the same time. The beautiful part is with your name and the fact that, in spite of all that, you become a cop," said TJ.

"I'm in the fight with my dad every day for justice — just not in exactly the same way. I know he wasn't perfect but he was on the right track with his heart in the right place."

"Sounds that way to me."

"And honestly, I've told very few people that much of the story. I'm not sure why it all came out right now with you. I don't even know you. I guess with you losing your wife the way you did … I could."

They stayed another fifteen minutes talking about the specific next steps of what each would attempt to do with the case they now shared. They exchanged phone numbers so they could stay in touch with each other.

As they were leaving, they shook hands in a manly and meaningful way as the detective looked straight into TJ's eyes and said, "Please, drop the Detective Jackson and just call me by my first name … Justice."

# CHAPTER
# 25

The monster had another terrible night. Very little sleep. The whole PTSD thing was alive and well and at work.

For the monster, a number of shocking and unexpected life events had been the cause of his post-traumatic stress. One of these events began as a simple visit to see a doctor when Leah became pregnant after three years of marriage.

---

"Hello Dr. Kimberlin. Thank-you for seeing us. We have heard you are one of the best in your field so we are happy to put our baby in your hands," said the monster.

"Well, thank-you for the kind words and I'm happy to get to know you both. My understanding is that this pregnancy has been a long time coming. That it was not an easy road to get to this point. Is that correct?" asked the obstetrician.

"Yes, all of that is true. It took a lot longer than either of us thought it would once we decided to have a child," said Leah.

"Well, we are here now. Before I examine you, I just have a few questions to ask. First, what is your blood type, Leah?"

"It's A negative."

"And have you ever been pregnant before?"

"Well ...."

The monster jumped in and said, "This is the first, doctor, and we are so excited!"

"Okay, then there's no problem. It's just with having a Rh-negative blood type, although fine with the first pregnancy, it can be life-threatening with following pregnancies if not dealt with properly."

"Just out of curiosity, could you explain that to me?" asked Leah.

"Sure. Your blood type tells you about markers on the surface of your red blood cells. The red cells in your blood can be A, B, AB or O. The red blood cells also have a protein that is called Rh on the surface of the cell. So, your blood can be Rh positive, which means that you have the Rh protein, or Rh negative, which means that you don't have the Rh protein. The letter of your blood group plus the Rh makes your blood type. Any questions before I go on?"

Leah was intensely still. The monster looked a bit disinterested. The doctor continued his explanation.

"So, being Rh negative means that you do not have Rh proteins on your red blood cells. Leah, if your baby is Rh positive and you get a small amount of your baby's blood into your bloodstream when you're pregnant or when you give birth, your body can make antibodies that hurt and kill red blood cells that are Rh positive. The most likely time you would be exposed to your baby's blood is when you give birth. This is why being Rh-negative will not harm your baby during your first pregnancy. But in your next pregnancy, the antibodies that you made when you were exposed to the Rh-positive blood at your first birth can cross the placenta and attack the Rh-positive red blood cells, if your next baby has Rh-positive blood. This is called Rh sensitization. Rh sensitization can occur any time the fetus' blood mixes with the mother's blood, which includes the times of miscarriage, ectopic pregnancy, or abortion.

"Now I hope I'm not getting too technical for you but since you asked for an explanation, I just want you to understand the situation fully."

The doctor had a suspicion that this was not Leah's first pregnancy. He continued.

"So, in other words, your body could respond as if it is allergic to the baby if the baby is Rh-positive. This can cause fetal anemia, miscarriage, stillbirth, or a serious illness in the baby called hemolytic disease. Obviously we don't want any of that so we give what's called a RhoGAM shot at twenty-eight weeks of pregnancy."

"So what exactly does that shot do, doctor?" asked the monster, trying to engage in the conversation.

"Well, RhoGAM is a very safe and proven medicine that would stop a person with Rh-negative blood from making antibodies that attack the Rh-positive blood cells. And like I said, we give it at twenty-eight weeks. This is because it's during the last trimester of a pregnancy when a woman's placenta is growing and the membranes that separate her blood from the baby's blood are very thin.

Now he spoke directly to Leah.

"Then, soon after you give birth, your baby's blood would be tested for Rh. If your baby's blood has Rh-positive blood, you will get another dose of the RhoGAM within seventy-two hours after you give birth. If your baby's blood is Rh-negative, you will not need the second shot. Does that all make sense to you?"

"Well, then ... to be honest, I have been pregnant before. I had an abortion when I was 19," Leah said very quietly, looking down at the floor.

"Okay. No problem, Leah. And since it's your first prenatal visit, we will test to be certain about your blood type," said Dr. Kimberlin.

This news was completely shocking to the monster. It had never heard about this part of her life. Inside its head and its heart, emotions were exploding. It stoically stared forward acting as if this was not really new news to him in front of the doctor but the doctor could tell that a massive internal explosion had just taken place.

Leah was quiet and in some kind of far-off world. The monster just wanted to get out of the doctor's office and find out the specifics of his world getting turned upside-down.

---

"What's this all about, Leah? I've never heard about you ever being pregnant and having an abortion. I thought we had 'the talk' about our past lives before we got married. I thought we had been honest with one another. I thought we could trust each other. You told me about your boyfriends. I told you about my girlfriends. You told me there was one long-term relationship and how he had cheated on you and how that had broken your heart at the time. As you can tell, I'm angry and I want the truth," said the monster.

Leah took a long pause before she spoke. "First, let me say I'm sorry. I just didn't want to lose you. I loved you too much to risk losing you. You had, and still have, such a strong opinion against abortion and about unwanted children. You told me how you had struggled with not knowing your real mom and dad. You told me what a nightmare it was for you to be adopted and then to never know why you weren't wanted and loved. Again, I'm sorry I kept it from you. That long-term relationship guy, Lincoln, got me pregnant and I had an abortion. That was when I was just 19 and a sophomore in college. I wasn't going to marry him. He wasn't going to marry me. I wasn't going to be a single mother. End of story. After that ordeal I completely stopped dating and concentrated on my studies. I graduated, moved to Boston for my Masters and I met you. I don't really want to discuss it any more than that!"

Day after day for many months the monster would have mental flashes of its wife in the arms of another man. It had seen a picture of Lincoln in one of Leah's parent's family photo albums on one of his visits to Leah's home. So, it knew what he looked like. That didn't help the mental torment. Night after night the monster would try to go to sleep as its mind blasted these kind of images along with thoughts about her abortion. It had always hated the idea that the love of his life had been with another man but he had at least thought he could be the first to give her a child. And it would be a baby who was wanted by its real mom and dad. It would be a baby who was deeply loved and cherished.

With the truth coming out into the open, a large degree of trust had been broken. The monster was questioning the woman he had married. It felt crushed.

---

After a period of time, the monster and Leah had successfully moved beyond past memories, painful hurts, and trust issues in their relationship. In fact, the monster had become more deeply in love with her as the years went by. But now, in the midst of deep and daily grief, the monster's rage had been resurrected as it uncovered more and more of the truth about Leah's life.

The monster kept looping painful images and painful thoughts in its mind. PTSD.

# CHAPTER
# 26

"Hello, my name is Amy. I live down the street and I'm selling the best cookies in the world. Girl Scout cookies! What kind and how many boxes would you like to order today?" said the slick seven-year-old salesgirl with her mother standing nearby.

"Well, I guess with that bold sales pitch I'll have to get eight boxes of the Thin Mints and two of the Samoas. The Thin Mints are my absolute favorite. I like to put them in the freezer and eat them cold," said the monster.

"So ten boxes in all. Thanks so much! Just print your name here and fill in the kind you want along with the number of boxes you want and I'll bring your cookies to you very soon. You pay at the time of delivery," said the cheerful little girl.

"Okay, thanks for coming by, Amy. And keep up the good work. You're a natural at this!"

The monster shut the door behind him on this sunny and unusually warm Saturday afternoon. It went back to reading the portion of Leah's diaries that always got him unsettled and upset. It was about her abortion.

*I HAD AN ABORTION! I can hardly believe I'm saying that. Here I am, a nineteen-year-old college student who has been gang raped and cheated on. I feel like I've been thrown out with the garbage. I had no heart to marry the father because I don't even know who that is! I certainly had no desire to be a single mother. Up until the time that I found myself pregnant, I had been opposed to abortion. My conviction had nothing to do about how God might feel about it; in my mind, abortion was morally and ethically wrong. WHAT A 180 DEGREE TURN-AROUND FROM THAT VIEW! Since abortion is illegal in Florida I went to NY where abortions were legal. I had no thought for the child. My only thoughts were on my predicament so I traveled to NYC for the procedure.*

*Only my EX-boyfriend and the woman helping me with the arrangements knew of my plans. I flew to New York by myself and was transported in a bus with other women who had flown in from all around the United States. Some of us began conversations, explaining how and why we got into the situations we were in. There was the girl who said, "I only did it once." There was the woman who had enough children already and did not want any more. Another woman was a repeater — she had visited the clinic before. We were pleasant with one another, encouraging, as if we were all on a trip to the dentist.*

*Upon arrival at the clinic, all of us were herded into waiting rooms where we filled out forms and had our blood tested. A nurse instructed us, in mass, about what the operation would involve. We chatted as we waited for our turn. One by one names were called, and women would put down their magazines and walk out of the room. When it was my name that was called, I went into a dressing room, removed all my clothing and jewelry, and put on a hospital gown. I walked barefoot into the operating room where the nurse instructed me to lie down on the table. She put my feet in the stirrups as the doctor entered, a surgeon's mask covering her face. I remember being surprised that the doctor was a woman but somehow it comforted me. A gas mask was placed over my mouth and nose, and I was told to count backwards. The last words I heard was the nurse saying, "We are ready to begin, Dr. Finch." Then there was a loud whirring sound, and at that moment I fell asleep.*

*The next thing I remember was being in a recovery ward with dozens of other women. Some were moaning, some were crying, some were vomiting. I awoke with no pain, no discomfort except for some minor cramping. There was a slight ache in my heart, but only slight. I was relieved. It was over. My "problem" was over.*

*The rest of the trip was uneventful. I returned to Gainesville, I went to classes, and life was normal. SORT OF! I find myself again drinking a lot and smoking pot a lot. I also find myself willing to be promiscuous, going from one guy to the next. WHAT A SLUT! WHO CARES? I feel ruined the way I am so I'll take what I want and need physically without getting emotionally close or staying around for very long. I am extremely careful not to get pregnant. I certainly do not want to go through another abortion ordeal again. I now take every precaution including "the pill." WHY DIDN'T I TAKE IT EARLIER? This seems to be the miracle helping to drive what's being called the sexual revolution. I remember seeing a picture of it on the cover of a TIME magazine when I was in eighth grade and then secretly reading the article away from my parents' eyes. But, I never thought that I would ever use it! My dream was to find my one, true Prince and marry him and raise a family together. I believed that would make me happy. NOW MY LIFE IS CRAP!*

*I am mad at myself for what I've allowed to happen to me. I feel like so much of it is my fault. I have an occasional twinge of guilt about having the abortion, but I quickly push it out of my mind. I have done what I had to do. And that's that.*

*The thing I've decided to do now is to study hard and to excel in all my coursework. I'm hoping this can be the path for me to still have a good and happy life. BUT IS THAT POSSIBLE? AND ... AM I GOOD?*

That night the monster tossed and turned in bed due to the emotional trauma that was stemming from its childhood of being the product of an unwanted pregnancy. It had learned that its birth mother had wanted an abortion until, at the last minute, her parents had stopped it. This story all came out after a moment of intense anger and frustration when the monster's adoptive mother shouted at him, "They should have aborted you!"

PTSD. To try and sleep the monster couldn't try counting sheep or any other animal or object because it would start counting the number of men who raped Leah. Then it would turn to counting the number of different men she had slept with. Finally, the monster would count the number of times she had sex with Lincoln. The monster had images of these things flashing and crashing in and out of its mind throughout the night. Much of this was from its own imagination but the mental pictures were projected because of the words found in the diaries. It was all ugly information that the monster had only recently learned. There was so much Leah had hidden from the monster. There were so may lies she had told and lived.

The two words she had used to describe herself in her diary were like daggers in the monster's heart. PROMISCUOUS SLUT. And, the word of what she had done with her unwanted baby tormented the monster. ABORTION.

# 1981

Leah and the monster were seeing Dr. Kimberlin again. They had lost their first baby soon after their initial visit two years earlier with a miscarriage. Now they had just gone through the agony of a third miscarriage and they were looking for some answers. After having the dilatation and curettage done four weeks previously, this was to be a simple check-up appointment. She hadn't needed the D&C done with the first two miscarriages but this time Leah had heavy bleeding and significant pain and so it was deemed necessary. Leah had been put under general anesthesia and when she was asleep, the procedure took only five to ten minutes. This brought Leah back to reliving the memories of her abortion in high definition clarity. It had been many years since traveling to NYC but with each passing year she would calculate the age her child would have been. Although her circumstances surrounding her initial pregnancy were abhorrent, it was no longer just a bit of remorse that was felt every now and then. It was so much more than that. It was like an ever intensifying storm of regret, shame, and disgrace.

"As you know, we have been trying to have a baby for a very long time. This is our third miscarriage. What do you think the problem could be? Is there any solution for it?" inquired the monster.

"Well, let me first say that I am very sorry about all that has happened with your pregnancies. I am sure it has been an emotional rollercoaster for both of you. Now Leah, as sensitive as this may be, have you told me everything about your abortion? Were there any complications that you know of either during the procedure or after it?" asked the doctor very gently.

"It all seemed to go well. I flew in and out of the City on the same day that I had it done. I was somewhat uncomfortable right afterward but nothing of any great note. I did have painful cramping and some discharge in the days following it but I just figured it was all a part of the ordeal," Leah said, matter-of-factly.

"Did you have a temperature along with the cramping and what was the color of the discharge?"

"Yes, I did have a fever that made me weak but I never took my temperature so I don't know what it was exactly. I know it was high. The discharge was yellowish-pink. Was this abnormal? I didn't want to go and see any doctor about it for obvious reasons."

"Those facts are very significant. One more question. How long were you pregnant before you had your abortion?"

"My guesstimate was eight to nine weeks. I missed at least two of my periods. By the way, I did hear the nurse talking as I was in the recovery room about my procedure being a little difficult but then she told me all was fine and there was nothing to worry about."

Leah had been counting the weeks from the time of being raped by her multiple violators to figure how long she had been pregnant.

"Why all these questions, doctor? What, if any, significance is there with the answers she gave?" the monster asked.

"Well, there's a lot that concerns me with this information. A person having an abortion should not have a fever, yellowish-pink discharge or prolonged, painful cramping after the abortion. All of that tells me something was going very wrong. A fever indicates there was an infection and this infection was never treated.

"Three possible issues come to mind beginning with the sad fact that in a first trimester abortion the doctor sometimes performs what is known as an incomplete abortion. It's rare but it happens. This is when some of the tissue is accidently left in the uterus. When fetal tissue is left behind in the womb it can rot and cause a severe infection that can cause permanent damage to the female reproductive organs. This can result in sterility or miscarriage of future pregnancies.

"Another thought, although this usually happens due to having multiple abortions, is having scarring at the top of the cervix or inside the uterus. Any procedure that dilates the cervix, which is a necessary step in most abortions, can weaken it. It can affect the ability of the embryo to implant into the uterus or the ability of the cervix to support a pregnancy.

"One other possible issue would be PID or Pelvic Inflammatory Disease. This is an infection of the upper part of the female reproductive system. The disease is caused by bacteria that spreads from the vagina and cervix. Infections by Neisseria gonorrhoeae or Chlamydia trachomatis are present in 75 to 90 percent of the cases. Having multiple sex partners increases this risk. This is usually accompanied by fever and lower abdominal pain," said Dr. Kimberlin.

"That's a lot to take in," said Leah.

"My best guess, unless you had multiple sex partners and then had a diagnosed venereal disease yourself, is that you had an incomplete abortion."

"I didn't have multiple sex partners or multiple abortions or a venereal disease so you can rule those out," stated Leah, feeling bad about lying about the multiple sex partners.

"Then most likely, the doctor doing your abortion did not do a complete job. Again guessing; I think you were probably pregnant for eleven to thirteen weeks instead of the eight or nine. With later abortions, thirteen weeks and over, the risk of complication is five times as great. The fetus literally doubles in size between the eleventh and twelfth weeks of pregnancy which means a greater amount of fetal material must be removed. As you experienced, the cervix is dilated and then a suction device is placed in the uterine cavity to remove the fetus and placenta. Then the doctor inserts a curette, which is a loop-shaped knife, into the uterus. The curette is used to scrape any remaining fetal parts and the placenta out of the uterus. Some must have been missed."

"So we can't have a baby?" the monster asked sharply.

"Most likely not. We can order some tests to be sure but it looks like Leah's reproductive organs were damaged in the aftermath of the abortion. I am so sorry."

The monster could only think about wanting to find and then to inflict pain upon the abortionist who had ruined his Leah and who had ruined his dream of a family.

Leah was looking out the window thinking about what she had just learned. If she was eleven to thirteen weeks pregnant, it would mean it was Lincoln's baby. Therefore, it was a baby made in love, not in lust. It was conceived with the boy she had genuinely loved, at least at the time. It was not conceived with the lions who tore her apart.

With this new understanding, the storm of guilt feelings were intensifying all the more for Leah. They left the doctor's office in silence.

# CHAPTER
## 27

TJ's main focus was on the two victims when they were University students. There was no doubt in his mind there had to be some kind of connection that would lead to the ultimate answer of the identity of the killer. The words exterminator, butcher, executioner, and assassin were also running through TJ's mind to describe the murderer.

TJ got a large cup of coffee from the kitchen and came into his main living area. He sat down on his comfortable couch and started making phone calls. He knew this was the beginning of some very long days. He made calls to UF's Dean of Students Office, Office for Student Financial Affairs, Office of the University Registrar, Office of Student Conduct and Conflict Resolution, the Student Health Care Center, Student Legal Services, UF Health Services, the Campus Police and to the UF Sigma Alpha Epsilon Fraternity. With each call he was hoping for the miracle of finding people who would be willing to look up school records concerning Joe Hiller and Troy Wilson. He was also hoping to talk to people who were working in some capacity around the University thirty to thirty-five years ago or to get some leads on people who had been there he could talk to.

TJ spent many hours and many days on this project. As the first week was ending, he thought of even trying to contact Stephen O'Connell, who had been the UF President from 1967 to 1973, but found out he had died just a year earlier at the age of eighty-five. While making his calls, he was able to acquire a small list of fraternity brothers who might be willing to share their insights and knowledge of the two murdered men.

Overall, most people were pleasant but not helpful. Just telling people he was with the FBI did not prove he was with the FBI. But the few he found who were willing to talk and look up records allowed some important insights to surface. Additionally, by talking to a few of the fraternity brothers, TJ was able to start seeing and feeling who Joe and Troy really were as people.

Both came from very wealthy and influential families and the two victims were apparently spoiled rich kids. TJ knew that money itself was neither good nor bad. It was neutral. But having it either humbled a person or filled a person with pride, arrogance, and entitlement. The vast majority of rich people skipped becoming humble. A Bible passage that TJ's granddad had made him memorize as a teenager was from the book of Deuteronomy: *"You may say to yourself, 'My power and the strength of my hands have produced this wealth for me.' But remember the Lord your God, for it is he who gives you the ability to produce wealth."* These words had helped to center TJ later in his life.

The Wilson family, extremely rich, had great wealth passed down through numerous generations coming from the automobile and railroad industries. Not to be outdone, the Hiller family was mega-rich. They had even given a boatload of money to the university, which financed a wing at Shands Hospital and a building on campus. Both structures proudly displayed the Hiller name. After hours of trying, TJ could not figure out exactly where their family fortune had come from. He did find some online articles saying they had added to their riches in an enormous way during the recent dot-com boom. Their financial advisors apparently knew when to cash-in before the burst of the dot-com bubble hit.

In speaking to three different frat brothers, all had an overabundance of flattering words for their old friends. He sensed they were reluctant to speak candidly, openly, and truthfully. He even felt they were somewhat fearful to say what they were actually thinking. The one phrase that stuck out from all the conversations was when he was told that privileged people consider themselves above the law and beyond the law. When asked what was meant by that, the individual hung up.

The people who were willing to discuss university records about the two boys all disclosed very positive, if not glowing, reports about them. Good grades. Good conduct. Good participation in the university's social scene and in student affairs. Joe had become the president of his fraternity for both his junior and senior year and was highly praised for the job he did. The only negative was a quick mention concerning some kind of conflict with a professor during Joe's freshman year. TJ wanted to find out more about that.

When TJ was speaking to a woman in the Office of Student Conduct and Conflict, she revealed there were records that were listed as confidential concerning Joe Hiller. After the helpful woman had time to read through the confidential report, TJ made a follow-up phone call. The woman decided she could inform TJ about its contents since the incident had occurred so far in the past. According to the report, Joe Hiller made a complaint early in his first year at UF against his English Literature professor, Dr. Conor Casey. The complaint specified that Joe had been invited to the teacher's home for private tutoring, where the professor tried to pressure him to have sex. Joe was still seventeen years old when this happened which made the case even more explosive since he was a minor. There were three boys who had given written, sworn testimony against the professor — Joe Hiller, Troy Wilson and

Pete Fox.

The result was the quiet removal and conviction of Professor Casey as a sexual offender. Since it never went to trial, the boys were kept out of the spotlight and their names out of the newspapers. Casey had pleaded guilty with the understanding he would serve no jail time. It was obvious to TJ that the wealthy parents had their hand in all of this. It was interesting that the money for the university was donated during this same time.

Another important piece to the puzzle was put in place when TJ contacted a fourth fraternity brother. TJ asked him if he knew anything about the matter with the fired English Literature professor. Only after getting TJ to promise that his words would be off the record and would not be repeated was the man willing to talk.

"The boys all boasted that they took the professor down using the fact that he was gay, at least to some extent, even though he had a wife and a son. Professor Casey bragged in class about his open marriage and about being bisexual like the English poet, Lord Byron. Joe was failing the course miserably and tried to bribe the professor with a large amount of money to get a strong passing grade. Joe was later confronted by him and told his conduct would be reported and that it could lead to expulsion from the university.

"So Joe made a plan. He went over to the professor's home when the rest of the family was not there. He made sure he was seen by neighbors as he entered. Later he put on a show as he came running out of the house looking scared and embarrassed. Joe got two frat brothers who were in the same English Lit class to join him in the lie about being approached or inappropriately touched. They bragged how their parents put pressure on the university and how Joe's father had offered a huge financial sum if all of this would be taken care of out of the eye of the public. With high-powered lawyers and with much money, influence, and power behind Hiller, the professor could see the writing on the wall and took the deal of a quiet conviction with no jail time. Of course, it ruined the professor's life and livelihood. This event bonded those three guys together and they became inseparable friends. They even formed a group they called THC — exclusive to the three of them. But that's another story. You're not asking about that and I don't have anything to say about it."

TJ was super grateful and excited about all this information and thanked the man profusely. He wasn't concerned about the apparent drug club they had started. Pot was everywhere on the campus. He had personal knowledge of that. He now believed he had a probable motive for the murders. He knew he needed to dig deeper and he knew he needed to talk with the third frat boy: Pete Fox.

# CHAPTER
## 28

The monster was on the prowl again. This time it landed at Atlanta Hartsfield-Jackson International Airport. It was happy because it had two stops to make in the same city. It felt it was achieving the proverbial goal of killing two birds with one stone. It got its rental car and sped off to the city center. It checked into a Hilton Garden Inn and then walked the short distance to the World of Coca-Cola museum located between the Georgia State Capitol and the Underground Atlanta shopping and entertainment district. It spent a few hours strolling around and enjoying the interactive exhibits, Coca-Cola artifacts, and video presentations of Coca-Cola advertising. Most fun was the 'Spectacular Fountain' where visitors were allowed to sample various Coke products. Overall, the experience was relaxing and soothing. It helped the monster focus and get ready for the reasons it had come. The reasons were Pete Fox and Lincoln Hart. On the way back to the hotel it grabbed a hamburger, fries, and a chocolate shake at Johnny Rockets. Then it returned to its hotel room and waited for darkness to fall.

The monster felt ready. It was well after midnight as it drove the fourteen miles to Sandy Springs. The monster was amazed how easy it was to find people now that the internet had been well established. He even found out that Pete had been divorced for a third time very recently. This was not surprising to the monster, considering the way Pete treated women. And this latest divorce would leave the man all alone in his big house in the serene suburbs of Atlanta.

After the monster's two previous revenge killings, it felt confident about doing the third one without any trouble. It had its backpack with all the needed items. It silently cut through a huge floor-to-ceiling window that overlooked the large kidney-shaped pool. There was a waterfall cascading through decorative rocks at the top of the pool. This soothing babble covered any disturbance that might be heard by the neighbors although the lots were large and any listening ears were a long way away.

The monster found Pete drunk and passed out on a couch in an amazing man-cave in the basement of the house. There was a curved, old fashion mahogany bar with matching stools. Behind the bar was a large mirror with the Florida Gator symbol etched in it. The monster was thinking that the multitude of Georgia Bulldogs in the area would not appreciate it. There were many bottles of expensive liquor on decorative glass shelves, along with glasses for every kind of drink imaginable. On one side of the basement expanse was a slate pool table with dark blue felt. There was also a very professional looking dartboard in that area. The walls were all filled with Gator sports memorabilia. On the opposite side of the room was an enormous brown, leather couch that faced the largest flatscreen TV the monster had ever seen. It laughed out loud when it saw Grace Kelly and realized that the old Hitchcock movie, *Dial M for Murder,* was playing.

The monster helped the inebriated man, who was unaware of what was really going on around him, move from the couch to the pool table. Soon, he was lying on his back completely nude as the monster used ropes to tie his hands and feet to the four legs of the pool table. He looked like an X marking the spot ... the spot to alleviate the monster's pain. It used the silver-grey duct tape to keep Pete's mouth shut and to wrap around his body to immobilize him. With that accomplished the monster went to the couch and watched the movie while he waited for Pete to come out of the alcohol stupor. It wanted him to be fully aware of what was happening to him.

After a while, Pete began fighting against the ropes and the tape. He understood enough to know he was facing imminent danger. The monster smiled and pulled out its syringe, vials of lidocaine, bypass pruner and the IV drip paraphernalia. It started the IV slowly, dripping Pete's blood from his body.

"Hey, Pete. Great to finally meet you. I've been staring at your picture for months now. It belonged to my wife. You know, one of the girls you raped back in college with your buddies. Oh, and by the way, she's dead. She died a slow death that began with a Homecoming party at your frat house. I guess you got some points, or digits as you boys liked to call them, for nailing a virgin. So I've got a slow death for you tonight. You can't really see it but your blood is slowly dripping out on the floor. It's a beautiful red. Just like the red Leah found on her sheets the morning after she was raped by all of you."

With this news, Pete came completely out of his alcohol daze. He was wide-eyed and struggling in vain against the ropes and the tape. He tried to make a life-saving noise but no sound penetrated the air.

"And Pete, I'm not done yet. See this bypass pruner? We've got some work to do. And you know, although your buddies, Joe and Troy, got some lidocaine shots, I don't see any reason why you need that done for you. We're in this lovely, large basement in a house set far away from your neighbors. Therefore, let's just go for it! You liked collecting digits so now I'm going to collect ten digits from you. Let's get this party started!

"This little piggy went to the market. One digit.

"This little piggy stayed home. Two digits.

"This little piggy had roast beef. Three digits.

"This little piggy had none. Four digits.

"And this little piggy went wee, wee, wee all the way home. Five digits.

"So much fun collecting digits, Pete! Were you having fun collecting your digits? I see that you were losing a bit of consciousness a moment ago so let's put some cold water on your face to wake you up. I wouldn't want you to miss a thing. Now, let's do some more work on those toes.

"This little piggy went to the frat house. Six digits.

"This little piggy lied. Seven digits.

"This little piggy had psychotic pills. Eight digits.

"This little piggy got high. Nine digits.

"And this little piggy cried no, no, no all the way home. Ten digits."

The monster put the toes into a baggie. It then put everything it had come with carefully back into the backpack. On the spur of the moment, it decided to write on the wall where Pete could easily see the letters ... a large capital T, a large capital H and a large capital C.

"Pete, you see what I wrote on the wall with your blood? THC. Now as you slowly die alone in pain, ask yourself the question: Was it worth it?"

---

With tears pouring out of Pete's eyes and blood dripping out of his veins, Pete held the vivid image from his memory of forcing himself on Leah as she cried out in her drugged bewilderment, "No, no, no! Please, please don't!" And blasting through his brain was the critical question: "Was it worth it?" ... "Was it worth it?" ... "Was it worth it?"

# CHAPTER
## 29

D riving back to the monster's hotel was a simple task because there wasn't much traffic in the early morning hours. But before arriving, it hit a twenty-four hour Waffle House for some artery-clogging Southern cooking. It was feeling good about what it had just accomplished but was famished after all the work it had performed during the night. There were numerous customers even at this raw hour. Too many were overweight but they didn't seem to care. The monster ate a medium rare steak, two eggs over easy and greasy hash browns with a waffle on the side as big as the plate it was on. Three cups of coffee washed it all down. After woofing down the food it paid the surprisingly inexpensive bill. When it finally reached the hotel, the bed was welcoming and the monster was asleep almost as fast as its head hit the pillow

No news was good news. No one had found the body yet. The monster left again very late the next evening going the opposite direction from the night before. This mission took him six miles from the hotel to Decatur. The neighborhood was much less pompous and more typical middle-class America than the mansion-like houses it had been surrounded by during the previous night. Making the night much easier for the monster, Lincoln's wife and two children happened to be out of town visiting her parents in Charleston, South Carolina. This was Lincoln's second family. He had an older child from his first wife but he had married a younger woman so the two kids were relatively young. And so, the monster's target was all alone.

Everything was dark except for the flicker of light emanating from a television located in a room toward the front of the house. The monster entered by a back kitchen door after cutting a small round hole with the glass cutter in the door window. The opening was just large enough to put his hand through to reach the lock and doorknob, allowing it to infiltrate the home. Fingers were crossed that an alarm had not been armed. As it opened the door, all that was heard was a beautiful silence.

The monster crept through the house to the television room. It found Lincoln half asleep watching porn. After subduing him, taking him to the bedroom, unclothing him and restraining him, the monster went to work.

"Hello, Lincoln. Remember Leah? You got her pregnant in college. She became my wife a few years later. You cared so little for her that you cheated on her which broke and crushed her heart. You just wanted it to all go away so you supported her having the abortion. Did you know she was in such pain caused by you that she got herself in a horrendous situation where she was drugged and gang-raped? This was all part of her slow death. It was many years of painful agony before she died but you were part of what had poisoned her emotions. Did I mention she killed herself? Did I mention that the abortion messed her up so she couldn't have kids? All that broke and crushed MY heart!"

It was a one-sided conversation. Lincoln was only able to listen, because his mouth was duct-taped securely shut. He started profusely shaking his head side to side. Again and again, he kept shaking his head in an attempt to say "NO!" to what the monster was telling him. This intrigued the monster. It put its finger to its mouth signaling Lincoln to make no noise if the tape was removed. Lincoln nodded his head up and down signifying agreement.

"Okay, what is it that you're wanting to tell me?"

In a scared, hushed voice Lincoln rapidly said, "It wasn't me. I didn't get her pregnant so don't do this to me."

"And why would I believe you? And how do you know it wasn't you?"

"I can't have kids. Never could. I didn't know it back then."

"Now I know you're lying; I found out about your life. I know you have a kid with your first wife and that you've got two kids now."

"But they're not my kids. I mean they're mine but I'm not their biological father. After not getting pregnant ... first wife and I went to a doctor ... he said my testicles were damaged so I couldn't produce viable sperm ... B-ball in high school ... had a massive collision ... a big guy's knee came down on me ... his full weight smashed my balls ... we adopted," Lincoln explained in spurts of words feeling the stress of the situation.

"And your two other kids? What about them?"

"Met second wife when already pregnant with twins. In a physically abusive marriage ... left her husband. We found each other and fell in love. Her ex-husband wanted nothing to do with her or the kids. I couldn't have kids but wanted them and I wanted her."

All of this unbalanced the monster. It put new duct tape over Lincoln's mouth and went looking for something to drink. It found some liquor in a cabinet in the dining room and removed a glass from the hutch. After pouring two fingers of whiskey in a glass the monster sat at the dining room table. After downing the golden liquid, it walked back to the struggling man's bedroom.

"Let's say I believe you. And, let's say I'm willing to make a deal with you. You assert you can't have kids therefore there was no way you were the father of Leah's baby. I'll check and find out about all your kids. If you're not their biological father, I won't kill them. If you have lied to me, I will find them and I will kill them. That's the deal," pronounced the monster.

Lincoln labored to get loose. It was impossible. The night had become full of unexpected terrors. He was cold, shaking and found it hard to breathe.

"So what to do with you? Well, like I told you before, it was you who greatly attributed to Leah's slow emotional death leading her to take her own life. You were a major destroying factor even if it wasn't your child. So I'm going to slowly take your life by extracting your blood with this IV device. In this way you can experience a little of what it was like for Leah to slowly have her life taken away through lies, deception, betrayal, rape and a botched abortion."

The monster packed up everything, including the liquor bottle and glass it had used, while the bedroom floor was turning red. Then it said a casual good-bye to Lincoln and walked out into the darkness. It was glad to be flying home in just a few hours but its mind was spinning out of control with this new information. The monster fully believed Lincoln about being unable to have children. He had no reaction during the pronouncement of his children being killed if it was a lie.

It was now remembering the conversation with Dr. Kimberlin when Leah had come to the new conclusion that Lincoln was the father of her child. This had thrown her into one of her emotional downward spiral times. But it wasn't Lincoln — it was one of the rapists!

---

Lincoln couldn't believe that his past had caught up to him in such a shocking and life-altering way. As he shuddered in panic, all he could feel was the cold hand of death pressing in on him. Help was not on the way. The cavalry was not coming.

# CHAPTER
## 30

TJ couldn't believe it. After tracking down Pete Fox, who was living in the Atlanta area, a report came into the FBI office that he was killed in the same manner as Joe Hiller and Troy Wilson in Florida. His toes were cut off and his blood was dripped out of his body. This linked the three together. This made it clear that the same monster murdered all of them, unless there was a copycat killer. That was quite doubtful considering all three were UF students who were in the same fraternity at the same time.

After learning about the devastating scam these three victims had pulled off against the English Literature professor, TJ was certain it was all connected. He believed it was the hidden motive behind the slayings. This made him determined to find out what happened to Dr. Conor Casey following his conviction and how it affected those around him. TJ was thinking these were revenge killings. He called Justice with the news.

"I believe I've figured out the motive for the murders. You already know about the third one down in Georgia and I've spoken to a witness proving that the three frat boys got a professor fired and convicted of sexual advances with a minor — the minor being Joe Hiller. He was still seventeen years old when he made the accusation. He got the other two, who happened to be in the same class, to lie and corroborate the story. It was all because Joe was failing the class and had tried to bribe the professor for a good grade but the professor was going to report him. Joe and the other two boys decided to strike first," said TJ with the excitement of a kid on Christmas morning.

"Hey, just slow down a little. You could be on to something and it needs to be explored but let's not jump to any conclusions just yet," Justice said.

"Yeah, I hear you ... but this has to be it. It connects what we know and I'll bet you it will connect everything else we find when we dig deeper."

"I hope you're right, but again, let's not be too hasty," warned Justice.

"I hear you, but let's get started right away. I'll find out about what happened to the professor and his wife and you check out his immediate family, close relatives, and longtime friends. Sound good to you?"

"Sounds like a plan. Let's talk in a couple of days to compare notes."

TJ went to work right away. He found that Dr. Casey had been fired from the university immediately after he admitted to the charges brought against him. The words in the conviction were harsh. They stated he was a sexual offender, which would mean to many that he was a danger to kids.

After a number of inquiries, TJ found current information that allowed him to reach out to the professor's wife. He was surprised to learn that she lived in Burlington, Vermont. Since it was just a couple hundred miles away, he contacted her and made an appointment to talk to her in person the next day. TJ called and left a message for Justice telling him what he was doing.

TJ found the trip relaxing once he got out of the bedroom communities of Boston. Traffic became sparse. The mountains in Vermont were beautiful and quiet. TJ could think clearly as he got ready to interview Sarah Casey. He pulled up to a small, white house with dark green shutters. Both the house and the yard were cared for and in good shape. The person who lived there wanted to live in nice and ordered surroundings. TJ got out of his car, stretched his legs, walked up to the door, and rang the doorbell.

A petite, mid-sixtyish lady answered. She had shoulder length, dyed blonde hair. She was physically and mentally strong. She was blessed with a face and neck that didn't have many wrinkles or much sagging. The sincerity of her smile was disarming. Her green eyes looked directly at TJ. She warmly welcomed him into her modern furnished home. They sat in chairs that were fronted by a gas fireplace that looked better than it heated the room.

"Mrs. Casey, it's so kind of you to talk to me on such short notice," said TJ.

"Please just call me Sarah. And, it's no problem. These days I have a lot of time on my hands. Retirement is not all it's cracked up to be. That's something you might want to remember," smiled Sarah.

"Okay, will do. As a reminder, I'm a profiler with the Boston FBI and some suspicious things have come up with the boys, now men, who were involved with your husband and the circumstances back at UF in '69 when he was let go. Could you tell me what you believe happened and what the fallout was?

"I've been waiting for someone to ask me a question like that for thirty-three years! I'm happy to tell his story. I just wish he was here to tell it for himself. It's a rather simple tale. Three bad rich boys against one low-paid educator. I will admit our lifestyle left us open to criticism. It was the late 60's and although we were in our mid-thirties we bought into the idea of having an open marriage with both men and women partners. We also enjoyed the drug culture of the day. Grace Slick in her Jefferson Airplane song, *White Rabbit,* said it all for us. She truly was the voice that launched a thousand trips. Or maybe I should say it was the dormouse who said it best: 'Feed your head.'"

"Yes. I know the song. It's a classic. Please go on."

"I know Conor was innocent. He got railroaded by those three boys. The worst one was named Joe. He was the instigator of it all. My husband was offered $10,000 to change his grade. That was a whole lot of money back then. Of course, he wasn't going to take it. In fact he told this boy, Joe, he was going to report him for trying to bribe him. That was his big blunder. He should have just reported the bribe attempt. Joe and the others made their accusations before he notified anyone. He did report it later but he was never believed."

"And what happened next?"

"Well, they had all these highfalutin' lawyers and we hardly had any money in the bank. He was told by our hire-on-the-cheap lawyer to just plead guilty and that he would make a deal so there would be no jail time and it would go on the books as only a small misdemeanor. Therefore, it wasn't supposed to have any real consequences to his life … to our lives. So he did as he was advised. And there was no jail time but he was convicted of a felony instead of a misdemeanor. Sexual Assault of a Minor. Apparently this Joe fellow was seventeen and so was still a minor in the eyes of the law. So Conor became a convicted sexual offender. He was fired right away. We found out later that Joe's father made some huge donations to the university soon after all this went down. A little suspicious, don't you think? We also wondered if they got to our lawyer with some kind of payoff to mislead us with bad advice."

"And what was the fallout after Dr. Casey was fired?"

"For Conor, it was devastating. The shame and disgrace he felt was huge. He was blackballed from any teaching jobs because of his conviction. This meant he couldn't do what he loved and what he was so good at doing. In fact, he couldn't find any kind of real job. He lost his friends. He started drinking and drugging very heavily. To get a fresh start, we decided to move out of Florida and back to where I grew up.

Here in Burlington. That didn't seem to help, though. I was a CPA so I could get a job pretty easily. Conor just drifted into another world. After years of that nonsense we divorced."

"I'm so sorry all of this happened. It must have been a nightmare."

"That it was. But it didn't stop there. He just moved around from city to city until we finally lost all contact with each other for many years. Then, out of the blue, he wrote to me ... from jail. He wanted to know how I was doing and he wanted to know how his son was doing. Dylan, our son, is another sad casualty in this story. But getting back to Conor, he had been living in Southern California and was caught having sex for money with a minor teenage boy. Someone he hooked-up with at a public bathroom. The cops were watching it because the location had that kind of reputation. It's all so pitiful. His ruined life destroyed so much. His family. His profession. His morals. He never would have been paying money for sex, especially to an under-aged boy!"

Before continuing, Sarah had to take a moment to compose herself. Many emotions were being stirred.

"This was all happening in '95. Since it was his second conviction of a sexual crime, it came with jail time. He got out in the summer of 2001 for good behavior. At that point he was a registered sex offender due to the '94 law. He had restrictions about being in the presence of under-age persons. He couldn't live in the proximity of a school or day-care center. He couldn't use the internet. It must have all been too much for him because he took his life soon after he got out of jail. That was just ten months ago. They found my information in his wallet and contacted me."

"Again, so sorry to hear all of that. And you mentioned you had a son. How did he handle all of this?"

"Like I said, it's another sad story. Dylan was only ten when his father went through the Florida ordeal. It was hard on him. He essentially lost his dad at that point. Conor always assured him that he was innocent and, at age-appropriate times, told Dylan more and more of the story of the three boys who lied about him. Dylan grew up an angry young man. He dropped out of high school and took up with the wrong crowd. He's been in and out of jail. He even told me, more than once, that he was going to kill those guys who had destroyed his father's life. Honestly, we don't communicate that much with each other even though he lives in the area. It's another hole in my heart," Sarah said while dabbing a few tears with a tissue.

Sarah continued, "And to tell you the whole story, I'll need to share about a certain priest. You must be aware of the Spotlight articles in the Boston Globe that started coming out in January exposing the degree of sexual abuse by priests in the Catholic Church. It's been tearing me up inside. You see, after we had moved back to this area we started to attend Mass even though I hadn't given God much thought for years. I guess once a Catholic, always a Catholic. A certain priest took an interest in Dylan. He was only twelve, had lost a functioning dad, had moved away from friends and so was emotionally overwhelmed. I felt like this priest was a God-send. He would come by and take Dylan out for ice cream just to spend time together. He said he wanted to help Dylan feel secure and wanted. And then it all came out. I don't even want to say what he did to my boy. I was up in arms! Then a lawyer for the Church showed up with the priest, who apologized for what he had done. They said this was unusual and the priest would be disciplined and sent for treatment.

"Of course now with the *Globe's* exposé I know the truth. Sexual abuse was rampant and the higher ups, like Cardinal Law, knew all about it and covered it up. All they did was move the priests to another assignment allowing them the opportunity to abuse more kids. I was offered a small financial settlement along with signing a non-disclosure agreement. You see, I was talked into protecting the Church's reputation instead of protecting my son and other vulnerable children. I don't think he has ever forgiven me for that. I just didn't know."

"All I can say, again, is that I'm so sorry all of this has occurred in your family's life," TJ said. "The extent of the sexual abuse and cover-up is absolutely abhorrent. When a child is molested it can emotionally scar that child for a lifetime. I know this has not been a pleasant or easy conversation for you to have, but I do so much appreciate your taking the time to share all of this with me. You have been very helpful. At this point, I think it's best if I go on my way."

TJ said good-bye and again thanked her. He left feeling the high of having solved his first case by doing more than just being a profiler. He got on the phone to set up a time with Justice to put their heads together.

# CHAPTER
# 31

Back at the same Starbucks and in the same comfortable chairs, TJ and Justice were meeting on a Thursday mid-morning. It was a time when the customer traffic was light. TJ had an unsweetened Venti iced coffee while Justice sipped on a Grande Dark Roast Coffee with a mix of almond milk and a packet of Stevia. TJ proceeded to give a detailed account of his conversation with Sarah Casey. He concluded by making a strong case that the only real suspect was the son, Dylan Casey. Justice was impressed but kept pressing the point that he was the actual detective and that TJ needed to follow his lead and not get out in front or just do his own thing.

"So here's where I'm at with what I know," Justice said. "So far, looking for plane tickets and rental cars have not panned out. About the Casey family, the professor had only one son. Dylan. Both parents were only children so there was no large extended family. No aunts or uncles. No nieces or nephews. As far as close friends who might know something, either I couldn't find any or there aren't any. As you've already said, Dr. Casey just floated around for years and then spent time in jail. His wife is an older woman and couldn't pull off the killings herself. She could have hired someone to do it but, from your interview with her, that seems unlikely," stated Justice.

"And what about the son?" TJ interrupted. "I've already told you about the sexual abuse he endured by the priest in Burlington when he was twelve. That certainly had a huge effect on him. For starters, it destroys a person's trust in authority figures, it causes shame and guilt, it produces anger, rebellion, and acting out in various ways. So, what about the son?"

"I'm getting to what I know and it makes a lot more sense now with what you've told me. Just give me a chance to get there."

"Will do."

"The son is very interesting. In his teen years he was your basic juvenile delinquent. A troublemaker. He dropped out of high school in his Junior year. He was almost eighteen because he had failed a grade. He was into the usual. Alcohol and drugs. He's got major anger issues. He's got a pretty long rap sheet. He's been in and out of jail for theft, drugs, and aggravated assault. He's got two DUI's.

"In the midst of all that, he's had EMT training. I'm not sure how he pulled that off but he did. Probably got his GED while he was in jail. He's divorced with no kids in the mix. I did get hold of his ex. She's not a happy camper. She said he's a bit of a loner and has a history of disappearing. But the most helpful information was about who his friends, or at least his business associates, have been. He's got ties to the Winter Hill Gang. By the way, that name came from the Winter Hill neighborhood of Somerville. I would think Dylan is just a small fish in the organization but he's with the bad boys of Boston."

"Some good alliteration ... b-b-b!" laughed TJ. "But seriously, this is sure ticking off the boxes for being our guy. Don't you think?"

"It's looking positive at this point."

"Can you tell me about this Winter Hill Gang and why it was the important piece of info from the ex-wife?"

"Sure. It's got a history. They were most influential from '65 to '79 when they were ruled by Buddy McLean and Howie Winter. Fixing horse races and shipping weapons to the IRA is what they were most known for. Then it became Whitey Bulger's mob. The gang members and leadership have always been predominantly Irish and Italian descent so with a good Irish name like Dylan Casey, he would fit in perfectly. Bulger, as you should know, is on your FBI's Ten Most Wanted list. He disappeared in '94 due to a pending federal indictment. Kevin Weeks, his lieutenant, took over until he was arrested in '99. Since 2000 the boss has been George "Georgie Boy" Hogan. They're headquartered in South Boston but their reach is throughout New England."

"And what are they into now?"

"The better question is: What are they not into? The list is long and ugly. Racketeering, loan sharking, drug trafficking, weapons trafficking, prostitution, assault, bribery, illegal gambling, theft, fraud, corruption, extortion, money laundering and, of course, murder."

"That's incredible! And it's fitting together perfectly!"

"Two more things. First, Dylan was a rabid Pats fan. He attended all the home games. Second, his landlord says the rent is past due since he's not come home since mid-February. Like the invisible man, he has disappeared."

"So, even more boxes ticked. One: A Patriots ticket holder. Two: He's on the run. Three: He has medical training for the use of the IV and access to drugs. He would also know how to avoid leaving a trace of himself at the crime scenes. Four: He has huge anger issues emanating from how his father was treated and how the priest abused him. Dylan was even arrested for aggravated assault. Five: It makes sense he wanted to hurt the men who hurt him so he cuts off their toes possibly showing that there was nowhere for them to run. Six: He is associated with murderers and so it's likely he had already committed murder in the past. He would know how to execute a solid plan of execution. Seven: He straight-up told his mother he wanted to kill Joe, Troy, and Pete. So this has been a desire growing inside him for many years. Eight: The murders started soon after his father committed suicide. That had to be the tipping point that put him over the edge. His rage was like a volcano no longer dormant. It came alive and erupted with a vengeance!"

"All of that sounds very plausible. Let's keep running with it. There's a lot more to do, like checking out his alibis for the times of each murder," said Justice.

———

TJ didn't listen to Justice. He called the detectives in Florida and the lead detective in Georgia. He exclaimed with certainty that they knew who the monster was that had so gruesomely killed the three men. He gave the impression that a huge manhunt was already in progress. And, to give himself greater sounding authority, he freely used the names of Special Agent Darius Mitchell, Superintendent Chip Thompson and Detective Justice Jackson. This news got released to the national press along with the names TJ had mentioned.

———

A few tense weeks went by. TJ was called on the carpet for running ahead on his own, acting like he had authority where he didn't and for using the names of Darius, Chip, and Justice. Darius especially was furious with TJ in a friend-to-friend kind of way. Chip said he had been severely reprimanded by his superiors but was quick to forgive TJ. Justice laughed until he cried and said, "I told you so."

It was bad that the papers had printed the story and named the supposed murderer. It would alert him to remain hidden. It was bad for the Boston FBI and the Boston Police Department to be put in the position of declaring a "win" to the public before the investigation was correctly completed.

A manhunt was eventually conducted for Dylan Casey. His body was found in a shallow grave in the woods behind his rented house located on the outskirts of Burlington. His mouth and anus were stuffed with dollar bills, which in the mob world symbolized greed.

At the time, the Boston Police had a certain Winter Hill Gang member under limited surveillance, including having his phone tapped. In one of the recorded calls, he was told to "blow down DC because he's got his fingers in the drug take up in Burlington." Although the caller was on a burner phone and never identified, the surveilled man was arrested for the murder of DC ... Dylan Casey.

In the coroner's report, the body had been in the ground for at least two months. The last victim, Pete Fox, had been dead for only a few weeks. Dylan Casey was not the monster.

# CHAPTER
## 32

TJ was deeply depressed. He felt lonely and he felt fearful about the future. Feeling like a complete failure, he again turned to alcohol for some deadening relief. He also considered, for much too long, the idea of taking his own life. It's one thing to have fleeting thoughts. It's in another realm when a person starts to make a serious plan with specifics of how it would be done. TJ had a plan ruminating from driving his commute from his apartment to the FBI office building using the Tobin Bridge. Late one night he took some action on his plan.

The three span, double-deck Tobin Bridge was a well-known jumper's destination. Yearly, six or more suicides occurred as people plummeted 200 feet before crashing into the Mystic River. At three in the morning TJ drove from Boston to Chelsea using this two-mile bridge. There was no traffic to speak of at that hour. He then turned around using a rotary so he could travel back into the city on the higher upper deck. He made a sudden stop, leaving his car on the side of the road in the middle of the bridge. He went to the railing and peered over the edge. There was no pedestrian walkway and no protective fencing, just a small sign advertising a suicide prevention hotline. He pictured himself falling into the deep darkness of watery oblivion.

TJ started asking himself a number of questions: *What are you doing here? Would it really be better to no longer exist? What would happen with Sky and E? Could I really leave my kids all alone? What would Granddad think of me? What would Suzo think of me?*

After a few precarious minutes TJ got back into his car and drove home, wanting to live more than ever.

Later that morning, TJ again drove across the Tobin Bridge making his way to the FBI building. He planned to quit. He felt he owed his friend the courtesy to do it face-to-face.

"Darius, thanks for seeing me. I wanted to let you know personally that I'm turning in my resignation."

"I didn't think you were a quitter, Mav. Maybe I read you wrong."

"I'm not so much quitting as I'm just trying to get out of your way. I've messed up and I don't want you to be caught up in my mess any more than you already have been," said TJ.

"Yeah, you screwed-up, that's for sure! But, that's to be expected to some degree. I threw you in the water hoping you could swim. And, while struggling not to drown, you've still shown good initiative and intelligence. Training is part of the job, especially when you begin. You have to learn what you're supposed to do — but you have to learn what you're not supposed to do, too." Darius leaned in closer and looked directly at TJ. "Failure is one of the great teachers in life. You're now better equipped to do the job than ever before."

"But I got down, got drunk and I thought about ending it all. I was even on the Tobin early this morning looking over the railing. If it wasn't for my kids, I think I might have ...."

"Stop it right there, Mav! You didn't jump. That says a lot. And yes, you blew it in a big way. It only proves smart people can do dumb things. So what? You learn. You go on. And, although unplanned and fortuitous, it ended up allowing law officials to arrest and indict the Dylan Casey murderer which then provided another step toward taking down Georgie Boy and the Winter Hill Gang. That's huge, in case you didn't know it!"

"You're just trying to make me feel better, I think."

"Yes, I'm trying to make you feel better but I'm not just blowing smoke. There were some very positive consequences to your actions so don't go and quit on me. Better yet, don't quit on yourself. I still want you on this case. I still need you on it. I had even decided to extend your contract for an extra month to give you more time and, hopefully, to make some sense of this case I've got you on. So stop feeling sorry for yourself and get to work! I expect your updated report on my desk in the next couple of days. You good with that?"

TJ took a deep breath. After a moment, he looked back at Darius.

"Yes, I think I'm good with that. And thanks for the straight talk, Darius."

"No thanks required. I insist that you get some professional support. See someone, talk to someone who can help solidify your emotions and your decision to move forward. I find one of the best cures to life's personal challenges is to make a difference in this world with whatever God-given talents you have. You're good at what you're doing and you'll only get better with time. You understand people. So get to work. Go make a difference!"

TJ left feeling measurably better than when he had arrived. Hope was starting to build in him again as he decided to head back to Florida.

# JOURNAL ENTRY
## April 21, 2002

Suzo:

It's been awhile since we've talked. Mud season is over and the flowers are blooming! I want to catch you up on everything.

First the high. I've apologized to the kids for my failures with them and I think it went as well as could be expected. Sky is relatively easy on me. E is working through it but we're making progress. I'm calling them often and I'm thoroughly enjoying the renewed connection.

Now the low. I messed up! I thought I was doing a lot of good until I hit a brick wall while going 100 mph — what a smash-up! What an Icarian fall from grace! I don't think people are going to respect or listen to me anymore. Some expert profiler I am! I was so sure I had it all figured out. I thought if I could just get this right, then in the process, it would somehow help heal me with my personal pain. I was so wrong!

I felt so foolish and embarrassed. Then all my pain returned with a vengeance so I gave in and ran to the liquor store and started to put down the better half of a bottle of whiskey. That was a stupid thing to do. In the hardest times I find myself destroying my body for peace of mind that I never get. I know that healing is creating a life in which numbness is no longer necessary for survival but knowing it and doing it are two very different things. Never have I dealt with anything more difficult than trying to let go of the tragic losses that have been defining me and defeating me, especially my loss of you. I've told many clients that new beginnings are often disguised as painful endings. I fully believe those words but it's so much easier to give sage advice than to embrace it.

When people say "heal," they typically think of returning to how they were before the pain. But true healing means there is no going back. You don't merely feel better, you recover who you were always meant to be. You become something completely different from what you were before. I know that's possible for others but I keep asking myself if it's possible for me. At the same time I know I shouldn't believe everything I think.

I've neglected our kids. I've failed at my new job. I've let depression get the better of me. I was hoping this new gig would have some of the answers I desperately needed for my life without you. I thought all the murders had to do with that professor and his son. And now, I'm feeling sorry for myself instead of facing the music and humbly admitting I was wrong. The job that was supposed to help me has only put more stress, failure, and pain into my life.

But I know I need to keep going forward instead of falling back to what is easy and comfortable. I guess courage is the power to let go of the familiar. I've found for myself that time doesn't heal emotional pain; I still need to learn how to let it go. Holding on is believing there is only a past; letting go is knowing there's a future. But what exactly is my future, Suzo?

I did get back in the Bible some. I know you and Granddad would want me to do that. I found a scripture in Psalms 34 that encouraged me: "The Lord is close to the brokenhearted and saves those who are crushed in spirit." I think

# Part Three

# WHO'LL STOP THE
# RAIN / PAIN

# CHAPTER
## 33

T J went back to Florida armed with an idea that might correct his earlier crash-and-burn defeat. He knew he should have stayed as Justice's wing man instead of going off on his own and so he resolved it would never happen again. He ended up way off track by sending investigators in the wrong direction with Casey's son, Dylan. Still, every time he mentally went through what he already knew about the case, he concluded that the biggest missing puzzle pieces were somewhere buried in the UF campus. He felt sure the fraternity was where some key answers were hiding. It was just a gut feeling but he was determined to find the secrets.

And, try as he may, he couldn't get the police from any of the victims' cities to investigate the UF connection more thoroughly. They had all been satisfied with the good grade records, the good behavior records and the good family backgrounds of the victims. They were also strongly encouraged by their superiors to move away from that part of their investigation. The influential families were being very influential. Beyond that, following the Conor Casey debacle they felt it would be a further waste of time, money, and manpower to dig any deeper. It was obvious that three of the victims were all together in the same fraternity at the same time but it wasn't obvious to anyone but TJ that it had to be the genesis of the motivation for murder. This took him back to his beloved campus where he had fallen in love with Suzanne. There were good memories found in so many locations throughout the sprawling grounds of the university. He now found himself in front of the SAE house standing by the white lion.

"Excuse me, but could you tell me where I could find your house mother?" TJ asked the first student who came out of the frat house.

"Sure, no problem. Just enter and go to your right. You'll find a hallway. Just follow it down to the last door. That's her living quarters. It's as far away from where all us guys live as possible. Gives her a bit of privacy. She's great. You'll like her. Her name's Rachel," said the boy.

"Thanks," said TJ.

As he entered the frat house, he was struck with the memory of having been there before dropping off some books for a friend in the middle of some party. He proceeded to turn right and entered the specified hallway. He knocked on the last door where a simple black and white sign read, HOUSE MOM. A woman with a cheery voice and caring smile opened it. She looked as if she were 35-years-old — but was certainly older than that. She had obviously taken very good care of herself. Apparently, being around young people kept her looking and acting younger than her true age.

"Hello, my name is TJ Maverick; I work with the FBI and wanted to see if you could help me in an investigation I'm involved with," said TJ.

He showed her some identification and she allowed him to enter her apartment. It was bigger than TJ had guessed her living quarters would be. It was a large room painted in a light grey with bright white trim. There was an off-white wall-to-wall carpet that flowed throughout, except for slate tile in the kitchen area. There were two very used blue leather couches facing each other with a stained coffee table in-between. Additionally there was an overstuffed gold and blue striped chair that looked relatively new. In a portion of the room, there was a small semi-circled bar with three stools. Behind it was a small kitchen with a compact stainless steel refrigerator, stove, dishwasher and microwave oven. The countertops and bar were grey granite with flowing patterns. Large windows allowed the space to be bright and happy. To the left of the kitchen was a closed door; TJ guessed it hid her bedroom. The house mom, Rachel, poured some coffee for each of them and they sat on opposite couches so they could look at each other face-to-face. She had obviously conducted many crucial conversations in this room. TJ opened it up.

"I am specifically a criminal profiler for the FBI and I am helping to find out what happened to three men who were murdered in the last seven or eight months. When they were college boys they lived in this frat house from 1970 to 1973. I am told they may have been friends with each other at that time," explained TJ.

"Well, I hope I don't look that old!" laughed Rachel.

"No, of course not. I was just trying to find out exactly what a house mother does and if she really gets to know the boys. Then I was wondering if I could find out who the house mom was back during those years. She may remember something about these specific individuals that could be critical to the case."

"All right. I understand now. Let me explain to you my role as a house mom or house director. I am responsible for opening the fraternity house at the beginning of the school year and closing it at the end. I maintain the place by hiring service providers, supervising cleaning staff, and paying vendors. The powers that be want a grown-up voice to talk to the kitchen and cleaning staff, strengthen alumni relations and help plan events, such as parents and alumni weekend. But the truth is it's a lot more than that. While house directors aren't expected to police students' behavior or play mom, they often do. In my mind, it's a lot of mothering, counseling, and friendship. Not everyone in this kind of job thinks that way, but I do. I know some who think of it more like a hotel management job where their duties are only with the physical operation. I've even heard some emphatically state they were not in this role to be anyone's mother. I think that's pretty cold."

"Sounds like you have a real connection and love for the boys in the house. I can respect and appreciate that. Is there any other info you think might be helpful?"

"Well, let me think. They usually look for unmarried, widowed, or divorced women with some age and life-experience. I'm 52 and divorced. My husband left me for his secretary. Typical scenario, I guess. Such a cliche. A pretty little thing fifteen years younger than him whom he got pregnant. He never wanted children. At least not with me. And I always wanted them so now I have hundreds of them."

"That's all very helpful."

"Sure, anything to cooperate with the FBI. You know, I've been here for ten years and plan to stay for more. I like to think I give wisdom, give a listening ear, and give a touch of female class."

"I'm hoping the house mom's before you had the same kind of heart and the same kind of connection with the boys you certainly have. Could I find out who the house mom was back in the '70's? And would you have any pictures of past members of the fraternity dating back to that time?"

"Pictures we've got. That's easy. We have a library room with framed pictures of the brothers from each year. The images of the faces are small but clear and the dates and names are on them. There are also archived pictures and articles from the many different events held at the house throughout the years. Everything has been digitized so it should be easy to access. There's a public computer in that room that you can use along with a printer. And the house mom you want to know about is probably listed and pictured in there somewhere, too. I'll take you to the room and let you have at it," said Rachel.

After expressing much thanks to Rachel, TJ started searching. He wanted pictures of the three victims when they were students and any information he could find on them. He was also hoping the house mother at the time could be identified and would be able to be found and would know the boys in question. This was what he was really going after — the hidden pieces of the puzzle that lay beneath the surface.

TJ found all three boys in each of the composite photos of the fraternity members from their freshman year through their senior year beginning in the 1969-1970 school year. Joe Hiller. Troy Wilson. Pete Fox. All smiling. All confident. All content. And now, all dead. They looked different from their recent photographs that had been given to the investigating officers and were now found in the police reports. Aging had done its thing. And they looked very different from their ashen pictures in the coroners' report.

Looking through the computerized files, TJ also found the name of the house mother who had served for sixteen years from 1965 to 1981. Her name was Dorothy Whitlock. There were pictures of her retirement party along with many kind words from a large number of the boys. The caption below one of the pictures read, "Sixty-Four Years Young With A Family Of Hundreds—ALL BOYS!" TJ was doing the math and figured she was forty-eight when she started as the house mom and would now be eighty-five. TJ was praying she was still alive and coherent.

As a shocking bonus, he happened on photos taken the night he had dropped off books. There was one with him on a couch sitting with a pretty girl he didn't recognize. Although he had forgotten all about it, he now remembered she was stoned and needed help getting down the stairs. He had sat with her for a while to make sure she would be okay. Scrolling through more photos TJ's heart skipped a beat: A picture of four guys helping this same girl down some stairs. TJ did a double take — he was one of those guys! Looking more closely gave him another shock — the others were the faces on the composites of the three victims. This blew TJ's mind! Although for only a few short minutes, he had actually been with Joe, Troy, and Pete!

As TJ was leaving the frat house, he longingly looked down Museum Road. He and Suzo had strolled along it many times together. He started walking. He passed the Reitz Union where he had eaten too many Gator Cheeseburgers. He walked past Constans Theatre where he and Suzo had seen a few plays together. The most memorable one was entitled, Butterflies Are Free. He remembered he and Suzo talking about the main actress wearing only her underwear for much of the play. Suzo had kidded him about not taking his eyes off her and that she had never seen him pay such close attention to a play before. She had been right.

He kept going farther along Museum Road until he came to the Florida Museum of Natural History. He stopped and then went down the concrete steps to the large, open, and quiet space behind the museum where there were benches and beautiful landscaping throughout the different levels of terraces. It was still a place of serenity and peace. TJ and Suzo had met here more times than could be counted to talk and to hug and to kiss. This was their spot away from everything and everybody. TJ sat on a bench where they had both been sitting years ago and imagined being with his young Suzo who was so full of starry ideas about love along with a fire of determination to conquer life. In his mind he could smell the sweetness of her fragrance and see the graceful beauty of her body. They had danced together here. They had dreamed together here. They had prayed together here. They had embraced each other here, saying they would never let go. All of a sudden, TJ felt very alone.

He climbed back up the concrete steps and started walking again. This took him past the tennis courts where he and Suzo had played tennis together. For a moment, he could see her wearing her light blue, short shorts and a white tee shirt with the words Outta Sight on the back of it. When the road ended at SW 13th Street, he found himself staring through the traffic at a large white anchor. It was in front of the Delta Gamma house. It was the place he had often dropped Suzo off when they had been students. This is where they said their long good-byes as their dates came to an end.

*If I could only go back, I would love her more and love her better, thought TJ. If I could have only kept her from getting on that doomed plane!*

He turned and started walking back to the SAE house to pick up his car and to drive to his hotel. He called Justice and filled him in. He was now on the hunt for an eighty-five year old lady named Dorothy Whitlock.

# CHAPTER
# 34

"You must like this Starbucks a lot, TJ. Same corner seats too. So you're back from that quick Florida trip, right?" asked Justice.

"Yeah, just back from the University of Florida campus yesterday," replied TJ. "And like I told you on the phone before I left, we've got to locate and then interview a Dorothy Whitlock. She may know something important about the victims during their college years. She was the house mom for their fraternity."

Justice took a swig of his Starbucks' Espresso Frappuccino and said, "Before we get into the case, I want to know how're you feeling about everything?"

"That's a loaded question, I think. Well, first let me apologize to you again for running ahead and thinking I knew what to do. Obviously, I blew it big time. I get that. I felt very down about all of it and had to get my head straight. I'm getting there. I want us to work together. I'm happy with you taking the lead, giving me direction and only moving forward together."

"Okay, I've made you grovel enough. You've gotten some sense knocked into you by the School of Hard Knocks. I've attended more than a few classes there myself. I've been waiting for you to really come around to all of this. But, if we're going to be a real team with this case, I'll need more than just the right words from you; I'll need the right actions. 'Well done is better than well said.' That's a quote from Mister Ben Franklin."

"You've got my words and you'll see my actions. Right now you'll see me act on my thirst. Gotta get some iced coffee."

After TJ returned, he started the conversation with a question, but Justice broke in.

"First, I've got one more question for you. How do you feel, really feel, about partnering up with me, a black guy?"

"Why would you ask me that? Have I done something to offend you?"

"No, but I looked up some info on your beloved UF campus. You know my background with my Dad and so you should know where I'm coming from with this. Did you know that UF desegregated in '58 but in '71 it was 20,000 white students to 343 black students? And when the Black Student Union organized a sit-in that year demanding greater encouragement for black enrollment and black faculty members, sixty-six were arrested and sixty were put on academic probation. In the end a hundred and twenty-three black students and two black faculty members left the University. Coming from that environment, I just didn't know exactly where your head was at, TJ."

"Wow, you really did do some digging. Even got the stats memorized. But listen, I became more sensitive about prejudice during my college years. My wife, girlfriend at the time, took me to a place close to campus called the 14th Street Church. It was about the only religious thing going on at the time that was black and white on Sunday mornings. You gotta remember it was in the early 70's and it was in the South. We attended there because we saw people not just talking about peace and love, they were living it. You know, walk the walk and not just talk the talk. I loved it and I loved all the people. Black or White, it didn't matter and still doesn't."

"All right. That's cool. You see, I wanted us to really go total partnership with this thing. That takes trust. I gotta know you have my black back!"

"Ditto. Total partnership. And you make sure you have my white back, too. After all, you're the one with a gun! And by the way, in case you can't tell by most of my clothes and my car, my favorite color is black. And to quote Wesley Snipes from the Passenger 57 movie ... 'Always bet on black!' I'm betting on you, Justice."

They both sat back, took a sip of their drinks and then laughed so loud it had everyone turning their heads.

"And now my question for you. How about planning on coming to Florida with me, assuming that's where the Whitlock lady is and that she's still alive?"

"I'm certainly willing to do that. And to make it work, you can give me cover with your FBI badge since a Boston cop in Florida is a little out of bounds — and I'll give you my investigator's expertise."

"Okay, so that's settled. I'll get some of our people trying to locate the Whitlock woman," said TJ.

"You know you jumped to your conclusions last time and never really looked into the Atlanta murder. And as you now know, there was a second murder around the same time that has to be connected."

"I've read the reports that were sent. With the first one, again, no trace left by the killer. Toes cut off. Blood dripped out of the body. The one big difference was the writing on the wall with the victim's blood. THC. Any thoughts on that, Justice?"

"Just the obvious one. Something having to do with drugs. But, whatever it means, it was either a message to those who would find the body or a message to the guy while he was dying. I'm thinking it was something meaningful, maybe even the reason, about why this Pete Fox guy was losing his life. He was made to face it during his demise."

"And then there's the other guy that wasn't even associated right away with the death of Fox. A Lincoln Hart. But, there were no toes cut. Why? Maybe interrupted. But more likely there was a different reason for him to die and so the cut toe message wouldn't mean anything to him. Blood loss was in the same manner, using the same kind of equipment. That's what ultimately connected the two deaths together. Also, he was found to be a UF student at the same time as Joe, Troy, and Pete. It's got to be intertwined in some way," added TJ.

"Agreed. And during every city's media coverage about the murders, nothing helpful came through on the tip lines that panned out. The canvass results going from house to house in each location have also come up with nothing useful. Surveillance cameras. Nada."

"Anything on phones, computer, etc. that show the guys were in touch with each other?" asked TJ.

"Nothing so far that I'm aware of. Seems like when they left college they must have drifted apart. There could be something on the dark web with encryption but nothing has been found. And that's just total conjecture on my part."

"You know, I would also like to interview the parents of the three with cut toes. There's something that bonded them together at least during their college years. Something more than partying together and getting high together. Of course there's the lying about that professor they all participated in. But maybe that was just their beginning. Could they have stolen something together? Were they selling drugs together? Were they selling grades? Or, did they kill someone together? So many possibilities," said TJ.

"Eliminating possibilities. That's the job we do."

Justice and TJ left their Starbucks' office as true colleagues. Justice went to check-in at the police station. TJ went to work on his report for Darius.

# CHAPTER 35

"This is all good stuff in your report, TJ. I'm going to call a number of people together who are in the office today so you can share your thoughts. I'd like to use your report as a continuing professional education training session. It will mostly be the same people you addressed the first time so you know them and they know you. I'll set the meeting for 10 a.m. which is thirty minutes from now. Sound good to you?" asked Darius.

"Whatever the boss wants," said TJ.

The thirty minutes went fast and TJ found himself scrambling to pull his thoughts together.

"Hello again. For anyone who wasn't in my last report, my name is Dr. TJ Maverick. I'm the criminal profiler on the case dealing with the two murders in Florida and the two murders in Georgia. The only solid connection to New England that we have is a portion of a dropped Patriots ticket from the crime scene of the second murder.

"Before I get into the specifics I need to make an apology. I'm new doing this work but that doesn't excuse me from personal responsibility. You are all aware that some of my actions put the Boston Field Office in a bad light. I didn't listen to the seasoned detective I was assigned to work with. I jumped to conclusions without a full and thorough investigation of the facts. I overstepped my authority. I jumped on the first motive or scenario that seemed to fit. I'm thankful some good came out of it but I feel bad that some reputations were damaged and dragged through the proverbial mud because of my actions. So, I just wanted to say I'm sorry to all of you."

Someone from the back of the room said, "Rookie mistakes, TJ."

Another person yelled out, "We've all gone down the wrong rabbit hole on cases … so welcome to the club!"

The group started snapping their fingers with big smiles on many of the faces. TJ was both encouraged and embarrassed. But mostly he was feeling accepted after he had failed so miserably.

"That response was very unexpected but very much appreciated. Now, let's get into the case.

"Hurt people hurt people. Let me say that again. HURT PEOPLE HURT PEOPLE. How a person handles their pain determines their life. I believe the killer is a hurt person who has chosen the path to hurt those whom he perceives has hurt him or has hurt someone he loves. That's the reason for cutting off the toes and the slow draining of the blood.

"I also believe the killer is experiencing some form of PTSD. Post-Traumatic Stress Disorder. The mental disorder is developed after experiencing trauma. The trauma could come in many different shapes and sizes. What may constitute a traumatic event for one person may or may not trigger it for another. It would all depend on how a person emotionally digests the event. PTSD could come from sexual assault, traffic collisions, child abuse, warfare, or other threats to a person's life. It can occur when something upsets a person at the core of their being. Something terrifying. It moves them from what centers them and grounds them. It comes when something deeply emotionally upsetting shocks their world.

"This does not automatically excuse a person's actions, it just helps us understand why those actions exist. Often the reaction to trauma is to cause pain — either pain to themselves or pain to others. It's not always easy to get into the internal programming that proceeds horrific outcomes like murder but that's what I'm attempting to do. Things get twisted in a mind full of pain. After all, trauma is not what happens to a person; trauma is what happens inside a person as a result of what happened to that person. A person's trauma gets expressed in a myriad of ways. Memory loss. Panic Attacks. Flashbacks. Disturbing thoughts. Upsetting feelings. Recurring dreams. Changes in how a person thinks and feels. An increase in the flight-or-fight response. Physical attacks. Trauma comes back as a reaction, not simply as a memory. And there are different triggers for different people that bring about different symptoms or reactions.

"When a person is coping with a traumatic past there is often dissociation and compartmentalization. They tend to not feel feelings correctly. To complicate matters further, if a person chooses more and more to do what they know is wrong, they break their moral fiber. This isn't like breaking a bone. When you break a bone, it heals stronger. It's more like tearing a ligament. It only gets weaker with time.

"In other words, a person destroys or sears their conscience. It would be like having a bad burn on your skin. When it heals, it will be a scar that is numb to the touch. The conscience also can scar up by the repetition of choosing what is morally wrong. It becomes numb. And so to the degree a person's conscience decreases, to that same degree wrong-doing increases. They no longer feel bad about doing what's wrong. This person has been very deliberate, with very good planning. As the moral fiber or moral integrity gets more broken and destroyed, the killer will likely become more reckless in his actions.

"Here are some new and interesting facts in this specific case. One: THC was written on the wall in sight of the third victim, Pete Fox, as he died. He was in the same fraternity at the same time as the first two victims. Two: The fourth victim, Lincoln Hart, had his blood removed, but did not have his toes removed. He was also a UF student at the same time as the other victims. Three: I found a photo taken at the fraternity house with the first three victims and I was in that photo. I actually had contact for a brief moment with three of the victims when they were in college. I'm not sure how that fits or if it's important but I have to say it shocked me. Four: After another quick visit to Florida, I have found the name of the fraternity house mother during the years the three victims were there — Dorothy Whitlock. I think she might be able to give us some needed background information on the three victims."

TJ passed around the pictures he had just spoken about so all could see. Not knowing he was going to address the larger crowd, he didn't have time to make up a fancy board with colorful arrows and photographs.

"Now, in light of both of my reports, let's add or deepen a few conclusions. One: Our killer is experiencing a PTSD condition. He is reacting to trauma that he has experienced. The way he has decided to deal with his pain is by killing those who have caused him pain. Two: A major key to the story has to be in the friendship or partnership of the three frat guys. Three: As far as we know, the three were not in touch with each other after college. Therefore, whatever activity they were involved in together must have ended when they left the university. Four: The fourth victim, the one whose toes were untouched, had no contact with the others. We can't find anything that puts them together when they were all students. Five: All four victims meant something significant to the killer. They caused enough pain to be killed for doing it — whatever 'it' is. And six. I still believe the Patriots ticket points to the killer as being a New England resident, not just a Pats fan attending the game from out of the region."

TJ took a few gulps of water, then continued.

"We have many questions that still need to be answered. One: What does THC mean? Two: Why were there no toes cut off the fourth victim? Three: What connected the three frat boys and what did they do that made them deserve to die, in the mind of the killer? Four: Where is Dorothy Whitlock? Five: What's the connection with the fourth victim and why did he deserve to die, in the killer's mind? Six: Why the big time gap between the college years of the victims and the time they were murdered? There are always more questions but these seem to be the top ones at the moment.

"The next steps will be these. One: Find Dorothy Whitlock. Two: Detective Justice Jackson, who is with the Boston PD, and myself will interview the Whitlock woman when she is found. Hopefully she is still alive. Three: Detective Jackson and I will also attempt to interview the parents of the three frat guys. Four: There was a girl coming down the stairs with our three victims. Who is she? Is she important? We should try to find out. And Five: For me not to jump the gun in any direction since I'm just the new kid on the block and only the profiler! Once we have further defining information, we will decide where to go from there."

The short meeting ended. People said a few words to TJ, along with a few pats on the back. Everyone went back to their assigned workspace. TJ was relieved it was done and over with but he kept thinking that, in some of his points about PTSD, he could have been talking about himself.

# CHAPTER
## 36

orothy Whitlock was found. TJ and Justice caught a plane out of Logan to Orlando so they could interview her. They rented a car and drove the fifty miles to Orange City. They learned she was a resident of John Knox Village of Central Florida — a retirement community. The kind of place where people were supposed to be able to age with dignity. They also learned she had recently suffered from heart issues and could not live independently; she was in the long-term care center.

When they arrived to talk with Dorothy, they were informed she had a small heart attack the day before and was rushed to the hospital by ambulance. They proceeded to Florida Hospital. There they showed their badges and received information about Dorothy. She was in the ICU. No family members or visitors had arrived to see her. She was stable but weak. She could talk but only for a few minutes at a time. The doctors advised no more than twenty minutes. Regrettably, her outlook was not favorable, as she was also dealing with slow-growing tumors in her digestive track.

Dorothy was a small woman who had shrunk with age. She was barely five feet tall and weighed only ninety-two pounds, according to her chart. Her hair was white and matted from lying in bed. Her face held deep frown lines, crow's feet and accordion lines. She had a turkey neck and the skin on her upper arms was sagging. Her eyes had a glazed-over look. Her wrists and hands were tiny and delicate with many age spots. Yet, she presented a strong countenance and a winning smile.

"Hello, Dorothy. My name is Dr. TJ Maverick and I work with the FBI. This is Detective Justice Jackson. We are engaged on a case and would appreciate your help," said TJ.

"Sounds important. I'm all ears. What can I do for you?" said Dorothy.

"Are you're sure you're feeling strong enough at this time? We could come back later."

"Don't listen to those doctors. I'm fine. I've got a very weak heart and it's going to give out soon but don't put me in the grave just yet. I also have some slow-growing cancer but I'm dealing with it."

"Okay. Thanks for doing this," said Justice. "And do you mind if we record the interview?"

"Do whatever you need to do," answered Dorothy.

Justice placed a small recording device on the adjustable side table and turned it on.

"Our understanding is you were the University of Florida SAE house mom for sixteen years. From 1965 to 1981. If my calculations are right, since you were sixty-four when you retired, you're eighty-five right now. We were wondering if you can remember back when you were the house mother at UF?" asked Justice.

"Listen son, I may be eighty-five years old but there's nothing wrong with my mind; it's my heart that's the problem at the moment. Who do you want to know about?"

"There are three boys we would like to talk to you about. Joe Hiller, Troy Wilson, and Pete Fox," said Justice.

"Well, it's sure taken you a long time to finally deal with them. What have those arrogant monsters done now?" inquired Dorothy.

Both TJ and Justice were a little taken aback by the description of the boys being arrogant monsters. Justice wasn't going to stop the interview until he found out what she meant by that comment.

"It's not what they've done; it's what been done to them. They are all dead. They've been murdered and we think it has to do with something from their college days."

"Serves them right!"

Suddenly Dorothy turned her head away from TJ and Justice and started crying. Tears came rolling down her cheeks onto the ultra-white hospital linens.

"I feel a lot of shame about this. I did things that I'm not proud of out of a need for self-survival. I knew a lot of what was going on and I kept my mouth shut and turned the other way. It'll be good for me to get it all out to you, the police, before I leave this world. So, I'm glad you came."

"That's a good thing to do since confession is freeing for the soul. Could you tell us now what you knew back then?" asked TJ.

Staring off in the distance, Dorothy began her story: "I was pressured, intimidated, bullied, threatened and bribed. I was in fear for my life. When I knew too much, I was told to remain as the house mother or those I cared about would die along with me. I guess they figured they could control me but they weren't sure about how a new house mom might react. In the midst of all the threats, I was offered a large sum of money and, regrettably, I took it. I felt trapped, so I figured I might as well take the cash. I have always believed I'd be killed if I ever opened my mouth.

"Those three kids were haughty and entitled because of their family money. They felt like they were beyond the law — you know, that double standard of justice for the rich, white-privileged and politically connected. Their actions started out relatively harmless but their behavior moved into hurting and damaging many people — especially young co-eds," said Dorothy.

"Could you get more specific?" asked Justice.

"Sure, no problem. I'll give you some examples. There was the alligator incident. They pulled Albert the Alligator from the pond next to the Rietz Union building. It was ten feet long. They got it by the tail and pulled it into the union building. Many knew who did it. It was written up as a prank with the idea of no harm, no foul. Their names were kept out of the public arena. Someone made sure of that. Others would have been severely disciplined for endangering the lives of others. In the end, antics like that were relatively harmless.

"Then there was the incident with the English Lit professor. They lied about him sexually assaulting them and got him fired. I overheard them planning it. It was all because Joe Hiller was failing the class and tried to bribe him for a passing grade. I was scared of them, so I didn't want to get involved. I've always wondered what happened to him. I hope he came through it all right."

"We know about the professor episode. Do you know what THC stands for? It was written on the wall at one of the victim's home," said Justice.

"Before I get into that I want to say that I knew it would all pass. I just had to get through the years they were there. I held on by counting down the days until they'd graduate and be gone," Dorothy said in a whisper.

"THC. Was this something to do with drugs?" asked TJ.

"Yes and no. This is what I most regret. I was a coward. I allowed this to keep happening to the girls. I feel so guilty and dirty. I protected myself instead of protecting them."

Dorothy looked away and let out several loud moans of pain and shame. She didn't speak for five minutes as the words just wouldn't come out. TJ and Justice waited and gave her space. After composing herself, she continued.

"They wanted others to think it was just a special pot club between the three of them but it wasn't that at all. It stood for The Harvest Club — THC. It was their little private joke. They would harvest cherries, tangerines and lemons. These were their code words for the girls they would gang-rape. There was the Lemon Drops, the Tangerine Ops and the Cherry Pops. The nerve of them! Joe Hiller arrogantly told me about all of this when I confronted him about my suspicions. He turned it around and confronted me, with a knife at my throat."

"I'm sorry that happened to you. Who do you think was the leader of this club?" asked Justice.

"Joe was the leader. He definitely called the shots. He was full of charisma and full of himself. He was even the president of the fraternity for two years. Pete and Troy were followers. I can't be sure but I think some of the other boys knew what was going on. But, like everyone else, they would've been harassed and threatened if they even thought of opening their mouths. On a side note, whenever Joe's dad came for a visit, I never felt completely safe around him for some reason. I could never put my finger on it exactly ... just a feeling I had. I did wonder if the saying was true for the two of them, that the acorn doesn't fall far from the tree. He fiercely protected his son but I guess, maybe, that's just being a dad."

"Can we get back to The Harvest Club? What more can you tell us?"

"The Lemon Drops were worth one point, or digit, as they liked to call them. These were the slutty women. Those who were already promiscuous. I'm sure many said no when three guys showed up for a good time but a 'no' would not be accepted. They figured a girl filled with alcohol and drugs along with a reputation of being loose wouldn't be believed. Just her word against theirs. I'm sure she would be threatened in some way if she started to make trouble. Then there was the

Tangerine Ops. Worth five digits. These were the more innocent type girls but sex wasn't a completely new thing for them. With these girls they would lace their drink with LSD, tripping them out of their minds and then raping them. Joe said they got the name from some song. And then there was the Cherry Pops. This earned them ten digits. You can guess what that was all about. Pop the cherry — virgins.

"They would use alcohol and Rohypnol. Sometimes Ecstasy or Ketamine. Of course these would impair a girl's mental functions with confusion, loss of coordination, slurred speech and, most importantly, amnesia. I don't know how many women they took advantage of and raped. I don't even want to think about it. I've tried to shove it out of my mind for all these years but the horror of it never goes away for me. I'm so, so sorry."

TJ and Justice were stunned by this heinous information. They could only sit quietly while being inwardly enraged as they tried to take it all in. They no longer felt any pity for the victims. All they wanted to do was expose the truth. Justice wanted justice.

"You've been incredibly helpful and we deeply appreciate that. I have just one more question for you. Do you know anyone named Lincoln Hart?" asked Justice.

"No. That name does not ring any bells. Sorry," answered Dorothy.

"Okay. Just checking. You were obviously under duress with this terrible situation with your life being threatened. And now, to bring all this out into the open, I need to know if you're willing to have what you've told us written up so you can sign it in front of witnesses?" asked Justice with his fingers crossed. "That would give us a sworn statement that could be used as evidence in a court of law."

"Yes. Yes. And yes again," said Dorothy. "I'm not sure how long I'll be around so I think that's a very good idea."

"By doing that you can feel good, even if it's years late. Your testimony will make a difference. Truth always makes a difference," said TJ.

TJ almost finished this last statement with even from the grave but he caught himself before it came out of his mouth.

As TJ and Justice were heading out the door, Dorothy Whitlock added, "You know, I told some of this to the other fellow who came to see me last July. He came once but there was no follow-up. He claimed to be an investigative reporter. Like you two, he was also very thankful to learn about The Harvest Club."

Justice and TJ stopped in their tracks and looked at each other. Then turning around quickly, Justice asked, "Who was it? Can you describe this person to us?"

"Didn't you know? I can't really see. Just shadows now. I lost my good vision years ago so I can't describe him. His voice seemed sad but very serious. Like you guys, he was a man on a mission. He said his name was John Dee."

TJ and Justice were again stunned by yet another critical revelation. They walked wordlessly out of Dorothy Whitlock's hospital room, down the hall to the elevator and then out to their rented car in the visitor's parking lot.

# CHAPTER
## 37

TJ and Justice were on their way by car to interview the parents of Pete Fox. Justice had been catching a few Z's but both were still reeling from the explosive information they had gleaned from Dorothy Whitlock.

"Unbelievable! 'John Dee' instead of 'John Doe,'" exclaimed Justice.

"Not exactly super creative," laughed TJ.

"He's our man. It's got to be him. He went and saw Dorothy in July. Found out all about The Harvest Club and planned his revenge. We can only speculate about the motive of why he wanted to take them out. He's careful. He's deliberate. He takes his time. The first murder was in September. It fits," said Justice.

"It seems to. I was once told by a friend not to jump to conclusions. But ... I'm with you. I'm jumping big time!"

"While I was snoozing, did you hear back yet from John Knox Village about surveillance cameras in the long-term care center?" asked Justice.

"Yeah. First of all, they said she was still in her independent living space last July. It was an attached home, one bedroom, one bathroom place. Small but plenty of room for a single, legally blind person. She had help come in a few days a week but she was basically on her own. Bottom line, no cameras in that area of the senior living community. I've asked for the neighbors to be questioned to see if they know anything. I've also asked if the person helping Dorothy happened to be present when the, so called, 'investigative reporter' showed up. They're trying to find that person as we speak."

"Disappointing about the surveillance cameras. Maybe somebody will remember something," offered Justice.

"What should we do about Dorothy Whitlock? Surely she's culpable. She knew the truth about the professor. She allowed women to be raped for years. She even took money to stay quiet."

"All true. Also true; her life was threatened along with those she loved. Or, so she says ... but I believe her. And with what we now know about Joe, I'm thinking that's exactly what would have happened if she had come forward with the truth. It's a tough call but I'm thinking she's suffered enough with her guilt and shame. You did notice how relieved she was to get it all out, right? She'll sign the affidavit admitting everything, and the powers-that-be can decide what, if anything, they want to do with her. In the end, she'll be dead soon and any consequences to her actions won't matter anymore. For what it's worth, that's what I think," said Justice.

"Makes sense," responded TJ.

"How long until we get to our first stop, Marco Island, to see the parents of Pete Fox?"

"It's about 250 miles from Orange City and we've been driving for about three, so another couple of hours, I'd say."

"And what do we know about this family and the others we're interviewing, TJ?"

"Not that much. We know the first parents are around seventy-five years old and are in good health. They're reported to be quite rich. Then the family after that, the Wilsons, are in Key West and are described as being even more wealthy. They're the ones who made all the stink and got this sent up to the Boston FBI field office in the first place. The final family, although the wife is deceased, is in Miami Beach. It's the father of our illustrious Joe Hiller. He was a Junior. The father passed on his name to his son so we'll be meeting with a Joseph Hiller Senior. When I was doing some research on him, the articles listed him as mega-rich and a man financially behind many powerful political candidates. That means he's got listening ears in influential places."

"Yep. That'll make for a fun time!" quipped Justice.

Justice closed his eyes for the rest of the trip while TJ listened to a 60's and 70's station.

# CHAPTER
# 38

"Wow, what a beautiful place this Marco Island is. I'd never heard of it before making this trip. Obviously it's pretty exclusive and the real-estate prices must be sky high," said Justice.

"No doubt about that," replied TJ.

They pulled into the driveway of an $8 million, 8,500 square foot ocean-front estate at the end of Caxambas Court where they had an appointment with Ron and Pat Fox, the parents of the deceased, Pete Fox. The massive home was bright white stucco with a grey tiled roof. The palm-strewn grounds were immaculate. The house seemed to lovingly embrace the huge pool in the back as it stretched out toward the soft blue ocean. TJ and Justice were met at the door by the Fox couple. The entrance was grand, with 30-foot ceilings, marble floors, and a curved staircase. They were invited into a huge living area with facing couches and wing-backed chairs.

They spent an hour doing the interview. In the end, they both felt it was a waste of time and effort. To the parents, Pete was a wonderful son, a successful architect who had no enemies and who wouldn't hurt a fly. If they only knew the truth.

After a hotel night, their next stop was Key West. They were both psyched about traveling on the 113-mile highway carrying U.S. Route 1 through the Florida Keys to Key West. This included the famous Seven Mile Bridge. They argued over the music in the car, the places to stop for food, and the all-time best football players but they were, at the same time, enjoying each other's company.

Key West was very different from Marco Island; only six square miles and isolated from population centers by distance and ocean. They went to Fleming Street and found the Wilson family home. It was located in the area known as Old Town where small properties went for huge amounts of money. This particular property reached back an entire city block. The white, wooden mini-mansion, originally built in the 1920's, was elegant and impressive, yet understated. The architectural style was unique to Key West and was known as "eyebrow." The pool area was a private sanctuary with a multitude of mature palms, along with flowering trees and bushes. TJ and Justice sat in a comfortable, outdoor, shaded area next to the serene pool with Tim and Carol Wilson.

Tim's age was in the high seventies while Carol must have been in her mid-thirties. TJ was thinking it was amazing what money could buy. They found out Troy's mother had died of pancreatic cancer when he was only eleven. Carol was the fourth wife. Justice was wondering who the fifth one would be.

Mr. Wilson was aggressive and pointed in his questioning about his son's death. He raised his voice more than once and demanded that the killer be brought to justice. Again, they were told the son had no real enemies, although he admitted the construction business could be brutally competitive, as Troy was a prosperous developer. In the course of the interview, the father threatened to speak to some very important people who would then speak to TJ's and Justice's superiors if they did not accomplish their jobs to his satisfaction. He said there would be consequences to their upward mobility. TJ worked hard not to laugh in his face knowing he was only doing a short-term gig. Justice was working hard to hold back his anger and not strangle the old man. He felt like shouting out that his son was a serial gang-rapist and deserved to die. But, that information was not ready for public consumption.

They found a place for the night called the Casa 325 Guesthouse on Duval Street. After checking in, they went to the Hot Tin Roof Restaurant, also located on Duval Street, and had some of the best seafood of their lives.

Early the next day TJ and Justice made the 168-mile trek back up U.S. Route 1 to Miami Beach. They were to interview Joe Hiller Senior at three in the afternoon. He lived off Venetian Way on the very exclusive Di Lido Island, which was surrounded by Biscayne Bay, part of the Intracoastal Waterway. This was just minutes away from Rivo Alto Island where the younger Joe Hiller had lived. TJ found an internet article telling how the very private Mr. Hiller had bought four connected properties for a few million on the north tip of the island, tore down the beautiful homes and then built what amounted to a $15 million compound for himself. *Those were the prices in the late 60's so it's worth a lot more now, TJ thought.* Completing the rich and famous lifestyle was a magnificent yacht at his beck-and-call docked at the pier on the waterfront of his compound.

Seventy-nine year old Joe Henry Hiller was surrounded by servants and a bevy of young, pretty women in tiny bikinis playing and lying around one of the largest and most ornate pools TJ had ever seen. Some of the women had apparently forgotten the top half of their bathing suits while others had forgotten both halves. TJ was thinking Dorothy Whitlock was right ... that the acorn didn't fall far from the tree. Justice was having a hard time taking his focus off the women and concentrating on the conversation about the death of the junior Joe Hiller; he needed to have his back toward the large picture window that looked out to the pool and the decoration of feminine bodies instead of having it directly in his view. TJ was hoping his detective friend would be able to remember the content of the conversation and not just the bust size of the women.

Mr. Hiller explained he was a confirmed bachelor after the unexpected death of Joe's mother in a car crash during his son's junior year of high school. He called himself an Independent Investor and said he had inherited some family money and then done well in most projects and companies he had put his money in through the years. He said a number of times that only high risks gave high rewards. It was obvious to both TJ and Justice he had not just done well, he had done fabulously well. He shared he had been born in London, served as a foot soldier in the British Army and after World War II studied civil engineering. He was able to emigrate to America in 1948 where he later met the woman he fell in love with and married.

He expressed to TJ and Justice that the loss of his one and only son had been heartbreaking but somehow he didn't look heartbroken when he said it. He suggested the killing of his son was probably some kind of tragic, random murder. Maybe a deranged thief or just a person who had moved from torturing animals to torturing human beings. Both TJ and Justice got the feeling that he didn't really want them to dig for the truth. He embodied such a different demeanor compared to the other parents. They thanked him for his time and were escorted out by the same muscle-bound servant who had ushered them in. They were not only shown to the door, they were also walked out to their car and watched as they left the spacious driveway.

"Was that weird or am I off base?" asked TJ.

"Yeah, that was weird. Something didn't feel right," responded Justice.

"He said all the right words but the emotions, gestures, and facial expressions didn't match. And yet, there were no telltale signs of lying."

"I think he's hiding something. Maybe he knew about his son's activities, or at least had suspicions, and he doesn't want it brought out to the light."

"I think you're on to something with that, Justice."

They were catching a plane back to Boston in the morning but decided to splurge and check out Joe's Stone Crab for dinner. They were not disappointed. Then they found a nearby hotel, got two rooms and both were happy to immediately hit the sack.

# 2001

The date was June 7, 2001. It was the night before Leah's and the monster's 25th wedding anniversary celebration. They were to leave for Bermuda early the next day. It was a still night, hot and sticky. But Leah insisted they sit on their back deck to gaze at the stars, have a glass of red wine and talk.

"It's a beautiful night and you look beautiful too, Leah," said the monster.

"Thanks. And yes, it certainly is."

"You said you wanted to talk about something? Right?"

Leah took a sip of wine and said, "That's right. I have some things on my mind that I need to get out. I don't want to go through our next twenty-five years together without you knowing all about me. Do you think you can handle learning who I really am?"

"I know who you are and I'm in love with you. I look forward to our time in Bermuda. We'll go back to all the places we visited and saw on our honeymoon. I can hardly wait until tomorrow. Now, what's on your mind?" asked the monster.

"I've always been afraid of having this talk with you. I've been afraid you wouldn't love me if you knew the whole truth about me. But, I can't go on like this. I need to know that you can love me unconditionally. You see, I'm not who you think I am. I've lied about many things and it's those lies and half-truths that I believe have made me emotionally fragile and distant at times, along with the traumatic experiences that have invaded my life. You know some bits and pieces only because they came out years ago when we were trying to have children. I know that's been a huge disappointment in your life."

"But as painful as it's been not being able to have children, we've had each other and I've been happy being with you. I love you and ...."

"Please, just let me finish. Then you can talk. Okay?"

"Yeah ... sure. Go ahead."

"I was raped in my freshman year of college. I was a virgin and I

226

couldn't report it because I was drugged and had no idea who did it. I was never the same after that happened. I was broken. I was full of guilt and shame and I lost the joy of living for a long time. I got into alcohol and drugs in a way I never had before. I was medicating myself. Then, as you know, I found a boyfriend, Lincoln; for a number of months I became hopeful about life again. During that time, for all practical purposes, we were living together. I thought he loved me but I found out he had cheated on me. This tore me up inside and I wanted to hurt him the way he had hurt me.

"So I went to a party. Got drunk. Was drugged and yes, again raped. Then I realized that these were the same guys from my freshman year! I was so ashamed and humiliated and knew that on this occasion I was asking for it in many ways so, again, I couldn't do much about it although I tried. They were all from rich and connected families. I would only lose the he-said, she-said battle and drag my family through all that crap with me.

"And then I found myself pregnant. I really don't know who the father was. I told you it was Lincoln but it could have been one of the rapists. I think with what Dr. Kimberlin told us, it probably was my boyfriend but I really don't know. So I had an abortion. I did something I knew was wrong. I killed a baby that was growing inside of me. I've tried to tell myself it was an okay thing to do because of the circumstances but it never really felt like it was okay to me. I was advised to never tell anyone for any reason that I had an abortion; to just keep it inside forever. So I did that but I think stuffing it and never really talking about it has damaged me even more.

"After the abortion I did more and more drugs and alcohol. But my real medication was sex. I had one-night stands and short-term sexual relationships; too many to count. I felt guilty and ashamed. I was out of control but to feel in control I just wanted someone inside of me. It made me feel loved and secure for the moment. Orgasms always came, making me forget my pain for at least a brief period of time.

"I finally put myself together enough to concentrate on my studies, graduate, and come to Boston for grad school. I was going to make a life for myself away from all my mess. I dreamed of having one great love ... it became you. And just so you know it, I've always been faithful to you. But I'm so sorry I've never been honest about all of this before now. Please, please forgive me. Always know you saved me. Your love for me saved me. Although I've had my bouts of depression and anxiety, I've been so happy being in your life, in your arms and in your heart."

Tears and raw emotion had been pouring out of Leah throughout her night of confession. The monster looked like it had been hit in the head with a baseball bat. A cooling breeze had delicately started to blow across the deck. The moon was full and the stars were shining beautifully bright. Leah was fearful, yet optimistic, as she held her breath waiting to see how her husband would respond.

"YOU SLUT!" yelled the monster as he slapped her hard across the face. The monster strode into the house and slammed the back door behind him. He got the keys to his car, threw open the front door and blasted out of the driveway.

---

Hours later, smelling of alcohol, the monster returned home with a bouquet of flowers in hand. It walked through the front door and politely yelled out, "Leah, I'm so sorry for my unkind and uncalled for reaction." Wandering through the house he called out again, "Leah, again I'm sorry. I lacked compassion and was only thinking of myself. I was out of control and in a jealous rage. What I did was terrible and I beg for your forgiveness."

There was no answer. The monster made his way toward the bedroom. Leah was lying in bed with an empty bottle of sleeping pills on her bedside table. She was finally at peace.

# CHAPTER
# 39

"Dr. Simmons, thank-you for taking the time to see me here at your home office for a therapy session. I was so impressed and appreciative of the five-week grief therapy sessions we had together back in the Fall. Your words have guided me in a positive direction but I could use some reinforcement," said TJ.

"Happy to help and thanks for your kind words. I do remember you very well, TJ. In fact, for me, you were unforgettable. Now tell me what's been going on."

"Well, to be honest, I'm here because I was told by my boss I needed to see a professional to help deepen my commitment to live and to deepen my resolve for a productive life after losing my wife. I didn't know who to call exactly but, like I said, you were so helpful in that five-week grief group that I wanted to try and reach out to you."

"Well, I'm glad you've come. Can I get you something to drink before we get started?"

"You know, a glass of ice water would be good right now, if you don't mind."

"No problem. Back in a minute."

While TJ waited, he took in the diplomas, pictures, and books that were scattered throughout Dr. Simmons' study. One of the diplomas was for a PhD in Structural Engineering from Columbia. TJ wondered if they had been in New York City at the same time when he was getting his masters at NYU. Most of the pictures were of unique, spectacular-looking buildings located in different parts of the world.

"Here's your water and I grabbed a can of soda for myself. Now let me tell you a little about me before we get into your story. You might have noticed my doctorate is not in psychology but in structural engineering. That's my profession. All these pictures you see of different buildings are the special ones I've been able to work on. And yes, I am a licensed therapist but that really is more of a sideline. I went through some significant trauma in my childhood and so I sought some answers and ended up doing classes and getting certificates in the specialized area of grief counseling. You already know about my book. I never thought in a million years it would have such success. I wrote it more for my personal well-being than for others but I'm glad it has seemed to help many along their way. You see, I lost my parents when I was in my teens through a tragic house fire. Later I was told it was started in their bedroom by an overloaded electrical outlet. I was lucky that my bedroom was located on the other side of the house so I was able to walk away from it with only some smoke inhalation issues. Actually they were my adoptive parents but we were a close-knit family who deeply loved each other so the loss was devastating for me. A more recent devastation was the loss of my wife. We were married for twenty-five wonderful years. She had long-term health issues and passed last June."

"I'm so sorry to hear that. I'm sure she was a remarkable person and I'm sure it's been a difficult time for you, too, with such a great loss," said TJ sympathetically.

Now it was TJ's turn to open up his life. He started by telling about his new gig working for the FBI as a profiler and how much he enjoyed it and how it was helping him. Then he turned to more personal matters. He told him about his parents dying when he was a child and about the turbulent years of living with his grandparents. He told him of the three things that had rocked his world, ultimately, in a good way — having cancer, being forgiven by a boy he viciously beat-up, and finding the love of his life, Suzanne. He told about coming to the point of having a deep respect and love for his late granddad and how he had learned so much about life from him.

He explained about medicating himself with alcohol and drugs over the past months following the death of his wife. He opened-up about his kids and his lack of care, concern, compassion, and connection. He pulled from his wallet their pictures and proudly showed them to Dr. Simmons who took a long and careful look at them. TJ explained what he had done to try and make-up with them. Lastly, he told him all about his time on the Tobin Bridge. All his emotions. All his thoughts. All his hopelessness. He ended by sharing about his resolve to live his life and to make a difference with it.

After an hour of listening, Dr. Simmons expressed many encouraging and sage words that left TJ with an even deeper desire to live and make a positive impact with his life. Some of what he said that left the deepest impressions in TJ's mind were, "Not that time heals all wounds but the passage of the years lets us make peace with our grief in our way." ... "You see, you either move backward or forward. You never stay the same. After all, you're responsible for how long you let what hurt you, haunt you." ... "TJ, you and your life are entirely up to you. And yes, the world is full of suffering but it's also full of overcoming it."

The one statement that didn't make complete sense to TJ, at least not yet, was when Dr. Simmons closed the session with the remark, "Sometimes we have to make decisions that hurt our hearts but heal our souls."

TJ paid the $300.00 fee for the session with cash and, as he was being walked out of the home, he noticed some family pictures hanging on the wall in the hallway. There was a wedding picture of a woman coming down a curved staircase. For some reason it caught his eye. She seemed vaguely familiar to TJ. They stopped at the front door, shook hands and said good-bye.

# JOURNAL ENTRY
## May 23, 2002

Suzo:

I've been busy and it's been good for me. I'm staying in touch with the kids and have visited them twice. I believe I'm making progress, which is a very good thing in life. As Granddad used to always tell me: Perfection never, progress forever!

I am convinced that I either stay working on myself or I'll backslide into the ways I was coping. I've got to make sure I don't stumble over something I've decided to put behind me like that crazy Tobin Bridge experience. I will never stare into the face of oblivion again, Suzo. I promise. I have to remember that progress is made by choosing happiness over history and it's a choice I must make every day of my life. I know some days will be harder than others.

I've done something that has helped me recently. I had a private session with a professional grief counselor to get everything out on the table and to gain some additional direction, correction, and perspective. Dealing with the pain of trauma is not easy!

I heard an old '70s song the other day by Creedence Clearwater Revival. It's always amazing to me how feelings and memories are attached to songs. It was the one by John Fogerty, "Who'll Stop The Rain." It was attached to that movie of the same name starring Nick Nolte ... the one about Vietnam. I always believed it to be a war protest song so, in my mind, I would change the word 'rain' for the word 'pain.' I had thought that to be the song's original meaning and intent. But decades later Fogerty revealed it was just a song recounting his Woodstock experience — people dancing in the rain, muddy, naked, and grouping together to keep warm while it just kept raining. So, I heard that song and it continued to run through my mind for days and I kept asking myself the question: Who'll Stop The Pain? Who'll Stop The Pain? Who'll Stop The Pain? I've come a distance but I have a ways to go. That's for sure, Suzo.

Talk about memories. After visiting the ol' G-ville campus I went back to our Lexington home and got some pictures of us when we were at UF. I've definitely aged but you looked so much the same. I always loved how you took such good care of yourself. I was also reliving in my mind the time we floated down the Itchetucknee. Such picture perfect, crystal clear water. I was definitely reliving seeing you in that tiny, yellow bikini. WOW!

WAIT! … I just thought of something … picture perfect, crystal clear water. Crystal — Picture. Crystal glass — College picture. Crystal glass with a distinct pattern. College picture of a girl coming down the stairs — wedding picture of a bride coming down the stairs. THIS COULD BE THE BREAKTHROUGH WE'VE BEEN NEEDING! BUT HOW CAN THIS BE TRUE?

Suzo, how can what I'm thinking be possible? But thanks so much for helping me put these pieces of the puzzle together.

Sorry to go like this…
All my love, all the time —
TJ

# CHAPTER
# 40

As soon as TJ stopped writing he grabbed his phone and called Justice. After many rings he picked up.

"Whoever this is, I was asleep in case you were wondering."

"It's just me. Your partner," said TJ.

"You do know it's well after midnight on a Thursday night or, should I say, early Friday morning? I've got to get to work in just a few hours. What do you want?" asked Justice with a big yawn.

"Sorry about the hour but it just struck me. I believe a person named Dr. Jack Simmons is our man. Long story on background but let it suffice to say that I went to see him for some counseling. He gave me a drink of water in a crystal glass. The decorative pattern on it was a match for the decorative pattern on the crystal glasses in the photos sent up from Atlanta detailing the murder of Lincoln Hart. In the photo, there were only three glasses, as one was reported missing from the set of four. I don't know why he would have taken it from the house but there it was!" exclaimed TJ.

"Oh, come on TJ. A glass? Are you kidding me? Can I remind you of the time?!"

"Listen, it's not only that. I saw a picture of his wife in a wedding dress coming down some stairs. She's the same girl in the picture I showed you that I found at the frat house with me in it. She's coming down some stairs in that picture, too."

"Really?" Justice was wide awake now. "Are you sure about it being the same girl? Absolutely sure, TJ?"

"I wouldn't go all-in but I'd wager pretty heavy."

"Then let's not move too fast. We don't want to have the same debacle as before and I want to see that pic of the crystal glass. I can't remember even seeing that in the file."

"I'll send you the glass pic but you need to do a quick deep dive into Dr. Simmons' life. I want to compare it to what he told me. You know making a false statement to the FBI is a federal crime and felony; I would just need to go back in an official capacity with the questions. I'll get someone to find out about those glasses. If a zillion of them have been sold everywhere then it means nothing but if it's something expensive and unique we may have a winner."

"Okay. Let's just keep this to ourselves for now."

"For sure. Much to do tomorrow, so get back to sleep," said TJ.

"Like that's going to happen. We'll talk more later."

---

"Again at the Starbucks? TJ, you're in love with this place," said Justice.

"Good coffee and privacy in a public space. Can't beat it!" replied TJ.

"Okay, so much for the small talk. It's been a week, what have you found out about the glass? Is it really possible it's the one missing in Atlanta?"

"I called down and got them to ask the wife about the glasses, to research about the glass itself and to send some new close-up photos to us. It's all very interesting. First, they were a wedding gift from the wife's parents. Apparently they have been in the family since the early '50s, so they were treasured objects. The set was purchased when this particular pattern was first made available. It was a set of four Waterford Crystal glasses and one was definitely missing. The wife was sure it was in the china cabinet before the murder because they were not something they used much, if at all. She said they were in perfect condition.

"It was a set of four in the Alana pattern of cut crystal. This pattern was begun in 1952 in a series of designs named after Irish girls. By the way, in Gaelic the name Alana means 'darling.' They were nine-ounce Irish crystal glasses. These were older and so the company name was found on an acid stamp in a Gothic script without the seahorse trademark. Also, they still had their gold stickers with the Waterford's green seahorse logo on them. The acid stamp and the sticker helped to identify their age. And by the way, there was a sticker exactly like that on the bottom of the glass I used.

"So these are not cheap glasses and I would assume antique ones would be worth even more. I learned that Ireland's Waterford Crystal began in 1783. It was found that by adding lead oxide to the silicates that make up the molten glass the process achieved a softness that allowed the glass to be blown and carved while remaining hard and clear as it cooled."

"Way too much detail. Just need the bottom line," said Justice.

"Right. So, these are mouth blown ... not hand-pressed or hand-molded or factory-made pieces. What I'm saying is that these glasses are expensive with a distinct pattern and they are not in the typical home. And certainly, fifty-year-old glasses that are unchipped with the original sticker are rarely found. If the one in Dr. Simmons' house matches, then we've got our killer."

"Like I said, that's more info than I ever wanted or needed to know about glassware but I'm fired-up you had that glass of water during your session with the guy. You're certainly demonstrating your supernatural powers of clairvoyance," Justice said with a hearty laugh.

"You might call them my superpowers. It's all about my photographic memory and my special ability for puzzles and patterns. They do give me a nice edge."

"And I won't give you the pleasure of hearing me say I'm a little jealous. Just saying I wouldn't mind that same edge, if you know what I mean. But now it's my turn to amaze you with my detective skills. Dr. Jack Simmons has history. He was adopted as a baby. His adoptive parents and young Jack did not get along well. More than once the police were called to the house due to noise complaints, which turned out to be heavy-duty verbal and physical fighting between the parents and the son. There were also incidences of cutting and suicide threats by the young teenager. These were chalked-up to the boy having serious abandonment issues. The parents died in a home fire when he was still a teenager. The fire was under investigation as being suspicious, but was finally ruled as accidental. He ended up inheriting a very large estate although it was overseen by a lawyer until his twenty-first birthday. Also, he's an avid, maybe obsessed, anti-abortion person, giving large donations and participating in anti-abortion rallies. He even has an arrest on record for being at a protest that must have gotten out of hand."

"This is good stuff. He told me he had a close and loving relationship with his parents," said TJ. "Keep it coming!"

"He's a structural engineer, PhD from Columbia. So he's smart. He's the majority owner of an engineering firm that does very high-end stuff all around the world. Their name, I'm told, is well known in the building world and they get big bucks for what they do. He also, as you already know, is a renowned grief-counselor who has written the book, *The Journey Back From Loss*. It's a best-seller, so with the engineering company, he's certainly not hurting for money.

"He was married in 1976. Now get this. Dr. Simmons' wife, Leah D'Angelo Simmons, committed suicide last June. A sleeping pill overdose. Nothing suspicious about it in the files. She did her post-grad work at Tufts but did her undergrad studies at ... wait for it ... the University of Florida from 1971 to 1975."

"Really? That's almost unbelievable. So it was her, both in the wedding pic and in the frat pic, coming down some stairs. You know Simmons wasn't very forthcoming with the info about the suicide. Could have been covering for the sake of his wife — or for himself. So what in the world is the ultimate connection and motivation for the murders?"

Justice replied in a determined voice, "I'm not sure but we're going to find out. We need to get a search warrant as soon as possible."

"Great! And let me add one interesting fact. The name Simmons means 'victorious protector.' Sometimes our name defines who we become. You can relate to that, right, JUSTICE?"

"I feel ya, TJ. Now let's get on that search warrant!"

---

A day later TJ and Justice, along with ten police officers, arrived on Radcliff Road at a grand home overlooking the Charles River in Newton. This was the second time TJ had been to this location. In their hands was a very generous search warrant that included the house and the car belonging to Dr. Jack Simmons. The document specified the appropriation of an antique Waterford Crystal glass with the Alana cut-glass pattern, and a picture of a bride coming down the stairs who was believed to be connected to at least three of the men who had been murdered.

A lone, black BMW sedan was parked in the driveway. They moved past that to the front door. There was no answer from ringing the doorbell or from loudly pounding on the door. They entered anyway and proceeded to tear-up the house while looking for any evidence that would link Dr. Simmons to any of the killings.

The car was clean. Nothing of evidential value was found. They figured he had taken a taxi to escape to the airport or railway station. But what made him run? TJ surmised he must have stared in a too noticeable way at the bride picture that revealed his recognition of the girl or maybe Dr. Simmons took off simply because he was paranoid that TJ worked with the FBI. In the house they easily found the crystal glass and the picture of the bride. They also found mounds of anti-abortion information in books and leaflets scattered throughout the house. In the master bedroom, it looked like a quick packing job had recently taken place.

There were two huge finds. First, there were diaries belonging to the wife, Leah, stacked in the corner of the den. Glancing through them, it became obvious to TJ that they contained many of the missing pieces concerning the murder spree puzzle. TJ could hardly wait for the diaries to be processed so he could start to more carefully read through each and every one of them. Secondly, they found three packages of toes, ten in each plastic bag, stuffed in the back of an oversized, Sub-Zero freezer next to boxes of Thin Mints Girl Scout cookies. That was the coup de grace.

# CHAPTER
# 41

T J, Justice, Darius, and Chip met together in a small conference room with dark wood-paneled walls at the Harvard Club, located on the top floor of One Federal Street in the Financial District. TJ, an alumnus of Harvard, had arranged the meeting space along with some drinks and sandwiches, as the gathering was at the noon hour. They were looking forward to the discussion and update of the case.

"Great view, Mav," said Darius. "Thanks for arranging this. Nice to be out of the office and in a quiet place where we won't be disturbed or interrupted."

"Same thoughts here. A nice spot for this," said Chip.

"No problem. Might as well use my Harvard clout in some capacity," said TJ.

"I'm afraid my U Mass Boston alma mater doesn't quite have these kinds of accommodations available," laughed Justice.

"And Maverick, just run through it like you were presenting it to the larger group. I may have you do it again if I think it can be another further training opportunity."

"Okay, will do. Food and drinks are on the table so just grab whatever looks good to you and I'll get us started with my report," said TJ. "There's a ton of new intelligence but before I get into the specifics, let me offer some statistical and informational background on rapes and abortions because these were central traumatic events in this case. What has happened to the people surrounding this investigation confirms the truths that pain begets pain and monsters beget monsters. I'll explain what I mean by that statement in a few minutes.

"One out of six American women have been the victim of an attempted or completed rape in her lifetime. Eleven million women in the U.S. have been raped while drunk, drugged, or high. Seventy-five percent of college students who experience unwanted intercourse are under the influence of alcohol or drugs at the time of the incident. Fifteen to thirty percent of college women have been the victim of 'acquaintance rape' at some point in their lives and two thirds of rape victims between eighteen and twenty-nine years of age know their attacker.

"The sad thing is that acquaintance rape is rarely reported to the police ... reported less than two percent of the time. It jumps to only twenty-one percent being reported if it's a stranger. Every year, one woman in eight in college is raped and eighty-five percent of these women know their attacker. And because of the trauma of rape, thirty-one percent of rape victims develop some form of rape-related PTSD. And here are a couple more facts to digest over lunch. One in twelve college males admit to having committed acts that met the legal definition of rape and one in five college students abandon safer sex practices when they're drunk.

"Now maybe you guys are all familiar with these recent stats but at least they're a vivid reminder. These facts certainly move me to want to protect the women in our society in a much better way. The heartbreaking thing is that rape survivors feel guilty, for the most part, because they feel they did something wrong which caused them to be sexually assaulted. They feel guilty because rape culture makes it seem like their actions caused the assault. On top of this, the shame is what prevents many survivors from speaking about what happened to them. Shame lasts longer than guilt. And let me reiterate, the feeling of shame is so intense for rape victims that many never tell anyone what happened to them.

"Rape is what happened to Leah D'Angelo Simmons when she was a freshman in college. In fact it was a gang-rape and it happened again in her sophomore year. Alcohol and drugs were a part of both attacks. A probable consequence from the last attack was an unwanted pregnancy. This led to Leah having an abortion. So let's talk about that now.

"On April 10, 1970, abortion on demand became legal in New York for all comers. This allowed abortions to be performed within twenty-four weeks of pregnancy and at any time if the women's life was at risk. Some felt this was a breakthrough for women's rights and some felt it was the end of civilization. Overnight, a new industry materialized. In the first twenty-four months, 400,000 abortions were performed in New York; sixty-six percent were from women coming from out of state. Two thirds from out-of-state were women with first-time pregnancies. Nineteen thousand came from the state of Florida where abortion was still illegal in 1972. Leah was one of those girls. She was already fragile from the rapes but abortion is consistently associated with elevated rates of mental illness compared to women without a history of abortion. People are affected differently from the procedure but all are affected and now one out of four American women will have an abortion before her forty-fifth birthday.

"Of course, abortion was legalized in the U.S. in 1973 with the Roe vs. Wade decision. Since that time, 62 million abortions have been done in America at a clip of 13,000 per day. Worldwide it's 40 to 50 million per year, or 125,000 per day. Let me add that abortion is either the greatest act of compassion on earth, saving children from being unwanted while allowing women the rights over their own bodies; or, it's the greatest mass murder sanctioned by law in nations throughout the world. If that's the case, it pushes Hitler and Stalin down the list of some of the worst mass murders in history.

"And so, considering all of Leah's trauma, her last words found in her diary make a lot of sense. On the night of her suicide she closed her diary thoughts with eight words taken from the musical, *Les Misérables*: '*Now life has killed the dream I dreamed.*'

"Justice, why don't you take over and speak about the results from the search of the Simmons' home?" asked TJ.

"Sure. No problem. First let me backtrack on one thing. We did not find out anything from the neighbors of Dorothy Whitlock, the retired frat mother, at John Knox Village where she was visited by the fake reporter. We did find the nurse helper who happened to be with Dorothy on the day the supposed reporter visited. Her description matches Dr. Simmons perfectly. A little over six feet tall. Dark hair, graying on the sides and thinning on the top. Fiftyish in age but in good physical shape. Strong and distinguished looking. Bushy eyebrows. Green eyes. A large nose but not too large for his face.

"Now, about the search of the Simmons' home. I know you've already read some of this so I'll be as brief as possible. The house was unoccupied. It looked like Dr. Simmons left in a hurry. We found a lot of anti-abortion books and pamphlets. Additionally, it was obvious because of autographed footballs and posters that he was an avid New England Patriots fan. He also had Patriots hats, shirts, and hoodies so you can assume the dropped Pats ticket was his. We found the Waterford crystal glass and it checked out to be the one missing from the set at the murder scene of Lincoln Hart. We found the wedding picture of the bride, Leah, descending some stairs and it checked out she was also the one descending stairs in the frat house in the photo TJ had found earlier. The picture shows her being helped down the stairs by the three victims who had their toes cut off. Of course, TJ was helping her, too, but I think he's in the clear! We also found a cache of dairies written by Leah that have given us details revealing the probable motive behind the killings. I'm sure TJ will have more to say about those since he read every word of every diary book and he's got, at least, a half decent memory. And then there were the toes found in the freezer. Three bags with ten toes in each bag. After running tests, it's confirmed they do belong to our victims."

"Thanks, Justice, for that info," TJ said. "And, thanks for tossing me out as a suspect! Now, where to go from here? Well ... let me give you a twelve-point summary of where we are and what we know so far. Much of this info is from the diaries.

"First: Leah, the wife of Dr. Jack Simmons, was drugged and gang-raped twice in college. This was before Simmons and Leah knew each other.

"Second: We found and interviewed the frat house mom, Dorothy Whitlock, who was at the fraternity in the early '70s. She told us about The Harvest Club ... abbreviated to THC ... and how the three boys, Joe, Troy and Pete, would get points or 'digits' for the women they raped depending if they were virgins, sexually loose girls or somewhere in between. Ten digits for virgins, and Leah was a virgin at the time of her first rape. The removal of ten toes or digits now makes sense. We have a signed affidavit with all this information from Dorothy as she may only have a short time to live.

"Third: She called the three boys monsters. They intimidated and threatened her. They also paid her off to keep their secrets.

"Fourth: Leah never reported the rapes. She was stopped by the fear of coming up against rich, powerful, and connected families. My guess is she was also stopped by her overwhelming sense of shame.

"Fifth: Leah never talked about her abortion. She was even advised to keep her mouth shut for all time. Having no one to talk to must have led to more mental-health issues since she was already feeling guilty about having the abortion.

"Sixth: Dr. Simmons was very upset when he learned about the abortion. This was not helpful to Leah's emotional state. On top of that, the abortion was botched, which led to Leah being unable to have children. This would be additional guilt and trauma in Leah's life.

"Seventh: On the night before her twenty-fifth anniversary, Leah decided to tell the whole truth about herself to her husband and then she ends up killing herself. I don't believe suicide was her initial plan but because Dr. Simmons condemned her after hearing the confession, it crushed her emotionally and pushed her to become suicidal.

"Eighth: The diaries were a secret and Simmons found them after her death.

"Ninth: This gave him pictures and names of the rapists along with further info on her summer of '72 lover, Lincoln Hart. He was not in the rape club. He was only a lousy, cheating boyfriend who possibly got her pregnant.

"Tenth: Simmons learned the frat mom's name, Dorothy Whitlock, from Leah's diary. He then located her and presented himself as an investigative reporter. She could not describe him to us because she is legally blind. This fake interview gave him the inside scoop and the specifics about The Harvest Club. Lemon Drops — one digit. Tangerine Ops — five digits. Cherry Pops — ten digits. That discussion with Dorothy Whitlock happened soon after the death of his wife and then the first murder occurred soon after that conversation with the Whitlock woman. So it all fits the timeline and explains why the murders occurred so many years after the rape events. Simmons had only just found out about how the rapes and the abortion had hurt and damaged the woman he loved.

"Eleventh: As I've already mentioned, Leah's summer-of-love boyfriend was Lincoln Hart. He cheated on her and out of spite she ended up angry and drunk, which led to the second gang-rape situation. When she told Lincoln she was pregnant, he went along with her desire to get an abortion and even helped pay for it. Because he wasn't in The Harvest Club, his toes were not cut off. He had not been collecting digits from rapes so his digits were not collected by Simmons.

"Twelfth: As Leah had suffered a slow, emotional death he wanted those who caused her emotional pain also to experience a slow death. So no knife or gun. Just a trickle of blood dripping out of their bodies as they watched and considered what they had done."

TJ drew a breath as he considered what to say next. "Now let's dive deeper concerning the motive. I'll do this using the Bible with its truths about human nature. Solomon says jealousy arouses a husband's fury and he will show no mercy when he takes revenge. By reading through the diaries, it was obvious that Simmons was very jealous when it came to his wife, Leah. He had major issues concerning her past sexual life. He especially had issues with her having an abortion, which led to her not being able to have children. To further deepen his pain concerning all of this, he was an unwanted child who was put up for adoption, which produced trauma from major abandonment issues. So with Simmons, his pain moved him from jealousy, to revenge, to murder.

"As some of you already know, my granddad was a preacher and I was pretty much forced to listen to his sermons when I was growing up, so I got to know some of the more obscure Bible stories. There's one about a beautiful young woman named Tamar. Amnon, a son of King David, was in love with her. He devised a plan to get her alone in his bedroom and then proceeded to rape her. Absalom, also a son of David from a different wife, heard what had happened. Tamar was his virgin sister. So he hated Amnon because he had disgraced and traumatized her. After two years of resentment, anger, and hatred, Absalom devised a plan to kill his half-brother Amnon. This had been his expressed intention ever since the day Amnon raped his sister, Tamar. So sinful human nature says that if you hurt me or someone I love, then I'll hurt you back. This was a revenge killing.

"Once Simmons knew what had been done to Leah, he devised a plan to kill those who raped and traumatized the love of his life. He felt her pain deeply. He felt his own pain deeply. His way to deal with and alleviate that pain was to kill those who had caused the pain in the first place. That included Joe, Troy, Pete, and Lincoln.

"And so, as I stated at the beginning, pain begets pain. And the three rapists, all monsters, turned Simmons into a monster. Monsters beget monsters."

The group was silent for a moment, then Chip spoke up, saying, "Now all we have to do is catch this guy. Detective Jackson, I'm counting on you to figure it out. Do whatever it takes to get the job done. And watch Mav's back if you do this together. I've got a feeling he wants in on the chase."

"That's right. I'm all-in till we complete what we've started," said TJ.

"I'll watch TJ's back and we'll get the monster. To start, I think we need to take another look at his home for any missing clues of where he might have disappeared to," said Justice with confidence and conviction.

All were satisfied with TJ's report. Darius indicated he wanted TJ to use the report in the near future as a professional development tool. Chip was congratulating his detective, Justice, and TJ on their successful partnership. The four left together riding the elevator down — but everyone was feeling up!

# CHAPTER
## 42

Both an APB, all-points bulletin, and a BOLO, be on the lookout, had been sent out concerning Dr. Jack Simmons soon after the house search. The APB went out first with just some general information, while the BOLO went out with a substantial amount of factual information including the intention for apprehension. TJ and Justice drove together back to the Simmons' house hoping to find some kind of new lead.

"Hey, there's something I've been meaning to ask you about. Both Special Agent Mitchell and Deputy Superintendent Thompson call you Mav or Maverick while you call them by their first names. You all seem very familiar with each other. What gives with that?" asked Justice.

"Both Chip and Darius are friends through our shared loss of our wives in the 9/11 attack. Chip also lost his daughter. We met in a grief-support group where, believe it or not, the facilitator was Dr. Simmons. That's the reason I went to him for some further counseling. By the way, Chip and I also have history going back to high school, but that's another story for another day. Anyway, I initiated a poker night together with Chip and Darius and two others from the grief group and it became something we regularly do. Chip felt I needed a new name to help me make my new start in life so he started calling me Mav or Maverick. Soon they all did and it just stuck," explained TJ.

"I had no idea about all of that; I only knew what you had told me about your loss. That's just not right! I feel terrible for all of you," said Justice.

"Nothing you can't relate to. You lost your father in a terrorist attack of another kind. Racial terrorists. You know, you should join our poker group. We could make good use of your money!" laughed TJ.

"I'm not so sure playing poker with my boss is a good idea."

"Hey, I'm playing with my boss and it's working just fine," said TJ.

"Okay. I'll think about it. Now, let's get to the house and then find this monster."

As they arrived, they were stunned to see that Dr. Simmons' car, which had been parked in the driveway, was no longer there.

"Where's the car? Who would have moved it? It definitely wasn't taken in for any forensic work after it was found to have nothing of evidential value. We even had a boot put on it. What in the world is going on?" exclaimed Justice.

"Don't know but that's really strange. Let's get inside and take a look," said TJ.

After going room by room through the house and finding nothing new of any significance, TJ and Justice sat down at the dining room table. They were both a bit discouraged. They talked through all the evidence they had and made guesses as to where the perp had gone but they knew he could literally be anywhere by now.

"This may sound like a stretch but he could have actually been here during our search and then taken the car after a few days when everything was completed. After all, he's a structural engineer who has worked closely with architects so it would be simple for him to devise and build a priest hole of some sort. You know, the kind of thing they hid Catholic priests in back in the mid-1500's. Let's check with the city and see if a recent building permit was issued for this property. Can you make that call to the building department, Justice?"

Justice made the call and used his Boston PD credentials to get a quick result over the phone. There had been a permit issued for work done last summer. After further questioning, they found it to be for downsizing the large master closet by four feet. It included plans for a removable panel, the building of a small room with electrical outlets, the installation of a small corner sink with running water and an air vent with a fan. They both said at the same time, "Who would downsize a closet?"

What they found shocked both of them. The design was ingenious and flawless. The entrance was invisible to the naked eye. The space was bigger than they had imagined. There was a small built-in desk, along with a comfortable office chair. There was a bright ceiling light with a switch to turn it on and off. The sink was installed at a height so it could be used as a toilet. The walls were painted with baseboards and crown molding. A small refrigerator contained drinks and snacks. On the walls hung pictures with a black X across them of Joe, Troy, Pete, and Lincoln. There was also the photo of TJ and the rapists helping Leah down the stairs of the frat house along with the photo of TJ on a couch sitting with Leah. Furthermore, they found notes about a Dr. Carolyn Finch with an address in Manhattan on the Upper West Side.

"HE WAS HERE!" yelled TJ.

"No doubt about that. He must have seen us coming, grabbed his suitcase and entered his hiding place. After a few days when the coast was clear he, as an engineer, easily removed the boot from the tire and got away in his car. A car we haven't been looking for because the wheel-clamp was supposed to immobilize it while it was in the driveway. And who in the world is this Dr. Finch?" asked Justice.

"Don't you remember? It was in Leah's diary. It said, and I quote ... *I walked barefoot into the operating room where the nurse instructed me to lie down on the table. She put my feet in the stirrups as the doctor entered, a surgeon's mask covering her face. I remember being surprised that the doctor was a women but somehow it comforted me. A gas mask was placed over my mouth and nose, and I was told to count backwards. The last words I heard was the nurse saying, "We are ready to begin, Dr. Finch.'* Don't you see? She's the abortion doctor that botched the procedure when Leah was a college student in '72. Simmons is not done killing yet and that must be where he's headed!" proclaimed TJ.

"Nice photographic memory! I read through the diaries but I didn't remember that name. And one additional thought about all of this, but it's not a good thought. He's got two pictures of you on his wall, TJ. Could he be thinking you're one of the boys that raped Leah?"

Urgently, Justice called the NYPD, gave the police dispatcher the quick rundown about Simmons and the address for Dr. Carolyn Finch. The dispatcher said she would immediately attempt to reach the endangered woman and a car would be sent to her address in a New York minute.

# CHAPTER
# 43

The monster, dressed in suit and tie, slipped past the doorman and strolled into a high-rise apartment building on the Upper West Side of Manhattan. It was on the hunt for Dr. Carolyn Finch. With a briefcase in hand, it entered the first elevator that arrived and then pushed the button for the top floor. It rang the doorbell this Friday afternoon on the last day of May knowing, from a phone call to the abortion clinic, that it was the doctor's day off.

A tired-looking woman in her sixties answered the door. She was a small woman with small features. Her eyes were bright and her smile was honest. Her hair was short and dark with some grey at the roots. She was thin and wore no make-up. Dressed in a simple, long sleeved, cotton dress with comfortable pink slippers on her feet, she had been curled up on the couch with a throw blanket reading a romance novel.

"Hello, may I help you?" asked the woman.

The monster quickly shoved the door open, knocking the woman to the floor. It shut the door, opened the briefcase, took out the duct tape and placed a strip of it over the woman's mouth and around her wrists, then took her to an overstuffed chair and tied and taped her so she couldn't move. The monster noticed the beautiful view of the

Hudson River out of the floor-to-ceiling windows thinking it would be a tranquil scene to watch while dying.

"So you're an abortionist. I have to tell you that I'm not a fan at all. But, I'll give you a chance to tell your story to me and then we'll see what happens. I just want to talk to you. Sound good to you? It sounds good to me. Now do you think you can control yourself to not scream if I remove the tape? I'll tell you now that I can be brutal if you don't obey me. Can you nod your head and let me know you agree and understand your situation?" asked the monster.

The woman, now with wide and wild-looking eyes, nodded her head and agreed. The monster removed the duct tape from her mouth.

"So I have some questions for you. You're expected to answer truthfully. Now, first question. Can you tell me about you becoming an abortion doctor?"

"Okay. Um ... I went into family medicine and then received specialized training in abortions when it was legalized here in New York," said Dr. Finch.

"But why did you want to become an abortion provider in the first place?" asked the monster.

"I wanted to help women in trouble, in need, who felt they were in a desperate situation and needed to find relief and a way out of their predicament. I just wanted to help."

"But what motivated you so deeply that made you want to help?"

"Well ... that's very personal. You see, I got ... well, I got pregnant when I was just sixteen. I was ... was never sure who the father actually was," said Dr. Finch stumbling over some of her words.

"Tell me more," demanded the monster.

"My parents ... well they were incredibly angry and absolutely ashamed of me. My friends ignored and chastised me. That was late in 1951. And what I needed ... um... what I wanted was to have an abortion and just go on with my life but that was impossible to do. It was illegal and my parents had forbidden it. So, my baby was born and was immediately given up for adoption."

Finch blinked away tears of fear and regret and then continued.

"I didn't even want to hold the child, thinking that would only make it harder on me. I know what I went through and I just wanted to keep other girls from having to go through the same emotional mess."

"How many abortions have you done since 1972?"

"I ... I don't know!" she stammered.

"Well, approximately," he said forcefully.

"I do about forty a week ... work about forty weeks a year ... Okay, um ... thirty years ... so maybe about 48,000."

"And are there ever any complications with the abortions you do?"

"There's always a risk with any medical procedure. I'm sure there have been a few over the years ... but very few."

"Do you remember doing an abortion on a nineteen-year-old girl in 1972 named Leah D'Angelo?"

"Are you kidding me? I have no idea who that is."

"She became my wife. She wrote about you in her diary that I read after her recent death. Because you botched her abortion she had an infection that led to not being able to have children."

Finch starred in horror.

"If that's true, I'm so sorry that happened."

"Did you know the name, Finch, means to *swindle*? D'Angelo means *angel*. You swindled my angel, and me, out of having children. You didn't help my wife, you destroyed my wife! We were going to have a family. One with a mom and dad who loved each other and who loved their children."

The monster put the tape back on Dr. Finch's mouth and then stripped her clothes from her, put the IV in her arm and started slowly dripping out her blood. Dr. Finch was shocked by such horrid treatment.

"I thought you'd be most comfortable with your clothes removed just like all the women must do before you kill the life inside them. Forty-eight thousand murders! And people are put to death for killing just one person. So hypocritical! And did you know that it's illegal to destroy an eagle egg? It's punishable by a $250,000 fine and up to two years in prison. But it's legal to kill a human being for any reason and taxpayer money even funds abortion providers. Again, so hypocritical!

"You know you're not the only person I've come to kill in NY. My Leah was gang raped. That's how she got pregnant. And the final rapist is yet to die. But before he dies, I'll get the rapist's two children. He took away my possibilities of kids so I'll take away his reality of kids. I'll crush their skulls in pieces like you do during a second trimester abortion. Limb by limb you tear the baby apart and eventually the skull is crushed into pieces so that it can be removed. I'll crush their skulls into pieces with a bullet in their heads! Then I'll get TJ, the rapist!

Dr. Finch was breathing fast and her heart was racing. The monster kept a rather sad and sour look on its face.

"Some last thoughts, Carolyn. I've been found out, so I need to hurry and finish what I've started. Let me share some facts about me. I was unwanted by my real mother, therefore, I got adopted by a wealthy Boston couple. I was once told by my adoptive mother that I should never have been born ... meaning I should have been aborted. Apparently, that's what my actual mother had initially wanted. I've done research for years and only recently received a letter revealing the identity of my birth mother. And yes, Dr. Finch, who got pregnant in '51 and had a baby in '52 ... I was that baby!

"Hello and good-bye ... MOTHER!"

———————————

Shocked and overwhelmed, Dr. Finch was aware of what was going to happen to her. With the loss of fourteen percent of her blood, she would feel lightheaded and dizzy. At fifteen to twenty percent there would be nausea along with an increased heart and respiratory rate. To compensate for the blood loss, the blood vessels in her limbs and extremities would constrict. This would lower the amount of blood her heart would pump outside the center of her body. Her skin would become cooler and pale.

At thirty to forty percent of blood loss, it would cause a traumatic reaction. Her blood pressure would drop even further and her heart rate would further increase. She would become confused and disoriented while her breathing would be more rapid and shallow. When her body could no longer maintain circulation and adequate blood pressure, she would pass out.

Finally, when the blood loss reached more than forty percent, her heart would no longer maintain blood pressure, pumping or circulation. Her organs would begin to fail without adequate blood and fluid. She would slip into a coma and she would die.

Before slipping into unconsciousness, Carolyn Finch gazed out the window to the serene, blue waters of the Hudson River and wondered if she deserved to die.

# CHAPTER
# 44

The policemen ran into the Manhattan Westside apartment building yelling at the doorman to grab the extra key for Carolyn Finch's apartment. All three rushed into an open elevator to the top floor. They pounded on the door and loudly called out, "Police, open the door." There was only silence. So with guns drawn, the door was cautiously unlocked and opened. There they found an unclothed, unconscious women restrained by rope and duct tape in an overstuffed chair with thirty-four percent of her blood pooled around her. They checked her pulse and found a very weak one. One of the cops immediately pulled the IV from her arm and held the puncture spot to stop any bleeding while the other called for an ambulance. The paramedics arrived in nine minutes and twenty-three seconds, stabilized the patient as best as possible and had her in an ambulance on the way to a hospital minutes later.

The police dispatcher radioed the responding cops and found out the details of the physical assault. She in turn called Detective Justice Jackson of the Boston Police Department to share the good news: Dr. Carolyn Finch was rescued just in time. She was unconscious and had lost a lot of blood from some contraption the perp had rigged, but the paramedics felt confident that with a blood transfusion, along with intravenous fluids, she would survive the attack. They said another few minutes with continued blood loss and failing blood pressure she would not have survived. She was taken to Mount Sinai West located at 1000 10th Street. Justice would have hugged her but on the phone he could only thank her profusely.

With the great news Justice and TJ gave each other a high five along with exuberant yelling that could be heard a block away. After their celebration, they jumped into Justice's unmarked police car with blue lights flashing and sped off to New York.

---

Justice and TJ arrived at the hospital four hours later after battling the infamous I-95 corridor traffic. They were told they could sit outside Dr. Finch's hospital room to wait for the thumbs-up to talk with her. Grabbing a couple of semi-edible ham sandwiches out of a machine along with chips and sodas, they knocked out their hunger pains. It was already ten-thirty at night. All they needed was five minutes alone with Carolyn Finch, to hopefully get a lead.

# CHAPTER
# 45

The monster, Dr. Jack Simmons, left Dr. Finch's apartment on the Westside in a big hurry. Going down the elevator and rushing out the front door without a word to the doorman, he waved down a taxi. He headed for Skylar Maverick's apartment at 126 First Street. Locating the address was no problem. Just another easy find off the internet if a person knew where to look. He already could recognize the Maverick children thanks to TJ showing him their pictures during the private counseling session. He had taken a very careful look at those photos knowing he would need to identify them at a later time.

Upon reaching his destination he climbed the steps to the fourth floor and knocked on the door with gun in hand, completely ready for another kill. He could see in his mind's eye his bullets shattering Skylar's skull into tiny pieces. Instead, all he got was silence. There was no one home. He figured it being a Friday night, she and any roommates were probably out partying and having a good time. He was thinking it would be her LAST good time!

He ran back downstairs and tried to hail another taxi but the few that passed were all occupied. Fifteen minutes later he was telling a driver to go to 777 6th Street and to step on it for some extra cash. Now he was headed for Ethan Maverick's apartment. There he took an elevator to the fourteenth floor, went to apartment G and hit the buzzer.

To the monster's surprise, an unfamiliar face answered the door. It belonged to a friendly looking African American.

"Hey, what's up?" said the young man.

"Ah ... I was looking for Ethan. Is he around?"

"Nope. Out for the night. And you are?"

"I'm a friend of their father's ... so a family friend. My name is Dr. Jack Simmons. You've probably heard him talk about me. When I'm in town I usually try to take Ethan and his sister out for dinner. My meetings were close by so I thought I'd just drop by."

"Okay. By the way, my name's Jadyn. Sean and E, I mean Ethan, are out for the night and Ethan's sister is with them. I'm just crashing here for a few weeks. There's this incredible concert with Billy Joel and Elton John at the Garden and they scored tickets. After that, they're hitting a special dance party around 11 o'clock ... something called *The Abandoned Dance Party*. I think they said it's at the old City Hall subway platform, which sounds pretty cool."

"Well ... thanks. Just tell Ethan I stopped by and will give more notice next time I'm in the City. This was just a last-minute thing."

Smiling on the outside but furious on the inside, the monster left the apartment and headed for the elevator. He knew there was no way to find them and kill them at the crowded concert but he at least knew where they'd be at eleven that night. He planned to have a bang of a time with them in just a few hours.

Dr. Simmons imagined for TJ's kids a relatively quick but painful death, a bullet in the head. He imagined the thrill of seeing the splatter of blood and bone. He was sure a well-aimed bullet would suck out the lives of Skylar and Ethan as if they had never existed, just like an abortion sucks the life out of a fetus. After that, he could go after TJ, one of the rapists who ruined his and Leah's dreams in life. And finally, he could take care of the one other person who was on his list for annihilation.

# CHAPTER
# 46

It was 10:30 on Friday night, May 31st, and Madison Square Garden was rocking with 20,000 loud and devoted fans of all ages. It was the *Face to Face* Tour 2002 with Billy Joel and Elton John. As the concert was finishing, everyone had clapping hands, dancing feet and singing mouths. Everything about the extravagant publicity and promotion of this concert was absolutely true. The hype was all real! Sky, Sean, Ethan, Kari, Shari and Rayne had been holding tickets for months waiting for the show. No one was disappointed and no one was complaining about the sky-high ticket price. It was a once in a life-time show.

"Awesome is too small of a word to describe this," said Sky almost yelling in Sean's ear.

"Yeah. It's totally amazing! And now we get to go to that exclusive underground dance party to top off the evening. It's a night to remember!" Sean yelled back over the noise of the crowd and the music. "Sky, you set it up, what are the details?"

"It's sponsored by the New York Transit Museum and they were tough tickets to get! It's called *The Abandoned Dance Party* and their tag line is *Dance with Abandon!* As you know, Summer wasn't up for a Billy and Elton night but she'll meet all of us at the dance. We said we'd all arrive there around eleven. Doors opened at ten."

"So what's the best way to get there from here?" asked Sean.

"Well, since we're on top of Penn Station right now we can get there pretty easily. It's at the City Hall abandoned subway station. We just need to get to a downtown 6 local and get off at the Brooklyn Bridge-City Hall stop. Should be no problem!"

When the concert was done, the six exited along with a very large and very happy crowd.

# CHAPTER
## 47

TJ and Justice finally got the okay from the doctors to go in and talk to Carolyn Finch. They said she would be fatigued, distressed, and exhausted from her ordeal but was out of danger. The doctor added her mind was strong and clear. They were asked to limit their interview to about five minutes.

"Hello, Dr. Finch. I'm Detective Jackson with the Boston Police and this is Dr. Maverick who is with the FBI. We're sorry for what you've endured but we need to ask you a few questions so we can apprehend this monster."

"I'm weak and may close my eyes some but I can try to answer your questions."

"Great. We believe the person who attacked you is Dr. Jack Simmons and we believe he tried to kill you because he has information that you performed an abortion back in '72 on a woman named Leah D'Angelo, who became his wife a few years later. Apparently, something happened post-op that prevented Leah from ever having children," stated Justice.

"Yes, that's correct. He told me that was his name and he told me that was the reason he was there. He also told me he was ... my son," said Dr. Finch with tears pouring down her cheeks.

Both TJ and Justice were stunned. They looked at each other with wide-eyed wonder that silently said, "That explains a lot!"

Dr. Finch continued her thoughts. "You see, I was only sixteen when I got pregnant. I wanted an abortion but was forced to carry the baby to term and then gave it up for adoption. I wanted nothing to do with that baby. I just wanted to forget it happened and live my life the way I wanted to live it. He wanted revenge for what I did to him and for what I did to his wife ... and maybe that's what I deserve." This was said with even more tears and emotion.

"Did he say anything else to you that would be important for us to know? Did he give any indication to where he was headed?" asked TJ.

"Yes. He said he was going after someone named ... BJ ... or maybe TJ. He said his wife was gang-raped and that this guy was the last rapist to die. It sounded like he had already gotten to the others."

Justice and TJ exchanged knowing looks. There was no reason to inform the good doctor about who was standing beside her.

"But, I'm not finished. He described how he planned to kill the rapist's children. He said something like ... 'he took away my possibilities of kids so I'll take away his reality of kids.' Again, he wants revenge. To kill those children just like the rapist, at least in his mind, had killed his future children."

As soon as TJ heard those words, he shot out of the hospital room, pulled out his phone and called Sky. It just went to voicemail. He then called E. It also went to voicemail. He then called Sean, Kari, Shari and Rayne. No one answered. Last on the list to call was Summer. She picked up on the first ring.

"Hello, Dr. Maverick. What's up?" said Summer.

"Do you know where Sky or Ethan are? It's an emergency!"

"The gang should be leaving the Garden about now. They all went to a concert. I was just leaving a friend's place because we're all meeting up at a dance party in about twenty minutes ... around 11 o'clock. Is everything okay?"

"No, it's not okay. Their lives are in danger. There's a madman planning on killing my kids and I can't get in touch with them to warn them," said TJ almost shouting.

"Oh my God! Okay, they either turned off their phones in the concert or they just can't hear the ring because of the loud music being played. Or maybe they're underground without a signal. They'll take the subway to the dance and its location is also underground. It's at the abandoned City Hall station," said Summer.

"Got it. I'm on my way!"

TJ came back into the room feeling panicked. He grabbed Justice's arm and started pulling him out of the room.

As they were heading out the door, Dr. Finch lamented, "It's all my fault. I didn't want him. I didn't love my own son!"

TJ and Justice ran through the halls of the hospital as people yelled at them to slow down. They were desperately trying to save two lives and catch a killer.

# CHAPTER
# 48

T he dance party was going strong with a mix of songs through
the decades. The station had been resurrected, restored, and re-
structured to host exclusive events. It once again looked like the
showpiece and the crown jewel of the New York City subway system with
brass fixtures and skylights that ran along the entire curve of the station,
giving it a miniature Grand Central Station look. The tall tile arches and
the vaulted tile ceiling were amazing to behold with elegant chandeliers
of days gone past reinstalled. It became again the chosen place to hang
the commemorative plaques recognizing the great achievement of building the underground train system of New York City.

A special removable deck was placed over the tracks for safety and to
create a dance-floor area. Removable walls were placed on each end of
the station, making it an enclosed space. Although the number 6 train
would usually go through the station without stopping using it as a
turnaround track, it was always rerouted when the old City Hall station
was in use with an event. A stage and dance floor were in place. Extra
lighting, also elegant, had been brought in. A special air-conditioning
and return air handler system had been built to have fresh, clean, cool
air always circulating. Tables with white table cloths and white chairs

surrounded the dance floor and the DJ had the place rocking. Drinks were flowing and appetizer type foods were available. And people danced with abandon!

The Billy and Elton concert group of six arrived, showed their tickets and came down the stairs from the one allowable entrance. At the same time, TJ and Justice were speeding down 9A and turning off at Chambers with blue grill-lights flashing. Summer was still on the number 6 train as it made its way toward the Brooklyn Bridge-City Hall stop.

Meanwhile, the monster was approaching from the underground tracks. He had researched the location, knowing that without a ticket he couldn't come through the main entrance for the dance. Besides, the security would be tight for such an event and a gun would not be welcomed. He arrived on the local 6 train and got off at the Brooklyn Bridge-City Hall stop. He waited for the train to pull out and then, with flashlight and gun, he jumped down to the tracks. He found the path that would eventually lead him to the old City Hall subway platform.

As the monster got closer he could clearly hear the music, assuring him that he was going to the right place. As he approached the subway platform the song "Who'll Stop The Rain" was being blasted through a stack of speakers. He knew the words by heart and started singing along. He remembered seeing the movie back in the mid 70's but couldn't remember the name of the guy who starred in it, but he remembered the girl, Tuesday Weld, because she was sexy. He was thinking the movie was really all about pain, not rain — the pain of the Vietnam War, heroin addiction and drug smuggling. Now, he knew who could stop his own pain. The Maverick family — ALL DEAD. The song emboldened him to keep moving and to do whatever it took to kill his pain.

The concert friends all got drinks and found an empty table. The music was good. When the song "Who'll Stop The Rain" started playing they all got up to dance.

Justice and TJ skidded to a sudden stop and started running toward a large, lit-up sign reading, THE ABANDONED DANCE PARTY. They showed their badges, quickly told the security guys what was going on and ran down the stairs hearing the song "Who'll Stop the Rain." Justice rushed to the DJ platform while TJ frantically searched the dimly lit room.

Dr. Simmons squeezed through a small opening onto the platform and crashed the party. He had a Red Sox baseball cap pulled down to cover a portion of his face. He wore jeans and a Grateful Dead T-shirt. He wanted to fit in and blend into the younger crowd as best he could. He carefully surveyed the mass of people until he found his targets on the dance floor. Lighting was romantically low and many dancers were moving to the music as he purposefully walked towards his intended victims, his hand ready to grab the gun tucked into the back of his pants.

Summer was running a little late and just arrived at the entrance. She was told she couldn't enter at this time due to some kind of emergency. She turned as if she were leaving and then bolted past the two security guys and down the stairs. She heard the song "Who'll Stop the Rain" just ending.

Justice had been talking to the DJ and, taking the mic in his hand, he made an announcement.

"May I have your attention, please. There has been a viable threat and we need to move in an orderly fashion out through the exits. Please move safely but you need to move NOW...."

This startled and scared the crowd more than was intended. Images of the recent 9/11 terrorist attack flashed through their minds and the crowd became agitated and panicked with pushing and shoving.

TJ was intently searching all the faces in the crowd for his son and daughter. Finding Sky, he started making his way to her. Suddenly, TJ's eyes locked onto the monster and the monster's eyes locked onto TJ. A split second later, the monster took aim at Skylar and squeezed off two shots just as TJ jumped in front of her. A bullet hit his chest and another one hit the side of his head. He went down.

The monster yelled, "At least I got the rapist!"

Screams and hysterics exploded. Justice pulled his gun and tried to run to where it seemed the shots came from. At the same time people were stampeding toward him trying to get out. This confusion was blocking Justice from the monster. Without warning he was pushed to the ground where his head hit hard on the cement. At this same time, Sky was shoved and jostled by the crowd but was able to see the monster taking aim at Ethan.

Sky screamed, "ET get down!"

Although he hated to be called ET, it automatically got his attention and he moved his head enough for the bullet to miss by inches.

The whole situation was looking bad. TJ was down and without a gun. Justice had a gun but was on his knees trying to get up and was feeling dizzy and disoriented.

The monster could see Ethan and Sky backed up against the wall holding on to each other. He didn't know who the other people in the group of six were. It seemed to him like they were trying to protect each other. The monster now had clear shots at both Maverick kids. He lifted his arm, took aim and ...

BANG. BANG. Two shots were fired. Both bullets hit their mark. E and Sky were on the ground. Sean, Kari, Shari and Rayne were all reaching for them. Tears started flowing from their eyes as they took in what just happened.

E and Sky had pulled each other to the floor at the sight of the gun being pointed at them. The monster was on the ground bleeding profusely from two bullet wounds. One hit his shoulder and the other one entered his neck. Summer, having just come down the stairs saw a man with a weapon pointed at her friends. After firing two shots, she still had her gun positioned in the direction of the monster ... just in case.

TJ slowly got up. His face was bloody from the bullet that grazed the side of his head. The bullet that hit his chest was stopped by a Kevlar vest. That had been Justice's idea. He went over to Simmons, knelt down and placed his hands on his neck to try and slow the bleeding. The bullet had hit the jugular. It wouldn't be a slow death from blood loss like the monster's victims; it would be a fast death from blood loss.

"I want you to know I did not rape Leah," said TJ. "I've never raped anyone! I wasn't with, in fact I never knew, those other three guys in the photo — Joe, Troy, and Pete. I was in the frat house at that time just dropping off some books. I saw a girl unsteadily coming down the stairs and I wanted to help her. Then I sat with her to make sure she was okay. That's the other photo in your collection. Me and Leah sitting on a couch. I asked her if she needed any help getting home and she said no. So, she went her way and I went mine. I never even knew her name! I was only there trying to help her and protect her," explained TJ.

"If that's true ... sorry for this ... your kids. I know I messed ... messed up ... added to Leah's death. The last on my list to kill ... was me. Now ... no more pa...."

Blood kept pouring out. It couldn't be stopped. Only his breathing stopped.

Summer was now standing over TJ and the monster. "After you called, I went back to the apartment to get my gun. And, just so you know, being a bit rushed I actually missed my shot. I was aiming for his head!"

# CHAPTER
# 49

The night had been memorable, but not in a good way. The next day Skylar and Ethan, along with the rest of their crew — Sean, Rayne, Kari, Shari and Summer — all crammed into TJ's small hospital room. Justice was also there visiting even while nursing his concussion from hitting the cement. The shot that grazed TJ's head turned out to be worse than it had first appeared. Somehow the bullet shattered when it glanced off leaving shrapnel pieces that needed to be removed along with a slight crack in TJ's skull. The medical procedure had gone well. The doctors wanted to observe him for a day and a night before releasing him just to make sure there was no internal damage that might affect his brain function.

"That was crazy last night! It started out being one of the best on record and ended up being a nightmare!" exclaimed Skylar.

"That sums it up for me, too," added Rayne.

"I'm just glad everyone's safe. It was an especially close call for the whole Maverick family," said Sean.

"A very close call for me, for sure. If it hadn't been for my sister yelling, ET, my brains would be splattered on the subway wall. It made me move just in time. Sky, you're my savior!" said Ethan, as he hugged her tightly.

"Well, just remember you owe me for the rest of your life," laughed Sky.

Then Shari shared by saying, "I'm thrilled we're all okay but I have to say I didn't sleep too well last night. I kept hearing the gun shots and imagining what could have happened to any one of us. I know I just need some time to get to a better place but I wanted to be open about it."

"I think we've all been traumatized, at least to some degree, but that's pretty normal with what we all went through. Keep holding on to each other and keep talking to each other and you'll be just fine," offered TJ.

"How are both of you feeling?" asked Kari to Justice and TJ.

"I'm good to go. I'm sure my headache will pass. A few more painkillers should take care of the problem," said Justice.

"And, although it may not look like it, I'm doing great," said TJ weakly. "As long as my kids are safe, all is well in the universe! And what can I say about our hero who's just standing there without saying a word. Thank God for concealed weapon licenses! Summer, I am so thankful for you protecting the people you love. If you hadn't been there, I would have lost what's most precious to me in this world. You are the hero ... or heroine ... of this story!" said TJ, his emotions exploding inside of him.

At these words, there was clapping and hugging. Summer just smiled and graciously took it all in.

Like clockwork, as the hugging ended, pizzas and sodas arrived. It was time for a little party and a big celebration.

———————

A few days later, TJ and Justice were back in Boston. They met with Darius and Chip for a debriefing session, which went well. When

TJ walked into the FBI office, people got up from their desks and congratulated him on a job well done. Much the same occurred with Justice at the police station.

The scene in New York had become an international story of heroism of a young college student named Summer. The Boston Police Department along with the Boston FBI Field Office, were held up as superior crime-fighting agencies working seamlessly together making the streets safer for the people of America. The earlier negative press that had been received from the fiasco concerning the professor's son was long forgotten. To top it off, TJ and Justice had their names in the news as the team that brought down the killer. The exploits of the fictional police duos of *Miami Vice* and *Lethal Weapon* were alluded to probably because of the black-white correlation. Both were feeling good about the comparisons!

---

After another week had gone by, TJ and Justice met at their usual place — Starbucks on Beacon Street in two overstuffed brown, leather chairs . They talked and laughed. They were loud to the point of being obnoxious but they disregarded the staring public. After a period of time the conversation turned serious.

"So how-ya feeling about everything, TJ?" asked Justice.

"Overall, I'm feeling really good. I've been getting some R&R and healing up quickly. But I have to say there are some things about our case that are still bugging me."

"What do you mean? It's wrapped up pretty tight."

"Yeah, I know. But still … something's just not completely right. As best we can tell from the information we've received, Troy and Pete did not continue raping women after they left Joe's influence. Joe was the definitive motivator and ringleader. On the other hand, there have been a number of sexual complaints throughout the years that have surfaced against Joe. None of them got any real traction, but still, the complaints are real. My bet is Joe continued in his rape mode in some capacity and I'd sure like to uncover the whole truth about him for the sake of his victims. So, I think we need to dig deeper and not stop short. There may not be anything more to the story but ...."

"Honestly, I had the same feeling. Maybe we should talk to Joe's father again with all that we now know and see if we can find out any more about his son's activities. I just think it might be worth a closer look," said Justice.

"You sure you just want to take a closer look at the son by talking with the father or is it actually about taking a closer look at all the half-naked girls?" TJ quipped, grinning.

"Yeah, real funny, TJ. But I was serious about needing to talk to the dad. Something's out of whack. And hey, you've got that golden ticket of unlimited expenses so we could ...."

"Go back to Miami?"

"That's what I'm talking about!"

"If we do, we probably should do it on the sly. I'd rather ask for forgiveness than ask for permission with this trip. What do-ya think?" asked TJ.

"I'm in."

"Okay. Miami here we come, again! Black's my color but maybe I should pick up a white linen suit ... then just call me Sonny!"

"And call me Tubbs!"

# JOURNAL ENTRY
## June 12, 2002

Suzo:

Everybody is safe! We had a madman, mad with pain, after all of us . . . but we survived and we are now thriving. Not that I would ever have planned it this way but I'm closer to the kids than ever before and Sky and E are loving each other as never before. Nothing like a life-threatening crisis to bring a family together!

A quick update for you, Suzo. A highly educated and accomplished man bent on revenge became a killer. He was suffering from the pain caused by numerous traumas in his life. The way he chose to deal with his pain was to kill those who caused the pain. He thought I was in the mix of raping the girl who became his wife, causing a pregnancy, an abortion, and infertility. His plan was to kill the rapists, kill the abortionist, kill me and our children, and then kill himself. And get this . . . the abortion doctor turned out to be his mother and the monster turned out to be my therapist!

It amazes me how intelligent, gifted and sensible peo-ple can become monsters. But, this whole experience has taught me and brought me a great distance. I don't want my pain to turn me into some kind of monster by domi-nating my life. I've been tempted to want revenge against those who stole you from me. Yet, Granddad taught me not to take revenge but to leave room for God to deal with it. Not an easy thing to do! I thought about the cosmic trauma that Jesus endured on the cross. You know, the pain didn't have a negative effect on who He was — the pain allowed Him to display the beauty of who He was more fully. He overcame the evil that was perpetrated against Him with the good that was released from Him. That's pretty cool! Suzo, I want my pain to help me become more fully who I was created to be.

I'm making progress. Perfection never, progress forever. I'm finding that healing doesn't mean that the damage never existed; it means that the damage no longer controls my life. I have to stop cheating on my future with my painful past! Complete resolution has its steps: Reveal. Feel. Heal. I've been taking some giant steps in the right direction!

I'm heading for Miami tomorrow with Justice. He's been my partner and my newest friend. It's going to be hard when this gig is completely over and we're not working together anymore. I don't want to even think about that right now. We're going to dig a little deeper to see if there's something under the surface that hasn't been revealed yet about this case. Wish me luck!

All my love, all the time —

TJ

# CHAPTER
# 50

The plane ride from Boston to Miami was easy. TJ and Justice grabbed a rental car at the airport and drove to the Miami Beach Police Department on Washington Avenue. TJ had already been there so he was in the driver's seat. Before getting on the plane, TJ set up a meeting with Detective Luis Perez, who had been the lead detective on the Joe Hiller investigation. He was only too happy to meet with TJ and his partner as they were the ones who found the murderer and closed the Hiller case.

"Great to see you again, Detective Perez. This is my partner, Detective Justice Jackson of the Boston PD. And, thanks for making some time for us. I know you're busy," said TJ.

"Not too busy for my new heroes. I was going nowhere with the Hiller case and for you guys to clear it for me … well, that was exceptional work! Please, have a seat and let me know why you're here and how I can help. Has something come up I'm unaware of?" asked Luis.

At this point Justice took the lead in the conversation, thinking it best to speak detective to detective.

"We both have a gut feeling there are more victims from Hiller's activities than we're aware of at the moment. Now, I assume you've read the reports that were sent down so I don't have to go through all the details ... correct?"

"Of course. The reports told a good story and I really like the ending!"

"Okay, great. We're thinking the other two rapists who Dr. Simmons murdered, Troy and Pete, stopped their activities once they graduated and were separated from the influence of Joe. But Joe had women who have made complaints and accusations against him throughout the years. Nothing ever came of them but, with money, influence, and intimidation, those kinds of things go away. We'd like to help the women who he sexually abused and raped to have closure by knowing the violator who invaded their lives is dead and gone. That would include the UF coeds and anyone after those years. As we all know, often sexual offenders like to hold on to keepsakes such as photos, panties, or personal trinkets belonging to their victims. And so, we thought another look around his house would be in order. Initially, it was searched as the home of a victim. Now, it will be searched as the home of a sexual predator."

"I think that could be arranged without much of a problem. Last I heard, his house had been sitting there empty for the last nine months. You know, his dad lives close and is quite rich so I guess there's been no need to do anything with the property. Now we'd have to get a search warrant but since there's solid evidence he was a rapist, that shouldn't be difficult," said Luis.

"Thanks for your cooperation. It's very much appreciated. Additionally, we have a bit of a wild thought but we'd like it to be considered. We're looking for a secret room of some sort. We found what's called a priest's hole at Dr. Simmons' residence. It was a small hiding place and work space. So that gave us the idea of something hidden at Hiller's estate. I hear it's a big place so there would be plenty of room for something like that," suggested Justice.

"You know that may not be so far-fetched. Many of the rich folks around here have built a protective space, or panic room, for their safety. This gives them a fortified room in the event of a home invasion, hurricane, terror attack or any other threat. Did you see the movie, *Panic Room*, with Jodi Foster that just came out in March? It was a pretty good flick."

"Missed it, but I like how you're thinking!" replied Justice.

"We're going to need some engineers and building experts to be part of the search crew. This secret room wouldn't have been built legally so there won't be any paper trail with building permits. How quickly can we get the search warrant and the right people to the site?" asked TJ.

Luis smiled saying, "Let's go and have a nice, long lunch as my people work on all of this. I'm thinking we could be ready to go later this afternoon."

After a relaxing and delicious lunch at the Nikki Beach restaurant, South Beach's place for jetsetters and celebrities, the three were ready for some action. Unfortunately, it was taking more time than originally thought to pull everything together. So they ordered more drinks and listened to the live entertainment's happy music as they watched the waves roll in. After another hour, they got the call to meet the search crew at the Joe Hiller Jr. home.

Justice was amazed at the house located on Rivo Alto Island. TJ had already seen it from the outside. Luis had been through it as the detective in charge of the crime scene. It was a white stucco, 7,000-square-foot, six-bedroom, five-and-a-half-bath, two-story Modern-Midcentury waterfront home with breath-taking views of Miami Beach. It had a gourmet kitchen with an open-floor plan for both living and dining. There were floor-to-ceiling sliding telescopic glass doors and windows, which provided indoor and outdoor living. Additionally, there was a luxurious pool and private dock.

After many hours of searching the home, everyone came up empty. The engineers looked for discrepancies in floor spacing versus wall spacing in each room and searched for a disguised entrance to some sort of secret room. Nothing was found. The search for trophies from sexual assault victims ... also nothing. Discouragement was starting to set in. TJ wanted everyone to take another look before leaving, thinking and hoping something had been missed. He and Justice started going from room to room for one last look themselves. When they came to a large room designated for the home gym, TJ stopped in his tracks. It was full of weights and workout machines of every kind, but TJ was struck by the arrangement of wall mirrors — they weren't spaced evenly. Since the whole house was obviously decorated by an interior designer who would have an eye for detail, it didn't seem right to have one large mirror panel spaced differently compared to all the others. If the mirrors were a puzzle, the pieces would fail to fit together correctly.

TJ went over to investigate. Something was definitely different about the sound as he thumped on this one particular mirror and its surrounding wall area compared to all the others. There was a denser, deeper sound. But the mirror was immovable and seemingly attached in the same way as all the others. Still, something just didn't feel right to TJ. Both TJ and Justice started searching for hidden buttons or switches that might operate the mirror in some way. Soon they had almost the whole search team in the gym looking and touching and moving everything. After forty-five minutes of futile searching, Justice grabbed a thirty-five pound metal dumbbell and threw it at the mirror. Everyone in the room was startled as the mirror crashed into a thousand pieces. Wires could now be seen that would have electronically and seamlessly moved the mirror up and out of the way. And a locked, metal door was revealed behind the broken glass.

Once the door was unlocked, there was a spiral staircase that wound down to a secret room. What was found was shocking. It was a private theatre with an eighty-five-inch screen and two black-leather seats that fully reclined. The room was twenty by fifteen with built-in bookcases and cabinets and a small desk. But what took everyone's breath away was the Nazi flag, Nazi medals, Nazi military keepsakes and Nazi photos. Everyone was silent as they took it all in.

"This stuff is all genuine," said Justice.

"I've never seen so much Nazi stuff in my life," said Luis.

"And look what's beautifully framed and hanging on the wall, guys. It's a photo of Hitler signed by Hitler and a photo of Himmler signed by Himmler. I'm completely blown away!" exclaimed TJ.

Looking through the cabinets they found a huge stash of DVD's and videos. There was a girl's name with a date marked on each cover of each video. After a closer examination, there was always a matching DVD with the same girl's name and date marked on it. The name Leah was found on two of the videos and two of the DVD's. Finding the DVD player, they inserted the disk and watched a portion of it, which was extremely difficult to do. The girl named Leah was in some kind of alcohol and drug-induced state, reaching into the air as if to catch something as three boys took turns raping her. The camera angle was from above. In checking a few of the other videos, the camera angle was always the same. In them, girls were crying and pleading and struggling. A few were unconscious but the boys never stopped their groping and probing and abusing and raping.

"This is horrible! No more, no more!" shouted Justice.

Shaking his head, TJ said, "Guys, it gets worse. I found some DVD's with Post-It Notes that said, *Dad's Copy.* So here's what I think. The ringleader of the UF rapes was Joe Jr. but behind him, grooming him, was Joe Sr., his father. Copies of the rape videos would be sent to his dad. And I'm betting the other two guys, Troy and Pete, never knew anything about the camera. We'll have to get the frat room inspected to see if there's any remnant left of the hidden camera after all these years. I'm guessing the camera was somehow concealed in the ceiling and could be activated by remote control. And after finding the VHS to DVD converter on the desk, it seems obvious Junior Hiller was in the progress of upgrading the old VHS videos into the newer DVD format for Senior Hiller."

"It's great we found all this but it's terrible that it even exists," said Luis.

"Agreed. And I'll say this whole Nazi thing doesn't connect for me," said Justice.

"Yeah, I was thinking the same thing," answered TJ. "But we'll figure it out. It's gonna connect somehow. The puzzle pieces are falling into place so let's just take it one step at a time. When the news of these videos get into circulation, proving certain rapes actually took place, women will come out from their hiding or from their denial to get justice, compensation, and closure. They'll also take legal action to have any court records sealed and videos destroyed making it impossible for the general public to view them."

"So it's on to the house of Joe Hiller Sr.," said Justice. "But I'm betting this next search warrant will be more difficult to attain. He's probably got people loyal to him everywhere because of his money."

"No doubt, but let's get it done!" said TJ with both conviction and indignation in his voice.

Before leaving the premises Justice called the whole search team together for some final words.

"First of all, let me say thank-you to Detective Perez and to all of you involved in this search. Everyone was essential and each of you did an outstanding job. Secondly, you cannot tell anyone what we've found ... NOT ANYONE! Can't tell your wife or lover; can't tell your co-worker; can't tell your best friend. It's imperative to keep this completely secret. At this point, there must not be any verbal or written reports. We'll just say the search turned up nothing of value and that's what you need to say if anyone asks. NOTHING MORE! If our thinking is correct about Joe Hiller Sr. and if our findings were to get back to him, he'll either destroy any possible evidence or, with his great wealth, flee the country. Am I making myself understood?"

There were quiet yeses and headshakes all around.

Boosting what had just been said, Luis emphatically stated, "Let me add this. If anyone does do anything or say anything that lets this story out, I will make it my personal mission in life to have you fired without compensation and your reputation ruined by feeding your name to the news people as aiding and abetting a rapist. I hope I've made myself clear. Now, I would like all of you to be involved when we do the next search. You have done some important work here today, but our job with this case is not over yet. I'll put together a larger team but one that includes each of you. So get some rest and be ready to move quickly once we get the search warrant."

That speech bonded the two detectives and TJ in friendship. They grabbed some late night dinner together and planned their attack on the Hiller compound.

# CHAPTER
# 51

Detective Luis Perez announced with some swagger to TJ and to Justice, "It took the whole day but we finally have the search warrant and we're ready to go in. If there's nothing illegal or suspicious in the compound I'll have egg on my face. I'll be looking really stupid to my superiors, as they'll think this plan was complete overkill with the use of so many police resources. But, I've got a weird feeling about this situation after being in that secret room yesterday. That Nazi stuff freaked me out, along with the dozens and dozens of rape videos so I've got a S.W.A.T. team coming. Also arranged is a F.B.I. presence going in with us — thank-you TJ. It's nighttime so I've got spotlights available. I even have a police cruiser to block the yacht if it tries to make a run for open water. They'll be a forensic team, an engineering team, and thirty-five police officers to do the search of the house and property. Afterall, it's a huge compound."

"Sounds like all the right stuff. LET'S GO!" shouted Justice.

When everyone was assembled outside the compound on Di Lido Island, an intimate party of a dozen guests was in progress. The search warrant was served and the place was now under the control of TJ,

Justice and Luis. When the guests were told to leave, grumbling and complaining broke out as they were ushered out. Standing around were a number of Hiller's hired armed security men closely watching the entire police operation. They looked like they were ready for action if orders were given. The overabundance of police fire power that was brought along turned out to be a smart move.

During the search, Joe Hiller Sr. sat himself in a blue, leather chair with his legs crossed looking completely unconcerned and proceeded to smoke an illegal Cuban cigar. He arrogantly looked at the three S.W.A.T. guys who were making sure he stayed put. Everyone was expecting it to be a long night.

Out of nowhere, a young Slavic girl with blonde hair and blue eyes found TJ and asked to speak to him privately.

They walked into a hallway as TJ asked, "Yes, how can I help you?"

"I need protection. I shouldn't be talking to you. This could cost me my life!" said the girl shaking with fear.

"What's your name and what are you so scared of?"

"My name is Annika. When I was fifteen, I thought I was coming to work as a maid for two years to pay for my passage to America and to get papers for citizenship but it was all a lie. I've been here for almost two years and I don't see an end to it. Men come, powerful men, and I must service them sexually or I get beaten and starved. The armed security men are not here to keep the thieves out as much as they're here to keep the girls, like me, in."

"Then why are you roaming free tonight?" inquired TJ.

"Because I was ordered to accompany, and later to entertain, a certain guest at the party. I suppose with all of you showing up, they forgot about me. "

"And, you said, girls. How many of you are there?"

"There are six of us most of the time. Some are mysteriously taken away, maybe die, but replacements always come," answered Annika.

"Where are you kept?"

"I can show you but you have to promise to help me," pleaded Annika.

"I promise. You're safe now."

TJ found Justice and Luis and told them the story. Annika took them outside and started leading them toward a small concrete structure that housed the motors, cleaning equipment, and chemicals for the pool. As they were walking, a shot rang out and Annika went down in a bloody mess with a hole in the side of her head. TJ, Justice and Luis all dropped to the ground. Everyone went on high alert as spotlights were turned on looking for the gunman. More shots were fired which could now be determined were coming from the yacht. The engine came to life and started to pull away from the dock. The police cruiser was immediately on it with more gunfire coming from both vessels. The primary gunman fell overboard, riddled with bullet holes. The others onboard stopped the engine and raised their hands. By this time, all the security men had been rounded up and disarmed. TJ was brimming with anger and sadness, but mostly he was feeling guilty. He had promised to save Annika and now she was lying in front of him, dead.

When everything settled down and it was deemed safe, a whole team went to the concrete structure to investigate it. After a thorough inspection, an ingenious hidden entrance was found, leading to a large, underground bunker. Justice made the comment that it would never have been located without the girl's help. The bunker was spacious and luxurious. There were six beautifully decorated rooms, or cells, just off the main room. Women were found locked inside five of them, all young and blonde, with blue or green eyes. They each fit the description of the supposed Aryan master race. And they all had a story to tell.

Concealed cameras were found in each room to record sexual activity. This was most likely unknown by the victimizers of the women. Some of the men who had been recorded were well known celebrities in entertainment, in business and in sports. There were even a few royals in the mix. The fall-out was going to be like the aftermath of an earthquake, registering nine on the Richter scale. With video proof, the usual lies and cover-ups wouldn't work this time with the easily deceived public.

There was also a theater room, larger than the junior Hiller's theatre. There was a bigger screen with six comfortable, reclining seats. Ornate bookshelves lined one wall containing a collection of what appeared to be hundreds of pornographic DVD's and videos. These included those with covers having a hand-written name of a woman with a specific date, penned with an indelible black marker. The two Leah videos were part of the sordid assortment.

All of this was too much to take in. Everyone was appalled. TJ noticed there was one particular engineer, who had been helping the day before, who kept thumping walls and taking measurements. TJ came over to talk to him.

"What are you thinking at this point?" asked TJ.

"First of all, to have underground, concrete, fortified rooms like yesterday's and today's in the Miami Beach area is an engineering feat. Normally you can't build underground because of the water table. But, if you have the money, anything can be built. It's sort of like the Palm Islands being created over in Dubai. Money can make the impossible, possible. Secondly, after yesterday, I'm not believing my eyes. I can't stop thinking about all that Nazi stuff and the similarity of these two secret rooms with the theater and the rape DVD's and videos. It seems to me that the son is following in his father's footsteps, yet, there's no Nazi paraphernalia here. So, like I said, I'm not believing my eyes. I think Nazi stuff must be here somewhere," said the engineer.

"You know, I think you're right on the money. Keep looking and I'll help."

TJ assessed the room, thinking surely it couldn't be as easy as what he was contemplating. One of the walls was completely wood paneled with a series of built-in bookcases. He pushed and shoved and pulled on each bookcase. He removed the books and the decorative items off the shelves. He looked for something to press or push or pull. As he was sliding his hand across the top of one of the bookcases, his fingers felt a small indentation. He got up on a chair to take a closer look. He pressed down on the slightly indented area and a quiet motor started up and the bookcase swiveled open. All the workers in the room stopped and stared and started moving toward the newly opened passageway. TJ walked through the hallway-like ingress and flipped on a light switch. Nazi Germany had just been reborn!

"It's no wonder Hiller Sr. wasn't pushing for a closer investigation of his son's death," remarked Justice.

Nazi flags. Nazi uniforms. Nazi weapons. Nazi medals. Nazi insignias. Nazi books. Nazi medical notes. Nazi documents. Nazi photographs. Nazi propaganda films. Nazi medical experimentation films. Nazi death camp films. Nazi stuff filled the room. Luis, Justice and TJ spent the next many hours going through the stacks of papers which included legal documents, passports, photographs, and bank books with account information.

"Guys, if I'm understanding this correctly, his money goes back to Swiss bank accounts filled with Nazi gold and to Swiss safe-deposit boxes filled with jewelry and art pieces, which I assume, were all stolen during Hitler's reign of terror," said Luis.

"Incredible! Now, hold on tight," said TJ. "I'm about to blow your minds even more. I found another photo of Heinrich Himmler and it's signed: Zu Joseph, Der Party immer treu sein, Dein Onkel Heinrich. My German isn't great, but in English I think it reads: To Joseph, Always be faithful to the Party, Your Uncle Heinrich. Of course he's talking about the National Socialist German Worker's Party ... the Nazis!"

"No, that can't be! That's too unbelievable! Are you actually saying Joe Hiller Jr. had Himmler as a great uncle and Joe Hiller Sr. is Himmler's nephew?" asked Luis.

"That's exactly what I'm saying!" exclaimed TJ.

"And come over and look at these," said Justice. "After reading through each document, I would say that Joe Hiller Sr. paid big bucks for a false British identity including fake British Army discharge papers. Look at this picture of the two Himmler men together and note carefully the uniforms they're wearing. The nephew was in the SS along with his uncle Heinrich Himmler, one who helped devise and implement the final solution for the extermination of Jews. Another four million undesirables were also annihilated. Absolutely staggering numbers!

"And here are Hiller's German military papers. His birth name was Joseph Heinrich Himmler. Then over here are his original stamped papers for passage out of Germany after the war. His name was changed to Joseph Heinrich Hiller. Obviously Hiller is close to Himmler—just drop two m's and add one l. It's also only one letter different from Hitler. A devious way to remember who and what you really are. Then in England, he got a forged birth certificate with the name, Joseph Henry Hiller and that's the name he used with his immigration papers in coming to America. It's amazing that he kept all this stuff — so beautifully incriminating!"

It became an all-nighter for many on the team. Hiller Sr. was arrested, along with any employee who may have had knowledge of the evil that was taking place in the compound. The five women were removed and taken to safety and put in protective custody until everything could be sorted out. All the rape movies, legal papers, and photos were being processed and logged into evidence. The work that was necessary to unravel all the evil would not be a short task.

As the sun was coming up, TJ, Justice, and Luis headed out of the compound to their respective beds. They were completely exhausted both physically and emotionally. Their lives would never be the same after what they had witnessed and experienced during this one night.

# 1942

Gebhard Himmler and his wife, Mathilde, were suffering sleepless nights out of concern for their nineteen-year-old son's safety. Although both fully supported Hitler's expansion plans, they wanted their son, who was in the SS, out of harm's way. Gebhard was the older brother of Hienrich Himmler, the highest ranking SS officer in charge of the Nazi's foremost agency of security, surveillance, and terror. Gebhard's and Mathilde's son, Joseph Heinrich Himmler, was named in remembrance of Gebhard's father, Joseph, and out of affection for his brother, Heinrich.

"We know what it's like out there — death everywhere," said Gebhard to Heinrich in a solemn tone. "We've seen it firsthand. I've got three daughters but he's my only son. He's your nephew. You report directly to the Führer so you can make happen whatever you want. Isn't there a place he can serve that's away from the bullets?"

"Are you sure you want to do that? He tells me he wants to be in the thick of battle. Keeping him safe and away from the real action could do more harm than good in the long run," responded Heinrich.

"Look, he's my only son. If I lose him then our family tree has one branch that gets cut off. He's even named after you and our father. So keep our legacy alive! What can you arrange for him?"

"Okay, I hear you. I've got a new program I'm starting in connection with our labor camp in Mauthausen. It's a very safe place … just twelve miles east of Linz. We're starting with one brothel to serve the area labor camps and using it as a model to establish others. We believe this will ultimately increase productivity and decrease homosexuality in the camps. I need SS men there to supervise the operation. They'll be selecting the women, matching the women with clients and detailing the sexual activity in logbooks. Not a bad job for a young man full of hormones. I can write up the orders myself and then emphasize the importance of this work to Joseph. What do you think, Gebhart?"

"I'm very grateful and will always be loyal to you."

The Mauthausen brothel was functioning well for the last seven months. A group of young SS men were patiently waiting for their superior to come and give them their specific duties for the next monthly rotation. Quiet conversations were happening among the men.

"What a great assignment this is ... sex work organized bureaucratically. And I love the spy holes!" said Joseph.

"Oh, yeah! And this is so much better than where the bombs are dropping and the bullets are flying," said a young SS man who happened to be sitting next to Joseph.

As the ranking officer walked in, everyone stood with the Sieg Heil salute by extending their right arm from the neck into the air with a straightened hand saying, "Heil Hitler!" The officer proceeded to read what was affectionally called *The Ten Commandments.*

"Here's the list of reminders for you. Do not deviate from these in any way. One: No Jews can work at the brothel and no Jews are allowed to patronize the brothel. Two: Hours of operation are every evening from 8 to 10 and Sunday afternoons from 2 to 4. Three: Only German prisoners with German women and Slavic prisoners with Slavic women. Four: No more than ten men in two hours. Five: The women must be regularly tested for sexually-transmitted diseases. Six: All pregnancies end by abortion. Sterilization is an option. Seven: Two Reichsmarks buys fifteen minutes — absolutely no longer! Eight: Select only suitable women ... early twenties is best. Nine: Missionary position only — no exceptions! Ten: Supervise acts of intercourse and detail it in our logs.

The men were dismissed after more instructions about productively running the brothel so the prototype could be duplicated in other strategic locations.

"Hey, Himmler ... what rotation are you on this month?" asked one of Joseph's buddies.

"I'm on selection duty. Love it! So many of these women think they're the lucky ones. Some even beg to be chosen for the clean, heated, sufficient-food living situation. And I like seeing their faces light up when I tell them that if they behave and fulfill their duties as sex workers for their fellow detainees, they'll get early release from the camp. That never happens! We use them until they get exhausted or sick and then replace them. Most just get sent away to their deaths," laughed Joseph. "And what's your assignment?"

"I'm on the match-ups. Who goes to who. Pretty simple, really. Just have to make sure no Germans go with the Slavic women."

"I did that a few months ago. But you know what I enjoy the most in this place? Seeing women, especially virgins, who only come face to face with their fate when their first patrons are ushered in. I make sure I'm watching that!" proclaimed Joseph.

# CHAPTER
# 52

TJ and Justice, back in Boston from the storm they had stirred-up in Miami Beach, returned to their assigned seats at their favorite Starbucks.

"So where are we with the background research with the Himmler family," asked Justice?

"I've got it but are you really wanting to hear it?" asked TJ.

"Yep. Let it rip!"

TJ pulled out his notes from his backpack and began. "Joseph Himmler had three sons. Gebhard, Heinrich, and Ernst. Gebhard, the oldest of the brothers, was the father of three daughters and one son. That son was Joseph Heinrich Himmler or the one we know by the name of Joseph Hiller Senior. Gebhard, as an SS man, commanded an army battalion and became the inspector of Waffen-SS schools ... the military branch of the Nazi Party's SS organization. So he was all-in with the Nazi agenda, to say the very least."

"And what happened to him?"

"Believe it or not, he was only imprisoned for three years. He was given a denazification certificate and, eventually, he even got his pension returned to him. He died in Munich in June of 1982 at the ripe old age of eighty-three."

"How in the world did he get away with what he must have known, and possibly participated in, since he was the brother of the mass murderer Heinrich Himmler?"

"A very good question that will never have a very good answer. Now some info on Heinrich Himmler. He was two years younger than Gebhard and was one of the most powerful men in Nazi Germany, reporting directly to Hitler. He was a main architect of the Holocaust and he's the Uncle Heinrich in the photo we found. So the man we know as Joe Hiller Sr. is his nephew and he's the great uncle of the younger Joe Hiller, our campus rapist."

"This all still staggers my imagination," said Justice.

"Me too. Now here's the quick run-down through the years:

"1898: Gebhard Himmler is born.

"1900: Heinrich Himmler is born.

"1923: Joseph Heinrich Himmler or, as we know him, Joseph Hiller Sr., is born. And again for clarification ... he is the son of Gebhard and the nephew of Heinrich.

"1942: Joseph at age 19 is in the SS and gets assigned to Mauthausen's brothel. I'm thinking that being around those poor women who were pressed into being sex slaves is what set in motion his obsession for sexual gratification through pornography and rape. It's reported that the SS men were to observe and record the sexual activity that took place. With his hidden bunker, he basically rebuilt a Mauthausen brothel so he could keep reliving it.

"1945: The war ends and Heinrich Himmler is captured and commits suicide.

"1945-1948: Joseph escapes to London under the false name, Joseph Heinrich Hiller, and buys forged documents. This would include a British birth certificate and British Army discharge papers. With these new documents to hide his past, he's able to use the name of Joseph Henry Hiller. He goes to school for civil engineering.

"1949: Joseph immigrates to America and finishes his degree at the University of Florida.

"1951: He gets married to an American girl. He hides his wealth and his true identity. He gets an engineering job in Miami.

"1952: Joseph has a son and names him, Joseph Henry Hiller Jr. and calls him Joe.

"1967: The senior Hiller's wife dies in a car accident. Something about the brakes not working. It was a questionable death but there was no traction in the investigation about foul play, but I would say the timing is definitely suspicious. After her death he buys the four house properties on Di Lido Island, knocks them down and starts to build his compound which must have included the hidden bunker. Before that time he was living a middle-class lifestyle but at this point he starts to live the life of the rich and famous. It's only my best guess but I think his deceased Uncle Heinrich somehow gave him access to that wealth.

"1969: His son, Joe, now seventeen, becomes a freshman at UF ... his father's alma mater. Early in his college career he has the grade issue with the English Lit professor, Conor Casey. Soon after that, he starts his rape club ... The Harvest Club or THC. I'm sure his father groomed him for this kind of activity. One of the women they rape — twice as a matter of fact — is Leah D'Angelo who ends up marrying Dr. Jack Simmons.

"2001: Leah commits suicide in June. Her husband, Simmons, finds her diaries following her death containing the details of her rapes and abortion. In September, Joe Jr. is murdered by Simmons. Later he kills two other rapists — Troy Wilson and Pete Fox.

"2002: Simmons endeavors to kill the abortion doctor who botched Leah's abortion in '72. She turns out to be his birth mother. Then he dies of gunshot wounds when attempting to murder me and my kids, thinking I was one of the rapists.

"And that pretty much sums it all up. And like I've been saying all along ... there's always history with pain and there's always history with monsters," said TJ.

"But wouldn't his identity have been uncovered from some kind of communication with his father?" asked Justice.

"Well, there's no communication between them that we know of and we've searched for it. The father could have thought that his son was killed and not identified since he never heard from him again. Or, he could have known about his escape and cut off all contact with his son, believing their communication would lead to his arrest. And, I guess they could have been in contact in some covert way we'll never know about."

After more discussion of all that had occurred, Justice yawned and stretched and said, "Okay, I think that's about all the Nazi stuff I can take today. We need to celebrate our victory a bit. Let's go over to Harvard Square to Harrell's Ice Cream. It's the same as Steve's and it's the absolute best! They have the smoosh-ins and I want mine covered in jimmies!"

"I know Steve's Ice Cream. Used to be one in Lexington. Loved it ... Let's go!"

# 1945

"Do you know who we're bringing to you for a medical exam, Captain Wells? It's the Nazi monster, Heinrich Himmler!" exclaimed one of the soldiers in charge of guarding the top SS officer. "Everyone was on the hunt for him and we've got him right here!"

"Yes, I've been informed he was coming. Just out of curiosity, do you know any specifics of how he was captured?" asked Captain Wells.

"All I know is he was attempting to go into hiding. He had a forged document with a suspicious unit number and stamp and so, at a checkpoint, he was stopped and detained. That was just two days ago. And then, just a few hours ago during an interrogation he admitted who he was!"

"Thanks for the info. Have the prisoner brought in and then stay with us."

Himmler, handcuffed and bound by a chain attached to each ankle, reluctantly came into the doctor's office.

"My name is Dr. Wells and I've been asked to do a medical examination on you. Take a seat over there and I'll start the exam."

The doctor, with Himmler under the watchful eyes of two soldiers, went about the task that was assigned to him.

"I've taken and recorded all your basic vitals. Now I need for you to open your mouth wide so I can examine it."

The doctor moved in closer. Jerking his head away and refusing to open his mouth, Himmler then crushed between his teeth a hidden cyanide pill and collapsed on the floor. He was dead in fifteen minutes. His death was recorded by the doctor as May 23, 1945.

—*Two Weeks Earlier*—

Heinrich Himmler, feeling distraught and desperate, was trying to save himself, a number of fellow SS officers and his nephew.

"It's official, Hitler's dead and an unconditional surrender has been declared ... so all is lost!" announced Himmler to the handful of high-ranking officers standing around him. "Everyone needs to get out of Germany as fast as possible by using the fake documents I've arranged for all of us to have. I'm taking a new last name with a lowly rank so I can get through the checkpoints with little to no trouble ... and you can do the same. Best of luck to all of us."

Heinrich strode quickly out of the room to find and talk to his nephew. Months before, at the point when the Third Reich looked doomed, he had pulled his nephew out of Mauthausen and brought him back to serve close to him.

"You need to listen to me closely, Joseph. Here are the documents you need to get out of Germany. Your name has been changed to Joseph Heinrich Hiller. Hiller's an old Bavarian name, and since we are from that region, you'll be able to answer any questions thrown at you, proving who you say you are. The name is also close to Himmler and Hitler so you'll never forget where your true loyalties lie. You got that?"

"Yes sir. Absolutely. I understand," said Joseph.

"Also, I have a plan that I expect you to follow. I'm going to give you codes and numbers to my personal Swiss bank accounts and safe-deposit boxes. These contain riches you can only imagine — money, gold, paintings, jewelry. But, it only belongs to you if you don't hear from me.

"Go to London to learn English and take elocution lessons. You're still young so you can get rid of any German accent and sound completely British quickly and easily. At the same time, start your education, maybe in engineering, like your father. Then get the best fake British birth certificate and the best fake British Army discharge papers that money can buy. Pay whatever it takes to erase your past. Change your name on those documents to Joseph Henry Hiller. You see, Hiller is also an Anglo-Saxon name. Then immigrate to America. There's going to be a lot of confusion over the next couple of years and confusion is your best friend. Be sure to take advantage of it."

"Sir, how long have you been thinking about this plan? It's so elaborate and well-thought-out," said Joseph.

"I could see this coming for quite some time now. So listen. When you get to America, finish your schooling and find an American woman to marry. Preferably one with blonde hair and blue eyes. And under no circumstances get into the Swiss money in any kind of big way for at least fifteen to twenty years. If you spend the money too quickly, many questions will arise. Initially, only use the money to establish your new identity and for absolute necessities. Never tell your wife about the money or about your actual identity. Maybe even get rid of her before you really start using the money. And if you have children, be sure to teach them the Nazi way. Have them appreciate and applaud their real heritage."

"I promise to do all of this and to never forget who I really am!"

"I'll try to meet up with you in the near future," said Heinrich, lowing his voice. "I'll be going by the name of Sergeant Heinrich Hitzinger. Be sure to stand under the Big Ben clock every Friday at noon during the month of July. If I don't show up, just figure I'm dead."

They left by different exits and traveled by different roads.

# CHAPTER
## 53

After all the action and excitement, TJ was resting and hanging out alone at his quiet and peaceful apartment. So much had happened. He felt transformed, like a butterfly breaking out of its cocoon becoming something and someone very different. Reaching for the copies of Leah's diaries on the coffee table, he started rereading some of the pages he had marked as being most important. This included her description of the meetings with Dr. Kimberlin, her feelings about not being able to have children, her many painful interactions with her husband, her guilt from not being completely honest about herself and her depiction of the shame she carried throughout her life. It also contained expressions of good and happy times but these were overshadowed by devastation from the rapes. She expressed a constant struggle to feel safe. She had chronic insomnia and nightmares. She spoke of the need to double-lock doors and windows to keep any, real or imaginary, invading evil out. When he once again read her final entry, tears fell from his eyes and dropped onto the pages of the diary.

# June 7, 2001

*I'm going to kill myself. Jack just left me after slapping my face and slamming the door. He called me a SLUT! I can't take any more pain in my life. I was hoping tonight would change everything. I decided to be full of truth, hoping my husband would be full of grace. He is the love of my life but I could never really be the love of his life. Too much tainted history. I foolishly thought he could become my safe place in this crazy world. I was hoping I could be loved unconditionally, allowing me to finally leave my guilt and leave my shame. I guess I'm not very lovable once the curtain is pulled back.*

*I got raped and cheated on and then raped again. It left me pregnant. It left me empty. It left me hopeless. It left me childless. I had dreamed of being able to live in a state of fulfillment, satisfaction, and joy. I had dreamed of sexual love being a total-person experience and the cement that holds two people together. I had dreamed of marital love being the strongest, most steadfast and invincible force in the human experience. All those dreams were broken and crushed and destroyed and stolen by barbarous assaults of forced sex and by a ten-minute suction procedure that stopped a heartbeat and tore apart fingers, legs, toes, and fragile bones.*

*When you find this and read this, Jack, I want you to know it was you, and only you, I wanted to share my life, my heart and my body with. In my mind and in my heart I wanted to give myself to you totally, uniquely, and wholeheartedly. I wanted only you to cherish my body. I belonged to you and to you alone. But ultimately in your mind, even after all our years together, I was nothing but a promiscuous slut and baby killer. I now know you could never completely love me and so I must leave you — forever. These eight words from a sad song tell my sad story: "Now life has killed the dream I dreamed."*

When TJ finished reading Leah's last diary entry, he exclaimed with no one listening, "No wonder Simmons felt so strongly that he contributed to Leah's death and deserved to die!"

Reading this made TJ want to embrace, more than ever, a significant role in helping people move through their pain successfully, before they got to Leah's point of hopelessness and despair. He knew personally how awful that felt as the loss of loved ones had wreaked havoc in his own life. Thankfully, he now surrounded himself with friends, struggling through loss themselves, but doing it together so no one felt alone. Darius and Chip were strong people but they let down their guard more than once and shared how difficult their loss had been for them. Their extended families were a good support. Their work was a good and needed diversion from the pain. And yet, they pointed to their poker group friends as being the most helpful for healing the hole in their hearts.

As TJ put down Leah's diary, he thought about how true it was that hurt people hurt people ... pain begets pain ... monsters beget monsters.

# Part Four

# I MADE IT THROUGH
# THE RAIN

# CHAPTER
# 54

With all the publicity concerning this case and with Hiller Sr. behind bars and the three rapists dead, scores of women were coming forward with stories of sexual mistreatment, harassment, and rape. Included in a number of these testimonies was the use of intimidation and threats to their lives to keep them silent. Even in Europe, a few women in their seventies, who had been paralyzed by a lifetime of trauma and shame, came forward to identify Hiller Sr. as an SS soldier who had grossly mistreated women at the brothel in Mauthausen.

The news reports surrounding the events of the case again opened up a divisive national debate on abortion. Talking heads with their personal point of view were screaming to be heard. Women's rights. Genocide of the unwanted. Designer babies versus defective babies. Roe versus Wade. Law of man versus Law of God. All the noise was deafening.

Justice received the George L. Hanna Memorial Award for Bravery. He was recognized for his brave and decisive actions that led to the arrest of a sexual predator with Nazi and family connections to the mass murderer, Heinrich Himmler. The award was given with these words: "A man of exceptional heroism." TJ was also recognized for his outstanding and heroic acts that went far beyond the customary role of a profiler. He received the FBI Medal of Valor.

Following the ceremonies there was a reception where TJ was offered a full-time job as a criminal profiler with either the Boston FBI or the Boston Police Department.

"Maverick, both offers are on the table without a time tag. Take whatever time you need to decide what you want to do," said Chip.

"And get some special time with your kids. Go and enjoy life together before the next term starts for them," encouraged Darius.

"I can't thank both of you enough for everything. I'll consider your offers and will get back to you with my answer. And with the suggestion of getting some family time, my Granddad emphasized that how people felt about each other depended on the memories they made together. Good memories foster good feelings. So that's what I'll do first and foremost with this next month!" said TJ.

TJ went to find Justice. They found an empty table in the corner and sat down together.

TJ started the conversation: "So, how you feeling Mr. Award for Bravery?

"Probably about the same as you're feeling, Mr. Medal of Valor," laughed Justice.

"You know, what really feels good is to have so many women coming forward. Hopefully, this can close a terrible chapter in their lives. I certainly hope it won't turn into just a bunch of money-grabbing civil suits" said TJ.

"Don't hold your breath on that one but, if it does happen, at least the Nazi treasure will be used for healing instead of hating."

"By the way, did you hear they're stripping the Hiller name from the UF campus? I say, well done to whoever made that decision! Too bad the rapists are dead. They should have faced public ridicule while facing their accusers. They got off too easy," said TJ.

"And one thing I'd like to know … who's putting out the word about me getting my head slammed on the subway concrete floor? I found a cracked coconut on my desk with a face painted on it. Beside it was a note saying: Way to use your head in Miami, Justice!"

"Hey, you gotta admit that's pretty funny. Around the office I've got the guys telling me it's a good thing I've got a hard head. But, no painted coconut with a bullet groove on its side has shown up yet! You know Justice, your dad would be proud of you. Justice for the women at UF. Justice for the women from the sex trafficking. Justice for the used women in Germany. Justice, although never enough, for the racial hatred and persecution of the Jews, political dissidents and the unwanted. And the list could go on. I'm sure he's proud of his boy," said TJ.

"From zeros to heroes," quipped Justice.

"Hey, let me get serious with you for a moment. I need some advice. It's about my wife and my kids. As you probably know, they started to discover body fragments from Flight 11, which was my wife's flight, within days of the attack. Bodies were found strapped to airplane seats and there was even the body of a flight attendant found with her hands bound. As of today, medical examiners have identified the remains of thirty-three of the victims. I just got a letter saying one of those thirty-three is Suzanne. So here's my question. Should I tell my children about this discovery? Will it help or only open up old wounds?"

"Boy, that's a tough one. I'm sorry you have to even go through any of this. Let me ask you a question. Does it help or hurt you to know about it?" asked Justice.

"The answer is YES. It hurts and it helps. But, it's more on the hurting side."

Justice thought for a moment before saying, "Well then, I think you have your answer."

Both men got up from the table, gave a good sized man-hug to each other and then moved into the crowd of people who wanted to pat them on the back and tell them what a great job they had done.

# CHAPTER
# 55

Moving back to his Lexington home put a big smile on TJ's face. He was embracing all the beautiful memories of the love of his life, Suzanne. He roamed the house, moving from room to room touching things she had enjoyed and smelling things that still held her scent. He ended up in his study, pulling photo book after photo book off the shelves; trying to relive and feel the moments the photos depicted. And yet, these surroundings he knew so well didn't seem familiar and safe like they had before. There was an intrusion, an invasion that exploded into his life. Now, he was taken over by a new direction, a new outlook and a new understanding of life. Nothing felt the same because he was not the same.

Lifting one of his guitars and holding it without even strumming the strings caused a powerful creative desire — something he had not felt for a long time. He could hear music and words in his head and he felt strangely pulled to a notepad and pen. He envisioned people from all nations looking at each other, eye to eye, wanting to be free ... free from pain and free to love. He pictured in his mind the fall of the Berlin Wall and thought of the many walls people build and rebuild that need to be knocked down. He thought of the impoverished, abused, and unwanted children that need to be loved. He considered how planes used as bombs exposed how horrible and destructive prejudice and hatred really were. He desired people to be free in the same way he was feeling free ... and he started writing.

# ALL NATIONS
## TJ Maverick

I went to the wall
Where East and West call
To join in a world shaking ball
Skinheads and armies
Neo-Nazis and all
Maintaining and building a wall
Where was the fall?
Where was the fall
Of this deadly wall?
Where was the fall?
Where was the fall
Of this deadly wall?
Something broke out inside of me
As more and more people came out to see
All I heard them say to me
Is...Can you set me free?

*All Nations, Gotta go eye to eye ....*

The sunrise appears
The world is in fear
No food and no clothes and so many tears

Unwanted children aborted and trashed
Abused by the arms
That draw them near
Where are the ears?
Where are the ears
Of the people who hear?
Where are the ears?
Where are the ears
Of the people who hear?
Something broke out inside of me
·As more and more people came out to see
All I heard them say to me
Is...Can you set me free?

*All Nations, Gotta go eye to eye ....*

New York is a place
Where many a face
Shows the tragedy of the waste
Times Square and Sinatra set up the pace
Bin Laden and bombers
Take their place
Where was the case?
Where was the case
Of this terrorist's face?
Where was the case?
Where was the case
Of this terrorist's face?
Something broke out inside of me
As more and more people came out to see
All I heard them say to me
Is ... Can you set me free?

*All Nations, Gotta go eye to eye ....*
*See all nations going eye to eye — See all nations going eye to eye*

———————————

Anthony's Pier 4 was packed with people. In a private dining room, TJ was with a special circle of friends.

TJ stood up and, tapping on a water glass with his spoon, said, "Before we order I just wanted to say thank-you for coming. It's not a birthday or anniversary celebration or a graduation or promotion celebration ... it's just a celebration. A celebration of life. And, I know there are those here who don't know each other but I hope everyone will connect in a meaningful way tonight.

"Let me take a moment and introduce everyone. First, we have my incredibly supportive poker club with us tonight ... Darius, Chip, Marco, and Frank. Guys, thanks for believing in me. We also have my daughter's talented roommates ... Rayne, Shari, Kari and Summer. And by the way, Summer, do you have your gun with you tonight?"

Everyone laughed until she grabbed her purse and pulled out her gun. Then everyone clapped!

"So, we have our protection for the night! I'm forever thankful for you, Summer. We also have my daughter's awesome boyfriend, Sean. And let me say that if you don't treat my daughter right, then I'll ask Summer to pay you a little visit." TJ laughed at his own words and then continued. "Over here is my partner's beautiful wife, Diamond. And beside her is the man who's been my mentor and my friend, Justice. He's got the perfect name for what he does and you should ask him how he got it. Justice, I just want to say that it's been an honor and a privilege to be your partner on our two-man task force. And finally, these two are my children who are my life ... Skylar and Ethan. So proud of both of you and love you both so very, very much!"

TJ's voice was cracking as he spoke these words while more than a few tears flowed from his eyes. It took a moment for him to compose himself.

"All right ... enough for the intros. Let's order so we can eat and get this party started! And by the way, as you look at your menu and see the fabulous prices, remember you're not paying for it ... ... ... JUSTICE IS!"

The laughter just kept going, and going, and going. When it finally did end, almost everyone ordered the famous Anthony's Pier 4 lobster dinner. Ethan was one of the hold-outs, stating lobsters were the cockroaches of the sea. At the end of the evening, TJ cheerfully paid the sizable bill that seemed greater than the national debt.

# ST. BARTS

# JOURNAL ENTRY
## September 11, 2002

Dear Suzo:

Some things you never forget like where you were when Kennedy or Martin Luther King were assassinated. You don't forget how you felt when the Discovery space shuttle exploded or when the Berlin Wall fell or when the World Trade Center Towers went crashing down. You never forget the first person you made love to, the first time you're told you're pregnant or the first time you hold your newborn child.

People also never forget when they're told they have cancer or that their child is going to die. They never forget their parent's funerals. When our world is rocked or shocked it becomes unforgettable.

The slogan going around is "Never Forget." For me, Suzo, I'll never forget you. I'll never forget the first time I saw you in our Hemingway class or the first time I held your hand or the first time we kissed or the first time we said the words "I love you" to each other. I'll never forget our wedding night. It was the first time we made love together. I remember watching you in your white, sheer nightgown with your long golden hair falling onto your shoulders. I remember the blue ribbon I pulled that untied your gown and I remember finding that pleasing rhythm. Roberta Flack was certainly right with her First Time song.

TJ carefully unwrapped a delicate, platinum watch and removed it from its box. On the back of the watch was an engraved message that read:

**TJ + Suzo**
**Forever**

He also pulled out the poem "Remember" which was unchanged from when he first wrote it one year earlier. TJ held the watch and the poem in his hands. He looked out on the clear, blue, aquamarine Caribbean waters and watched the sun go down, surrounded by pink-brushed clouds. He then opened up the note Suzanne had written for him a year earlier. He had been unable to do so before now. He had never been ready to read her final words to him. Tears began to pour out as TJ got to the end of Suzo's words ... *Enjoy your time away from me but don't forget about me while I'm gone. Forever yours, Suzo.*

After a period of reflection accompanied with both pain and joy, TJ continued to write.

*I have your 25th anniversary present with me. It's about a year late. You were supposed to be wearing it already.*

*Suzo, I came here to be with you and to figure out life. In my heart I wish I could go back but the thing is ... even if I could go back, I'm not sure I would belong there anymore. I believe I've transformed, at least to some degree, to become who I was always meant to be.*

*So what do you think? Should I stay in our home or run away again from the pain of all the memories? I* think I'll stay. I need your memories. I'll forever carry you with me along with the pain of losing you. Seems like nothing goes away until it teaches us what we need to know and I realize I still have a lot to learn. Perfection never. Progress forever.

So what do I do with my life after all the mess, Suzo? I've been thinking about this for a while now. I've learned pain always has a consequence and monsters always have a face. So, I thought about permanently trying to deal with some of the bad guys in this world who create pain. I think that's who I've become. I think I could be good at that. I'm certainly motivated. I think it might keep me sane and satisfied at the same time. I was offered positions as an expert profiler with both the Boston Police Department and the Boston FBI office. Not too bad of a gig, I think. What do you think, Suzo?

The sun went all the way down. The moon had risen. The stars were doing their illumination show. The trade winds provided a soft, cooling, constant breeze. TJ was sitting on the pool deck feeling lonely and trying to hold himself together. He took out his guitar and started playing the James Taylor song "Fire and Rain." For Sweet Baby James, the song was about his friend Suzanne who committed suicide, about his personal struggle with his heroin addiction, and the depression felt about the demise of his band, The Flying Machine. For TJ, the words meant something completely different. In his mind they told of the crash of the September 11th flying machines that caused the tragic loss of his beloved Suzanne. The words of the song also seemed to describe for TJ his own battle with alcohol, drugs, and depression. And to TJ, it felt as if it all just happened yesterday.

*Just yesterday morning, they let me know you were gone*
*Suzanne, the plans they made put an end to you ....*
*Won't you look down upon me, Jesus*
*You've got to help me make a stand ....*
*Sweet dreams and flying machines in pieces on the ground ....*
*I've seen fire and I've seen rain ...*
*But I always thought that I'd see you again*

This song left TJ quite melancholy. He needed to stop strumming his pain with his fingers. His mind turned to some lines between Westley and Buttercup from *The Princess Bride*. This put a smile on TJ's face.

*Westley:* I told you I would always come for you. Why didn't you wait for me?
*Buttercup:* Well ... you were dead.
*Westley:* Death cannot stop true love. All it can do is delay it for a while.
*Buttercup:* I will never doubt you again.

He started playing another song that got him into a better mood. This one described the destination he had finally achieved. Along with Barry Manilow, he could say with certainty that ... *I've Made It Through The Rain.*

*We dreamers have our ways*
*Of facing rainy days*
*And somehow we survive ...*
*I made it through the rain*
*I kept my world protected*
*I made it through the rain*
*I kept my point of view*
*I made it through the rain ...*

He stayed there for hours. He took the time to think, and to hear his dead wife's voice of reason and wisdom. He thought about all the money he had received and he felt very guilty about it. A million-dollar policy from her workplace. A half-million policy he personally had on his wife. And on top of that, $2.35 million from the Victim Compensation Fund and another $230,000 from the September 11th Fund. Unless he did something with it for Suzanne, he knew he could never spend a dime of it. Then he finished writing for the night.

*If I decide to do this, Suzo, I'm doing it for us. I believe I want to help stop the monsters who inflict so much pain on people like you and me. This is how I could use your money and the time I have left on this earth. So, with your permission, my decision to one of these new job offers will be a strong YES! And with this embraced and decided, I've thought of a name for myself Suzo — just call me the ... Pain Killer.*

*All my love, all the time –*

*TJ*

# EPILOGUE

The temperature is getting cooler again throughout New England. The leaves have just started turning into brilliant yellows and reds. Later, they will change to rusts and browns. They will die. They will fall. The storms and the snow will come with the bitter winds. Everything will be touched and covered in white.

Although not noticeable to the human eye, the trees of every forest have grown bigger, stronger, wider, and taller. Sunshine and rain have done their job. And yet, some trees in the past year have sustained broken branches while others have been scarred with the unexpected strike of fiery lightning. Some trees even died. On the trees with scars or broken branches, great growth can be found in other portions of that same tree. Where dead trees have fallen, new saplings can be found.

Nothing is the same.

Rain, rain, go away.
Come again some other day.

Pain, pain, go away.
Come again some other day.

# Fact or Fiction?

1.  FACT: John Maverick and one of his sons, Moses Maverick, are New England historical figures. (Interesting sidenote: We got the word *maverick* in the English language from Samuel A. Maverick, a Texas descendent of John Maverick. He received 400 head of cattle for a $1,200 debt and proceeded to leave them unbranded and roam freely. Others started branding them and stealing them. When Maverick realized what was occurring, he branded the cattle that were left and sold them. During this time, his name became synonymous with such unbranded livestock. By the end of the 19th century, the term *maverick* was used speaking of individuals who prefer to blaze their own trails.)

2.  FACT: The timing and details of the 9/11 terrorist attack are factual.

3.  FICTION: The Boston FBI field office does not cover the state of Vermont. It does cover the states of Maine, Massachusetts, New Hampshire and Rhode Island.

4.  FACT & FICTION: The Florida Players did perform the play, *Butterflies Are Free*, but they performed it in the Spring of 1973, not the Fall of 1972. (Interesting sidenote: Kay Summers, who became my wife, was the Goldie Hawn look-a-like in the show, playing the leading role as the hippie girl.)

5.  FACT & FICTION: *The Florida Alligator* newspaper had to become independent after the act of adding mimeographed lists of abortion clinics in one edition but the specific articles detailing women who had abortions are fiction.

6.  FACT: The stats concerning rape and abortion are true.

7.  FACT: Background information about the Winter Hill Gang is true.

8. FACT & FICTION: Elton John and Billy Joel did have a concert at Madison Square Garden with their *Face to Face* Tour 2002 but it was on March 15, 2002 and not on May 31, 2002.

9. FACT & FICTION: The Old City Hall subway station exists and was the magnificent station that served for the opening of the New York City subway on October 27, 1904 with the arched Guastavino-tiled ceiling, brass chandeliers and cut amethyst glass skylights. It became obsolete due to the curving tracks that could only accommodate the original five-car subways and so closed on December 31, 1945. It is fiction that the abandoned station is ever used for parties or special events. (Interesting sidenote: Open for members only, The Transit Museum gives tours of the Old City Hall station for $50. The tickets sell out fast!)

10. FICTION: Gebhard Himmler, the older brother of Heinrich Himmler, had three daughters but did not have a son.

11. FACT & FICTION: The Mauthausen brothel was the brainchild of Heinrich Himmler and was used as a model for future brothels. Using the name, *The Ten Commandments,* is fiction but the specifics listed are all factual.

12. FACT: The specifics about Heinrich Himmler's life, attempted escape, capture and death are all true.

13. FACT & FICTION: The Victim Compensation Fund was real. It is true that a calculation was made according to the age and earning potential of the 9/11 victims. What is false is the calendar speed the calculations were made and accepted. The book suggests the money was transferred to the victims' families earlier than it actually occurred. For a full understanding and explanation of the VCF be sure to watch the excellent Netflix movie, *Worth,* staring Michael Keaton as Kenneth Feinberg, the Boston lawyer overseeing this emotional and controversial process.

# ACKNOWLEDGMENTS

Writing is a learning experience and I am thankful for what I've learned through this endeavor. I am deeply grateful for the help from Bill Worth with his excellent editing.

Also, a tremendous help to me was my longtime friend, Toney Mulhollan. His expertise in cover design, layout, and publishing moved this book to become a reality.

I am thankful for the insightful advice from my daughter, Summer, concerning different facets of the story making it more relatable and believable.

Thankful also to my son, Kent, who after reading the story and giving input encouraged me with the words, "It would make a great movie!"

And a shout-out to the friends at Ke Ali'i Ocean Villas who were my initial readers. They provided solid feedback, especially my next-door neighbor, Terry Dockins.

Finally, there is my wife, the love of my life, Kay. Her patience with me was epic as I hid away in my study hour after hour finding words to write the story I've wanted to write for many years. This book could not have been completed without her help, insights, and encouragement.

He has been using my new friends, Darius and Chip, to save me from myself. I don't have you but I'm not alone.

I realize I've been all over the map with my thoughts but you know my heart, feel my pain and believe in me. I promise I won't let pain turn my life into something ugly. I'll show you that surviving can be amazing. Healing is tough, but so am I!

Goodnight, Suzo. And thanks for letting me wade through my chaos.

All my love, all the time —

TJ